ANOTHER DAY, ANOTHER DALI

Center Point
Large Print

Also by Sandra Orchard and available from Center Point Large Print:

The Port Aster Secrets
  Deadly Devotion
  Blind Trust

Serena Jones Mysteries
  A Fool and His Monet

**This Large Print Book carries the
Seal of Approval of N.A.V.H.**

A SERENA JONES MYSTERY

ANOTHER DAY, ANOTHER DALI

Sandra Orchard

CENTER POINT LARGE PRINT
THORNDIKE, MAINE

This Center Point Large Print edition
is published in the year 2016 by arrangement with
Revell, a division of Baker Publishing Group.

The text of this Large Print edition is unabridged.
In other aspects, this book may vary
from the original edition.
Printed in the United States of America
on permanent paper.
Set in 16-point Times New Roman type.

ISBN: 978-1-68324-205-5

Library of Congress Cataloging-in-Publication Data
Names: Orchard, Sandra, author.
Title: Another day, another dali : a Serena Jones mystery / Sandra
Orchard.
Description: Center Point Large Print edition. | Thorndike, Maine :
Center Point Large Print, 2016.
Identifiers: LCCN 2016040398 | ISBN 9781683242055
    (hardcover : alk. paper)
Subjects: LCSH: Women detectives—Fiction. | Art thefts—
Investigation—Fiction. | United States. Federal Bureau of
Investigation—Fiction. | Government investigators—Fiction. | Large
type books. | GSAFD: Mystery fiction. | Christian fiction.
Classification: LCC PR9199.4.O73 A83 2016b | DDC 813/.6—dc23
LC record available at https://lccn.loc.gov/2016040398

To Jed—
for inspiring your namesake character
and making me smile when I'm stuck

I

I tore my gaze from the porch that wrapped around the drug dealer's house and cringed at the number on my phone's call display.

Mom said there'd be days like this.

Tanner, still decked out in his SWAT gear, peered over my shoulder as the phone vibrated insistently in my hand. "Good thing you're a field-hardened FBI agent, so you don't let little old ladies scare the pants off you."

I sent him a silencing glare. Ignoring his grin, I turned away from the rest of the team traipsing in and out of the building, and clicked Connect. "Hi, Nana," I said, injecting fake cheerfulness into my voice. "What's up?"

"I need you to come see me."

"You nee—are you okay?" My heart stuttered. If anything happened to Nana . . .

"Of course I'm okay. Stop stammering, girl."

Tanner, still hovering close enough to hear her strident tones, snickered.

I placed a muffling hand over the phone.

"Excuse me, *sir*," I said sweetly. "Don't you have a forgery to Bubble-Wrap?"

"Forgery?" His stunned look was so comical I forgave myself for rushing to a verdict before

7

my usual careful perusal. Not that I was in any serious doubt about this particular painting.

"Really?" he said, broad shoulders slumping. When I arrived on scene, he boasted they'd turned up art so hot it was still smoking.

"Yup. Fake." I, too, felt a pang of genuine regret that the "Renoir" hanging in the drug dealer's den wasn't the one on the FBI's Ten Most Wanted list.

But I'd left Nana hanging.

Straightening my shoulders, I put the phone back to my ear. "Sorry, Nana. Um, I have to be at the youth drop-in center by seven to teach the art class, so . . ." I glanced at my watch and cast about for a workable solution, but there just wasn't enough time. "I'm afraid—"

"Never mind," she interrupted. "Obviously, you're at work." *Where you shouldn't be taking personal calls,* her tone implied. "Call me when you get home."

"Okay," I said to dead air.

Annoyed at myself for the guilty feeling I couldn't stop from churning my stomach, I turned to study the front of the house once more. Something was niggling at my brain.

"Um . . . Tanner," I said, hesitating.

"Yeah?"

"There's something . . ." I squinted against the dropping September sun, mentally reviewing the interior.

He grinned. "Stop stammering, girl. Spit it out."

8

"Ha, ha." *Wait* . . . "Oh, that's got to be it!" I stuffed my phone in my pocket and headed back inside.

Tanner followed me. "What's *it?*"

I stopped at the door to the den and glanced at the window three feet from the side wall.

"Serena? What's going on?" Tanner pressed, trailing me to the next doorway, this one into a bedroom.

"The window is three feet from the wall, just like in the other room."

"So?"

"Where's the attic hatch?"

"Mason checked the attic."

"Humor me."

"Don't I always?" Tanner said. "I'm a funny guy."

"Uh-huh." He actually had the quickest wit of any guy I knew, even if he did run to cheesy puns sometimes.

Not that I'd admit that to him.

"Over here." He steered me toward a step-ladder set up near the back door. "But there's nothing up there except insulation and mice."

"Mice, huh? Are you trying to scare me out of looking?" I started climbing, and Tanner moved in to hold the ladder steady.

I pushed open the hatch and stuck my head into the attic.

"See?" Tanner said.

"Yes, I do." I stepped down a couple of ladder rungs and flashed him a grin. "A false wall six to eight feet in from the back of the house."

Tanner squeezed past me and beamed his flashlight around the vacant space. "Unbelievable. Mason should've caught that."

"The wall's covered in cobwebs and dust. It wouldn't have registered unless you were looking for it."

Tanner muttered something I couldn't make out, but having been on the receiving end of his displeasure during my FBI training—granted, always earned—I didn't envy poor Mason.

Tanner hoisted himself into the attic, then balance-beamed his way across a joist to the wall and examined every inch of it. "I don't see any way to access what's behind it." He shone the light over the attic's insulation-covered floor and then the shoe impressions he'd left in the dust on the joist. "It doesn't look like anyone else has been up here recently. There must be another ceiling access panel." He climbed back down, eyeing me with interest. "How'd you know to look for a secret room?"

I shrugged evasively.

Tanner followed me back to the room where the fake Renoir had been found and swept his flashlight beam over every inch of the ceiling. "There's no other way up there that I can see."

I maneuvered around the agent photographing

evidence. The wall between this room and the next was decorated in wood panels and elaborate moldings that looked uncomfortably familiar. I ran my fingers along the moldings.

Tanner studied me. "What are you doing?"

"Looking for a secret panel."

"Uh-huh. And you seem to know exactly what you're doing here, Nancy Drew, because . . . ?"

I expelled a breath. "There was one at my grandfather's house, okay?"

"Your grandfather? The one who was murdered?"

"Yes." I blew away a strand of long, blond hair that had escaped my ponytail. "Maybe you could be helpful instead of giving me the third degree?"

"Sorry." Tanner beamed his flashlight at the section of paneling I was running my hands over.

My breath caught as my fingertips made contact with the pressure sensor I'd been seeking. "Tanner, I've found—"

"Wait!"

Primed to open it, I tossed a frown over my shoulder. "Are you really going to pull the SWAT-clears-every-room-first rule on this one?"

"No, I thought I'd rock-paper-scissors you for the privilege." He motioned me to get out of his way.

My finger still on the sensor, I sidestepped two feet so he'd have a clear view as I pulled back the panel. "You ready? I'll slide it open and you can call the all-clear." I slid it three-quarters of an inch and froze. "Uh-oh."

Tanner cursed. "Please tell me you're messing with me."

I gulped. "You don't hear that ticking?"

He crouched down and shone his flashlight through the gap I'd opened. "Blast, Serena, don't move a muscle."

Yeah, got that.

"Blast!"

"Tanner, could you *stop* using that *word?*"

"Everybody out!" He shooed away the agents conducting the search. "We've got a bomb, people. Move it. Send Douglas in here. And call in the rest of the bomb squad. Now!" Tanner returned to my side. "You okay?"

Sweat slid down my temple and into my eye. My arm was trembling from the strain of trying to hold the panel still. "Do I look like I'm okay?" I said through gritted teeth.

Tanner squatted at my side once more and squinted at the gap. "The panel's been spring-loaded." He angled his flashlight in another direction. "And we're looking at enough C-4 to level the house if you make a wrong move." An expletive slipped out. "Tell me more about the setup at your grandfather's house."

I squeezed my eyes closed, then opened them again and looked Tanner in the eye without moving my head. "There was a secret staircase behind a panel exactly like this one. He figured it was built to aid the Underground Railroad."

"You mean like the caves under the cobblestone streets at Laclede's Landing?"

"Kind of, but his led to the attic, not a tunnel." I closed off the memories before they could—

"Hey," Tanner said softly, giving me the little half smile that crinkled the laugh lines around his eyes. "It's okay. We're going to get you out of here."

"I know." He'd never let me down.

I concentrated on his six feet four inches of solid muscle reassuringly standing between me and the opening, and an idea made its way to my brain. "If you can find something the same width as my two fingers, I think there's enough back pressure on the panel to hold it in place."

Tanner shook his head. "If you're wrong, we'd have less than two seconds to clear that window."

I squinted at the small slider.

"It's eight feet away. And painted shut. Not an option, Jones."

"What about tacky putty? That'll stay put."

Tanner looked at the gap and nodded. "That could work." He shoved a couple of squares of chewing gum into his mouth.

"No, it can't," Special Agent Spencer Douglas of the St. Louis Division's bomb squad said, entering the room. "The spring pressure could make the

13

panel squish it like a raisin. Give me a chance to see what we've got before you try any heroics."

I gulped. Okay, this was worse than I thought. Much worse.

"How are you going to access the bomb if she can't move?" Tanner demanded.

"Check the next room for another access panel," I said. I cleared my throat, embarrassed by the quaver in my voice.

"Did your grandfather's place have a second one?" Tanner asked.

"Yes."

Tanner shot Douglas a look. "Be careful. It could be booby-trapped too."

Douglas motioned Tanner out of the way, then fished a tiny camera through the crack and slanted the viewer so we could see it with him. "There's a staircase."

"Our access to the secret attic room," Tanner said, sounding pleased. "Just like Serena called it."

"Hello? Bomb, people!" I reminded them.

Douglas turned the camera toward the stack of C-4. "Looks like we might have a way in from the other side that's not booby-trapped. You two"—he motioned to Mason and a bomb squad member—"check the next room for another panel."

As the sound of heavy furniture being moved vibrated across the floor, Douglas moved the camera around the bomb. "The detonator appears simple enough to disarm."

He glanced up at Tanner and me. "I don't get it. The drugs were left in plain view. The money was stuffed in the wall safe. So why plant a bomb?"

"There's got to be something we're not seeing. What could be so important that they'd blow up everything to protect it?" Anticipation welled in my chest despite the scant quarter-inch of wood between me and an armload of plastic explosives.

Douglas pulled back the camera. "They're in. Time to get out, Tanner."

"Not. Leaving. My. Wingman," Tanner ground out. His eyes radiated sincerity, holding mine with fierce intensity.

My heart did a ridiculous flip. "Don't be an idiot," I said as Douglas shook his head and left the room to supervise the bomb's defusing. "There's no point in both of us risking our lives."

Tanner's serious look morphed into mirth, making me miss whatever Douglas had barked on the other side of the wall.

"I can't believe you didn't catch that reference, Miss Movie Buff," Tanner said, grinning.

"Huh?"

"*Top Gun.*" He leaned in close to me, taking distract-Serena-from-the-bomb to dangerously stupid levels, and smiled. "Tom Cruise, right?"

I blinked.

Oh for crying out loud. *Really?* "You think

now is an appropriate time for this?" My voice squeaked a little, to my mortification.

Okay, so I had a habit of connecting people to their Hollywood look-alikes. And I'd never told Tanner who I thought his doppelganger was. But was this really the time?

Tanner's calm was unnatural. "I can't go to my grave not knowing what movie star you think I look like."

"I—" *Wait a minute.*

Something was fishy here. I mentally reviewed what Douglas had said . . . and that I'd missed some of it. "Did he just give you the all clear?" I demanded.

Tanner's eyes widened into a picture of innocence, and my arm twitched as I quelled the urge to punch him.

"Hey, careful." His hand shot out to steady mine, and my heart tripped over another beat. "Your mother would kill me if I let you get blown to smithereens." He grinned. "And now that your Aunt Martha is buddy-buddy with that Malgucci mob guy," he went on, "your mom wouldn't even have to get her hands dirty. She could probably get Malgucci's *family* to do me in for free."

This time I did smack him.

Douglas pushed the panel open from the other side and held up the stack of C-4. "You're batting two for two, Tanner. Your Renoir was a forgery, and so's your bomb."

"I guess they hoped it would be enough to scare off any nosy parkers," Tanner said, and he must've felt me tremble because he wrapped an arm around me and gave me a brotherly jostle. "Hey, pull yourself together." He radioed in the rest of his SWAT team. "We have a secret room to explore."

The instant the musty smell from inside the wall reached my nostrils, memories assaulted me. Okay, I clearly hadn't been thinking straight when I'd been ready to traipse into the narrow, windowless, suffocatingly stuffy stairwell that led to the attic's hidden room.

Now that I'd come to my senses, I stepped back to let the SWAT team do their thing. I slipped outside to grab a breath of fresh air and escape the memories.

In the driveway, the drug dealer's 1960s Corvette had been ruthlessly disassembled by agents who'd slapped the search warrant in his hand within minutes of his return from a Kansas car show. They'd recovered thirty kilos of cocaine hidden inside the body.

A good haul, but they'd been hoping for a lot more—drugs and cash.

Itching to know if they'd found anything in the attic, I headed back inside.

Tanner whistled from the secret passage's opening. "Look what we found." He held up a painting of a ballerina. "A Degas and enough cash

17

to put you in Agent Dunn's good books for a long time."

I chuckled. Special Agent Dunn was with the drug task force and in charge of today's search. "Good, never know when I might need a favor."

Tanner set the painting down beside the forged Renoir I'd propped against the wall. "What are you doing?"

I accessed the FBI's database of stolen art on my smartphone. "Combing through descriptions of missing Degases."

Tanner peered at the forged Renoir. "How could you tell this was fake? I didn't see you use a black light on it or anything."

"We used to use black light to look for the fluorescing given off by new signatures added to old paintings. It makes them look like they float off the page."

"Yeah, I knew it was something like that."

I bit back a smile. "But nowadays, a good forger would use non-fluorescing paint or a masking varnish to counter the effect."

"Okay, so how did you figure out it was fake?"

"The cracks. As canvas ages, the paint cracks."

Tanner frowned at the forgery. "It has cracks."

"Sure, but a naturally aged piece has random cracks. See these?" I pointed to the predomi-nantly vertical cracks on the forgery. "Forgers, trying to duplicate the cracks, bake the finished piece, then roll it in various directions. But the deepest cracks inevitably show up in the first direction the canvas is rolled."

Tanner peered more closely. "Huh."

A member of the evidence recovery team handed me Bubble-Wrap for the paintings, then slapped Tanner on the back with a chuckle. "He thought we'd scored a major coup."

"You find anything on the Degas?" Tanner asked, ignoring the friendly goading.

"Not yet." I quickly wrapped and labeled the paintings for transport. "I'll have to follow up on it tomorrow. I need to get to the drop-in center."

Tanner scooped up the leftover wrapping materials and followed me outside.

Yvonne, an agent working the search warrant and fellow movie buff, flagged me down. "I got that movie you wanted to borrow in my car." She hurried off.

"You should watch *Top Gun*," Tanner said.

"*Ha!* For the record, you look nothing like Tom Cruise. You have black hair and have got to be four inches taller than him."

"But good-looking, right?"

I rolled my eyes.

"What? You don't think Cruise is good-looking?"

I restrained a grin.

Yvonne returned with the movie before I'd finished loading the paintings.

Tanner took the DVD from her. *"How to Steal*

a Million," he read aloud and chuckled. "The bureau not paying you enough?"

I plucked it from his hands. "I'll take that. Thank you, Yvonne!"

She waved, already heading back inside. "Anytime. Enjoy."

"A romantic comedy heist, huh?" Tanner went on. "At least it's not in black and white like the one you subjected me to when I was sick. I could probably endure it if we watched it over pizza."

"No need. I hadn't planned on subjecting you to it. Nate *wants* to watch it with me."

"Nate? Your *building superintendent* Nate?"

"That's right."

"He likes old movies?"

"Yes."

"That explains a lot," Tanner muttered under his breath.

"You have a problem with Nate?" If either of them should have a problem with the other, it should be Nate with Tanner, considering Tanner had mistaken him for a prowler and practically dangled him off the landing outside my door at gunpoint.

Tanner raised his hands and backed away. "No, no problem. You can watch movies with whoever you like."

My heart reenacted the crazy flip it had pulled when Tanner refused to leave my side during the bomb scare.

And men wish women came with a manual.

2

The youth drop-in center where I taught painting classes was housed in a former butcher shop on a sketchy street in the North End. My grandfather started the art program to give disadvantaged youth the opportunity to explore their creative side.

On something other than the sides of buildings, as Tanner liked to add.

The drop-in center sat between boarded-up shops that weren't always as vacant as they should be, so I liked to park my car where I could keep an eye on it through the center's large front window. But tonight, Nana's silver BMW occupied my usual spot. *This can't be good.*

Yes, Nana continued to sponsor the art program in Granddad's honor, but she never visited. The neighborhood made her acutely uncomfortable.

Not that I blamed her. I was a gun-carrying federal agent, and the hair on the back of my neck had prickled more than once when leaving at the end of a class. I pulled in behind her car, my stomach churning. Finding the secret passage had roused too many memories of Granddad's murder. I wasn't sure I could keep my emotions in check if I had to face her.

I inhaled a fortifying breath and cast a fleeting

glance at the men loitering in the alley. The bells above the door jingled as I opened it.

Nana grabbed my arm with a surprisingly firm grip and tugged me toward the office. "I need to talk to you."

I tossed an apologetic glance to my assistant, who was setting art supplies on the easels for the arriving students. Nana had never been one of those bake-you-cookies and read-you-stories types. Her elegant clothes and perfectly coiffed hair had made her seem unapproachable somehow. That and her sharp tongue. As a kid, I'd always been on pins and needles the second I walked in the house and caught a whiff of her flowery scent. Even at twenty-eight, I still harbored my old trepidation. And it was doubly annoying that Tanner had noticed how she pushed my buttons.

I hung my jacket and purse on the coat tree next to the office door. Nana closed the door behind us, then twisted closed the blinds in the window overlooking the main room.

Oh no, whatever bee was in her bonnet was worse than I'd feared.

She turned to me, her ruby-red lips quivering. "I need a favor."

Whoa! I'm sure I must've looked like one of those bulgy-eyed cartoon characters, because for a few seconds all I could do was stare at her. "From me?"

"It's for a friend."

I squinted at her skeptically. *For a friend* was usually code for *it's for me, but I don't want to admit it.*

Apparently reading my thoughts, she let out a disgruntled huff. "For Gladys Hoffemeier. Someone stole a painting from her house."

Ridiculously, my heart lifted. Not that I was happy her friend had been burglarized, but that Nana would actually come to me. She'd never expressed much regard for my career choice. "Has Gladys reported the theft to the police?"

"No." Nana's voice dropped to a whisper. "Her son is on the force and she doesn't want him to know."

"Why?"

"That's not important."

It was if she suspected him. "When did this happen?"

"She's not sure. It could've been more than a fortnight."

Intrigued, I sat behind the desk and pulled out a pen and paper. "Which painting was stolen?" I'd been in Mrs. Hoffemeier's mansion as a child. Her art collection was quite valuable, so chances were good the painting was worth over 100K and the investigation would fall under my jurisdiction. I hoped so, because I didn't want to face Nana's agitation if I had to tell her the theft was a police matter.

Nana pulled the paper and pen away from me.

"The investigation needs to stay off the record."

The demand wasn't one I hadn't heard before. Rich folks hated to admit to being hoodwinked in any way that might undermine their social standing, but Nana's friend or not . . . "Until I know the facts, I can't help her. Or make any promises."

Nana returned the pen and paper. "Okay, okay. It's her Degas."

No way! My insides did a little happy dance. Could helping Nana and solving the mystery of the Degas I'd recovered this afternoon be this simple? "Do you know the painting's title?" I asked, imagining pride in my grandmother's eyes as I presented her friend with her missing Degas.

"No. But the burglar left a forgery of it in its place, if that helps."

Wow, forgeries were turning up left, right, and center. It must've been better than the Renoir at the drug dealer's for Gladys not to notice the switch.

Then again, maybe she was having financial trouble and swapped it out herself. It'd explain why she was reluctant to report the crime.

"Were you the one who noticed the switch?" I asked. Nana had always loved to scrutinize what hung on others' walls. She might've trotted out the fact that her granddaughter was an art crime detective to elevate her ability to help, clueless that our help might be the last thing Gladys wanted.

"No, the appraiser did."

"An insurance appraiser?"

"No, he works for one of those big New York auction houses."

So Gladys had been hoping to raise some money. "Is she sure the painting she has now is a substitute? Unscrupulous dealers have been known to pass off forgeries to unsuspecting buyers."

Nana shot me an indignant look. "Of course she's certain. And the appraiser said the paperwork she had appeared in order."

Outside the office, the noise level rose, my students no doubt growing impatient to start. "Listen, I need to teach my class now. How about you make arrangements for us to visit Gladys tomorrow so I can examine the fake and get the full story from her?"

"No, that's no good. If you investigate on the bureau's time, they might ask questions. We'll visit her tonight after you finish here."

"Uh . . ." Any other night, my FBI agent alter ego—not to mention my little-girl desire to please my grandmother—would've pounced at the opportunity. But after today's bomb scare, I desperately needed downtime. "I can't tonight. I already have other plans."

"Work-related?"

"No."

"Then change them."

I stiffened at her demanding tone. "If I'm to investigate the theft, I do it officially. I can see her first thing in the morning." Sure, Nate would understand if I bailed from our movie night and I was eager to see if Gladys's missing Degas was the same one I'd found, but where the investigation was concerned, Nana needed to know I was in charge.

Nana let out a disapproving tut. "You always were a contrary child."

I ignored the sting and forced a smile. "You can let her know I'll stop by at nine tomorrow morning."

"Yes, yes." With a dismissive wave, Nana let herself out my office door and tripped over someone's foot. "Who are you?" she demanded of the guy crawling past the door on all fours.

By the time I hurried out behind her, the guy was sitting on his heels below my office window. "What are you doing?" I demanded. He looked like the beach-bum actor Owen Wilson with his shaggy, windswept blond hair, distinctive nose, and quirky smile.

"I'll tell you what he was doing. He was listening in on our conversation." Nana smoothed her hair bun. "I'll see you in the morning."

"Family," the man chortled once Nana was out of earshot. "They're always throwing how we acted as kids back in our faces."

So he had overheard the conversation, but was

it because he'd been deliberately listening? "And you are?"

He pushed to his feet. "Ted."

"Ted who?"

"Ted's Pest Control." He spoke in a southern drawl that even sounded like the comedic actor he looked like. He poked his head into my office and flicked the light switch, eyeballing the fluorescents. "I noticed the lights flickering and thought you might have mice chewing your wires."

I glanced at my assistant.

She shrugged, which I took to mean this was the first she'd noticed him. Our art students stood behind their easels, watching us curiously.

"I appreciate your offer to help." I walked Ted-with-no-last-name toward the door. "Do you have a business card? I'll pass it along to our board chair." *After dusting it for fingerprints.*

"Nah, sorry." He perused the students' artwork hanging on the walls as I urged him along. "These are good." He pointed to one by Tyrone, my best pupil. "That one looks like a Basquiat. Who did it?"

I pointed out Tyrone, whose chest had visibly swelled at the comparison of his work to that of the first black contemporary artist to skyrocket to success in the art world. Tyrone resembled a young Will Smith and was as gifted an artist as his likeness was an actor.

I snagged a couple of fundraiser brochures from the stack by the door and pressed them into Ted's hand. "Perhaps you'd be interested in being a business sponsor? Oh wait, I think I gave you two." I attempted to reclaim the top one, sure to sport a clean thumbprint, but he held firm.

"No problem." He stuffed both in his pocket. "I'll share them around."

Right. Or he was onto my amateur attempt to get his prints in case there was something to Nana's suspicions.

My stomach growled as Nate opened his apartment door in response to my knock.

His rumbly laughter welcomed me inside. That and the delicious aroma wafting from his kitchen. "Are you ranivorous?"

"If that's a new way to say *starving,* yes. I didn't have time to grab dinner before going to the art class."

"I guess Mr. Sutton didn't relay the word of the day to you yet?"

"Uh . . . no. Should I be . . . horrified by what I just said yes to?" Mr. Sutton was my elderly next-door neighbor on the second floor, a retired English professor who delighted in helping us expand our vocabularies with a new word each day.

Nate relieved me of my bag, still chuckling. "Only if you don't like eating frogs."

"O-kay." Not exactly the chicken wings I thought I smelled, but . . . "Can't say I have a position either way on that one. I've never tried them."

My Aunt Martha toddled out of Nate's kitchen. "Well, today's your lucky day." She held out a platter of—

"Ew, ew. *Ew!* They still have their little webbed feet attached." I suddenly didn't feel hungry.

"That's what *I* said," Nate replied. "They've got to feel weird going down the throat."

I shuddered.

Aunt Martha shook her head at us as if we were wimps. "You two need to learn to live a little." She used to live in the apartment I now shared with her cat, Harold, and often returned to visit everyone, especially Nate, her favorite apartment superintendent.

"In my day," she went on, "I was game to try just about anything. Sometimes didn't have much choice."

Aunt Martha was my mother's never-married aunt, of an age she wasn't willing to disclose. Once upon a time, she'd been the secretary to a wealthy business tycoon and, *if* the tales could be believed, had traveled the world with him. Not that Aunt Martha would lie. She just liked to embellish a little.

"It'll be good practice for you, Serena," Aunt Martha went on. "You never know when you might have to go undercover and pretend to be a wealthy, caviar-and-frog-leg-eating art collector."

I clutched my stomach. Caviar? Okay, now I just wanted to gag. "I'm pretty sure I could just say I'm allergic."

"Or a vegan," Nate suggested as if he had first-hand experience at getting out of such sticky situations. He lifted the movie from my coat pocket and grinned. "I've been looking forward to this all day."

"Oh my, look at the time." Aunt Martha set the plate on the kitchen table and hooked her coat over her arm. "I need to get home."

It was hardly a secret that if I let Aunt Martha pick a man for me, the movie-star-handsome Nathan Butler, with his pale blue eyes and sandy brown hair, would be her first choice. Thankfully, Nate seemed as comfortable as I was with ignoring the innuendoes and merely enjoying each other's company with no strings attached.

Nate handed Aunt Martha back the plate. "Why don't you take the frog legs up to Mr. Sutton before you go? I'm sure he'll get a kick out of them, given his word of the day."

"If you're both sure you don't want to try them?"

"We're sure," we said in unison as I opened the door for her.

Aunt Martha tsked. "Your loss."

After I'd closed the door behind her, Nate said, "People say they taste like chicken."

"Yeah, people say a lot of things. Doesn't mean they're true."

Nate ushered me to the sofa.

The table in front of it was filled with a platter of cheese and crackers, a bowl of popcorn, a pitcher of lemonade, and . . . a plate of chicken wings! "Can I kiss you?" I burst out, whirling about to thank him. I gulped at the sparkle in his eyes. *Talk about a Freudian slip.* No, what was I saying? That would mean I *wanted* to kiss him.

Harold wound himself around my legs, purring loudly.

I snatched him up. "Hey, big guy," I cooed, burying my heated cheeks in his fur. "Let me guess, Aunt Martha brought him down?"

"I don't mind." Nate must've guessed that I'd grabbed Harold to subvert any attempt to actually kiss me, because he popped the DVD into the player. "This way Martha doesn't have to choose between visiting me and Harold."

Harold had been Aunt Martha's cat and was one of the reasons she'd begged me to take over her lease when her temporary, post-hip-surgery stint at my parents' house turned permanent. My stomach grumbled once more, winning me a chuckle from Nate.

"I guess it's trying to tell me something." I tried to put Harold down, but his claw snagged in my long hair. "Ouch. Ouch. *Ouch.*"

Nate clasped the cat's paw and gently freed the

lock of hair, his warm breath teasing the wisps fluttering at my cheeks.

"Thank you." I looked up, and my breath caught. I teetered, our lips mere inches apart.

Nate tucked the lock of hair behind my ear, his dimples winking through the whiskers dusting his cheeks. And for an eternal moment, time seemed to be suspended.

Then the movie company's theme song blasted from the TV.

I sprang back, dropped the cat, and scooped up a cracker and cheese instead. I stuffed them in my mouth. "Mmm, thank you for this."

"I thought you might be hungry." Nate's wink did funny things to my already-flummoxed tummy. Now there was a word of the day for Mr. Sutton.

Nate reached for the lemonade pitcher. "Martha heard you almost got blown up at a drug bust today. That true?"

I shook my head in disbelief, surprised that she didn't stick around long enough to grill me about it herself. "Where does she hear that stuff?"

"So it's *not* true?" Nate paused in the middle of pouring a glass of lemonade, his gaze snagging mine.

I should've known he wouldn't let the evasion slide. I sank my teeth into my bottom lip. "I think I'll plead the Fifth on that one."

His chuckle sounded forced as he finished

filling the glass. "I'm glad you're okay. What were you doing at a drug bust anyway? I thought you were on the major theft squad."

"They thought they'd uncovered a stolen Renoir in the raid, but it turned out to be a forgery."

Nate's head cocked sideways. "So why the glint in your eye?"

"I don't have a glint in my eye."

"Yeah, you do. The kind you get when you're on a new art case."

"You're making that up." I didn't know how to read his mischievous look as he stretched out on the other end of the love seat, propping the popcorn bowl between us.

He grinned at me unrepentantly. "Tell me I'm wrong."

I shrugged. "It doesn't look as if it'll amount to a case for me. Like I said, the painting was a forgery." Except maybe for that Degas painting. Nana would be so pleased if I recovered her friend's stolen piece.

Nate tossed a kernel of popcorn in his mouth, still looking far too amused. "Uh-huh."

"What's that supposed to mean?"

Holding my gaze, he leaned closer. "That little smile you just cracked, not to mention the glint in your eye, tells me you're on to something."

I rolled my eyes and popped another cracker into my mouth. It was downright unnerving how adept Nate had gotten at reading me. Made me seriously question my aptitude for the latest undercover gig the director of the Art Crime Team had conscripted me for.

"Aren't you going to track down the forger? Chances are good he's local, don't you think?"

I gnawed on a chicken wing to rein in the smile tugging at my lips. It was too much to hope for to imagine the Renoir had been copied from the original. But if I could find out who forged Gladys's piece, chances were good that I could convince him to tell me who bought it.

Nate's eyebrow lifted expectantly as I took my time wiping sauce from my fingers.

"Copying paintings isn't a crime, but yes, I plan to try to find the forger. There's a professor at Wash U who's made a study of forgers. I'm hoping he might be able to identify my artist."

"You talking about Ledbetter?"

"You know him?"

"The newspaper had an article about him a few weeks ago. He's on a sabbatical in Italy for the fall semester, studying the masters."

My chest deflated a little too audibly.

Nate's expression turned sympathetic. "I guess the FBI won't pay for you to hop a plane to Italy to pay him a visit?"

"Hmm."

"Hey, I know where you might score a lead." Nate snatched up the remote and flicked off the TV. "Let's go."

"Go where? I thought we were watching a movie."

"We can do that anytime. You have to set the bait before news of the FBI's find hits the streets."

"Bait for what?"

"Your forger."

Now look who was sporting a giddy glint in his eye. "And where are we going to set this bait?" I asked, deciding to humor him.

"The Grotto. It's an underground bar popular with the avant-garde crowd."

"If it's so popular, why haven't I heard of it?"

"We're talking the kind of experimental art someone would need a crane to steal."

"Ah. And how do you know about it?" Hanging out at a bar didn't fit the impression Aunt Martha had given me of her favorite apartment superintendent.

"My brother went through a stage where he thought he might like to be an artist."

"Interesting." Nate didn't talk much about his family. I knew his brother was his only living relative, and that his grandfather had bequeathed them each a couple of valuable paintings. And that his brother had sold his to live the good life, while Nate held on to his. "What happened?"

"He realized the term *starving artist* was coined for a reason."

"Ha! But you think someone at the bar might know a good forger?"

"A guy's got to eat, no matter how *progressive* his views on art." He stuffed what was left of the chicken and cheese in his fridge and covered the rest of the snacks with plastic wrap. "Sometimes that means painting a portrait for a business mogul, sofa art for a furniture store, or a copy of a soon-to-be-ex-husband's six-figure Monet."

Goosebumps rippled my arms. "Do I want to know how you know all this?"

3

Nate didn't answer my question on how he knew so much about forgers. Instead, the corners of his lips twitched, and he lifted his shoulders in the slightest of shrugs.

He was baiting me, but I couldn't resist. I grabbed Harold and my coat and bag. "You know if anyone there recognizes me, word will spread that I'm a Fed and no one will admit to anything."

"You're right. You need a disguise." He rummaged through his hall closet. "Your aunt left a cape here one time, and I forgot to return it."

Harold squirmed in my arms. Maybe this wasn't such a good idea. The FBI had strict rules about working only one undercover case at a time, and I was currently involved in an ongoing one based in Boston. Not that this was technically an FBI op. More like a whim.

Nate pulled a batik floral poncho, reminiscent of the '60s, from the back of the closet. "What do you think?"

"Very hippy."

"Yeah, it's perfect. Add a floppy hat and some glasses and nobody'll recognize you."

I grinned, imagining one better. "Give me ten minutes. I'll meet you at your car." I grabbed the poncho and dashed upstairs to my apartment. First, makeup.

I dropped everything, Harold included, on the bed and started with the outlandish false eyelashes I'd bought for a costume party next month. Next I swiped a streak of glittery green eye shadow over each eye, then pinned dark brown hair extensions beneath my shoulder-length blond locks, added a floppy sunhat, and—Voilà!

I glanced at my shoes. Okay, they wouldn't work. Far too sensible. I dug my pair of knee-high black leather boots out from the back of the closet and grabbed my tan, distressed-leather courier bag while I was at it. I dumped the contents of my purse inside, then zipped the boots up over my black leggings. Then I chose the biggest and brightest necklace I owned, courtesy of my aunt, and fastened it around my neck. Scooping Aunt Martha's poncho out from under Harold, I twirled. "What do you think?"

He yowled something that sounded unnervingly like "Not good. Not good. *Not good.*"

"Yeah, well, you're not my mother. Or my handler."

With one last don't-say-I-didn't-warn-you yowl, he turned his back and pawed at the bed.

"Whatever." Flouncing out, I snapped off the light and cheerily called over my shoulder, "Don't wait up!"

By the time I reached the parking lot, Nate was leaning against the hood of his car. He sprang up and did a double take. "Wow, I scarcely recognized you."

I grinned. "Good. All those years of playing dress-up are finally paying off."

He opened the passenger door of his Land Rover, and I slid in. I usually drove my FBI-issued sedan whenever I went anywhere, in case I got called to an emergency, but I sure couldn't show up anywhere in that car, looking like this.

Nate kept glancing my way as he drove.

"What?" I felt my face. "Is one of the eyelashes falling off?"

"No, I was trying to decide who you look like. You'll need a new name."

"Call me Sara. It's close enough to Serena that if you goof up, you can easily catch yourself."

"Good thinking." He parked. "Here we are."

"You weren't kidding when you said *under-ground*." The Grotto's entrance was off a back alley near The Loop, known for its trendy boutiques and nightlife. Only "The Grotto" didn't seem to fit the billing. Nate led me down steep, poorly lit stairs into the basement of a dry cleaning business. "You sure the place is still open?"

"The shady appearance is part of the appeal."

"Oh? Patrons like to think they're above the law?"

"Let's just say they weren't the kinds of kids who liked to color inside the lines." Nate reached around me for the door handle. "Follow my lead, Mrs. Thompson."

"Missus?" And where did *Thompson* come from?

"Trust me. This will work."

"You know I'm not wearing a wedding band, right?"

"That's okay."

The lounge wasn't lit much better than the stairwell, and a haze hung in the air from more than just the smoky pillar candles in the center of each table.

"Let's hope the police don't pick tonight to raid this place," I whispered close to Nate's ear. As my eyes adjusted to the lighting, I surreptitiously surveyed the room, and apart from one art dealer and a real estate agent, who I only recognized because his face was plastered on all his For Sale signs, I didn't recognize anyone.

"Nate!" shouted a shaggy-haired guy standing next to the bar.

"You're a regular?" I asked, not managing to keep the surprise from my voice.

Nate snorted. "Look again, *detective*." He clasped my hand and drew me toward the bar.

At his touch, something far too pleasant I didn't want to begin to try to identify zinged up my arm. I dragged my attention from our interlocked fingers and scanned Nate's friend.

He wore designer clothes that complemented his slim build. And his well-manicured hands, without a hint of paint staining the cuticles, didn't look like any painter's or sculptor's I'd ever met. A dealer's maybe?

As our eyes met, his seemed curious. No indication we'd met before, although something about him seemed familiar. "Should I know him?" I whispered to Nate.

"No, I guess not." Nate shook the guy's hand. "Randy, good to see you. I'd like you to meet Sara Thompson." Nate turned to me as the guy extended his hand in my direction. "Sara, this is Randy, my brother."

"Your br—" I choked down my surprise and returned Randy's limp handshake with a firm one. Even if we'd met on the street, instead of at this dive, his handshake alone would've told me Randy and Nate were nothing alike. Reminding myself to doctor my voice, I said, "Nice to meet you."

"A Brit. Very nice." Randy motioned to the bartender. "What'll you have?"

"Just a cola for me, please," I said, wondering if

Sara Thompson would be expected to order something stronger. We hadn't exactly fleshed out my identity, let alone backstopped it.

"Make that two," Nate added.

"Same old Nate." Randy grabbed his bottle of beer from the bar and led us to an empty table in the center of the room. "So what brings you here?"

"I want to hire someone to copy a painting, and Nate said this was the place to come."

"What kind of painting?"

Recalling Nate's story, I smirked. "One my soon-to-be-ex-husband doesn't want to part with."

Randy laughed so hard, beer spurted from his mouth.

Nate curled his arm around the back of my chair and whispered close to my ear, "You're a quick study."

I took that to mean I needn't worry about his brother's laughing fit.

Randy wiped his mouth with his sleeve as if it were flannel and not a two-hundred-dollar Armani. He shook his head at his brother. "And you're okay with this?"

I tilted my head his way, inexplicably pleased his brother expected him to be more straitlaced. Okay, yeah, not so inexplicable. I didn't want Nate to be the kind of guy who'd stoop to helping a woman forge a painting so she could steal the original—even if it were from a make-believe, deadbeat husband.

Ducking my head, I rubbed my fingers back and forth on the polished, dark-wood table and injected a self-conscious wobble into my voice. "I'm sorry, Nate. It wasn't fair of me to ask you. You're a better—"

Nate stopped my performance with a warm touch to my jittering fingers. "Any man who uses his wife as a punching bag deserves what he gets."

I caught myself staring at him. Where did he come up with this stuff?

Randy snorted and tipped back the rest of his beer. "You better hope her husband doesn't spot you holding her hand like that, or you'll be the punching bag."

I jerked my hand out from beneath Nate's and slipped it into my lap. "My husband's away on business at the moment."

"From my experience, men like that don't leave their women unwatched. If you know what I mean."

I gasped and darted my gaze about the room, as he would expect. "You think he'd have someone follow me?"

"It's likely. And not too many painters are going to like the odds."

"There's no one following her," Nate said in a tone that, from a mob guy like Malgucci or SWAT guy like Tanner, meant he'd made sure of it. But coming from Nate, it made me want to burst into laughter. The man used no-kill mousetraps, for goodness' sake. Not exactly the kind of guy who'd take someone out, abusive husband or not.

But Randy took him at his word without so much as a raised eyebrow. Pushing up from the table, he scraped his chair backward across the scarred oak floor. "Let me get another beer and ask around. See what I can come up with."

"Thanks, Randy," Nate said. "I appreciate it."

"Did you know your brother would be here?" I whispered once he was out of earshot.

"No, but it'll make finding you a forger a lot easier."

"Sure, until he asks to see my painting."

"Show him one from today's bust. The forger's reaction would tell you in a second whether he painted it or knew who did. Then you tell him you want to think about it and send in Serena Jones to question him further."

"If he figures out it was a setup, it could ruin you for this place."

Nate looked around and shrugged. "No great loss."

His brother strutted back to our table. "The guy I have in mind isn't here tonight. I'll have him get in touch with Nate, okay?"

"Thank you so much," I said breathlessly.

Nate shook his brother's hand once more, then whisked us outside.

"Sounds promising," I said as we climbed the stairs to street level.

He grinned. "That British accent is so—" He coughed nixing whatever descriptor he'd been about to use.

"Nate?" Tanner stood at the top of the stairs, his gaze shifting from Nate to me.

My stomach plummeted. I dipped my chin so my floppy hat blocked his view of my face. What was he doing here? Had he recognized me?

And why did I care?

Tanner frowned. "What are you doing here?" he demanded, his gaze fixed on Nate. Not me.

I hid a smile. He didn't sound any happier to see Nate out with *another woman* than he'd been about him watching a movie with me tonight.

"None of your business," Nate said, not sounding like Nate at all and clearly not appreciating how sweet Tanner was being, worrying about me being two-timed and all. Tanner looked at us as if he'd like to say more, but Nate slipped his hand through the crook of my arm and guided me past him.

Oh no. What if Tanner recognizes my walk or something?

Nate opened his passenger door for me, and at the burst of light, I tugged my hat brim lower and dove into the car.

Except I needn't have bothered. Tanner had turned his attention to his cell phone.

Unless . . . I scrabbled through my purse for

my phone. Nate shut the door just as my thumb found Mute. I peeked at my phone's screen, and Tanner's name appeared.

Whew! Thwarted him catching me out just in time.

As Nate slid behind the wheel and the car's dome light went out, I peeked from beneath my hat brim.

Tanner held his phone to his ear, frowning at me through the windshield.

Guilt tightened my chest. What if I was wrong and he'd just been checking up on me, maybe thinking Nate had stood me up? I didn't need to lie to him. Not really. He might've been disappointed in my lack of judgment, but he wouldn't have reported me.

I let the phone go to voice mail. Ten seconds passed, then a text came in. *You okay?*

My heart stuttered.

Nate glanced across at my phone. "He telling you he saw me with another woman?"

"No. Just asking if I'm okay." I typed in *I'm good. What's up?*

His next text came back: *I thought you might have trouble sleeping after today's scare.*

Warmth filled my chest. He didn't mention seeing Nate, apparently more reluctant to risk upsetting me than to prove Nate unworthy.

Nah, I'll just dream about a hunky hero coming to my rescue, I texted back, expecting

45

him to respond with the latest movie star he figured was his likeness.

He texted back a smiley face.

Sometimes the man was hard to figure out.

4

I finished off my morning run through Forest Park with leg stretches on the stairs to my second-floor apartment.

Mr. Sutton's frantic voice echoed through the stairwell. "If she's not answering, you should unlock the door. She might be hurt."

"She's probably out for her morning run," Nate said, his voice the epitome of patient reason and, considering I was the only woman in the building under seventy, he was talking about me.

I sprinted up the stairs to my floor. "What's up?"

Nate's warm smile made my pulse forget it was supposed to be in cool-down mode. "See, she was running," Nate said to my elderly neighbor, then to me said, "Your phone has been ringing nonstop for the past twenty minutes, and Mr. Sutton was concerned something had happened to you."

I squeezed Mr. Sutton's elbow. "Thank you. I appreciate you looking out for me."

He huffed. "Lot of good it does when all this

young man does is stand there and gongoozle your door."

Gongoozle?

Nate must've seen my confusion. "Means to stare at," he explained. "Today's word of the day."

"Ah."

My phone blared through the door. Wow, I really needed to turn down the volume on that thing.

"See," Mr. Sutton said. "Someone's desperate to get hold of you." He turned back to his door as I fit my key into my lock. "Don't forget the new word." He lifted his chin toward Nate with a chuckle. "That one has gongoozling down to an art."

I shot a glance back to Nate and caught him gongoozling me. I fumbled the key in the lock. The phone stopped ringing, then started up again. I refocused on the key. "I'd better see who that is."

"Sure thing. Have a good day. I'll let you know if I hear from my brother."

"That'd be great. Thanks." I tumbled into my apartment, hoping he'd attribute my breathlessness to my run, and snatched up the phone.

"Serena, it's about time you got up," Nana scolded. "I've been trying to reach you for half an hour."

"What's the matter?" I asked rather than explaining where I'd been. Knowing Nana, I was pretty sure she'd think I was being disrespectful or something.

"Gladys doesn't want you to come to her house. I think she's afraid the neighbors will see you and tell her son."

"Nana, if I'm going to investigate a theft from her house, I need to examine the scene of the crime."

"Of course, of course, but I was thinking we could make it seem like we'd run into you."

Oh no. I had a bad feeling about this. This sounded like the kind of crazy scheme Aunt Martha might dream up. "Are you sure Gladys wants me to investigate the theft?"

"What kind of question is that? Of course she does." The scolding tone I'd thankfully developed a bit of a thick skin to over the years rattled through the line. "Now, we go to the MAC for lunch on Fridays, so I thought perhaps you could *happen* to pass by as we arrive. Then I would, of course, invite you to join us."

Of course. The Missouri Athletic Club—or the MAC, as everyone called it—was founded in 1903 as a traditional gentleman's club, a place where the movers and shakers of society congregated to discuss business and enjoy recreational pursuits. As my grandmother liked to say, "Everybody who was anybody was a member." Although it wasn't until 1988 that the female half of that equation was welcome.

"Then we can steer the conversation toward art and figure out a way to finagle you an invitation to her house."

I definitely didn't like the sound of this. "You know, I've met Mrs. Hoffemeier's son. He seems like a pretty levelheaded cop. Why is she so concerned about him finding out about the burglary?"

"Can you be at the MAC or not?" she snapped.

I muffled a sigh. "What time do you want me there?"

"Eleven forty-five."

"Okay, I'll do my best. I'll call your cell phone if an emergency comes up."

"Another one?" The tone of her voice underlined how inconvenient that would be.

"Impossible to predict," I said blithely. *"Official* cases have to come first."

Nana hung up with a huff, and I probably enjoyed the moment of satisfaction more than I should, but it was easier on the nerves than fretting over why everything I did seemed to irk her.

I showered and dressed, then plunked a couple of pieces of toast into the toaster for breakfast. But when I swung open the fridge door to grab the jam jar, my stomach revolted. A plate of frog legs my aunt must've snuck in last night sat on the top shelf. I clamped my hand over my mouth and tried not to lose what little supper I'd eaten.

Harold chose that moment to plop between me and the open fridge and meow his isn't-there-anything-better-than-kibbles-to-eat-around-here rant.

I grabbed the plate of frog legs and set it on the floor in front of him. "Today is your lucky day." I cringed as he trotted off with a leg in his mouth, doggie-bone style. But then . . . "Oh no, wait!" I raced after him and caught the frog's leg by its foot. "Let go. You might choke on the bone."

Harold swung his head like a dog in a tug-of-war and refused to yield.

"I'll give it back. I promise. But you can't eat the bone." I wrestled it out of his mouth and raced back to the kitchen to scoop the plate off the floor before he could grab another one.

He swiped at my leg.

"Don't you start with me." I looked at the mangled frog leg in my hand and staunched the urge to upchuck. "Be grateful I'm not dumping the whole thing down the garbage chute." Holding my breath, I quickly tore the meat off the tiny bones and into his bowl, then tossed the bones in a plastic bag. "There," I said, washing my hands. "They almost look edible now." I plopped the bowl back on the floor. "Happy?"

He sniffed at the meat, then sat back on his haunches and looked up at me.

"It's the same meat!" I snatched up my bare toast and my coat and bag. "I want that bowl empty by the time I come home," I called to Harold. "And I don't want to find any coughed-up frog feet later, either." Oh man, I was starting to sound like my mother.

The phone rang. Mom.

"Oh good, you *are* home. Did Nana get hold of you?" she asked before I could spit out a hello. "She called here in a tizzy because you weren't answering your phone."

"Yes, we talked."

"What did she want? Aunt Martha figures it must be something big for how fired up she was."

I could just imagine the wheels spinning in Aunt Martha's brain, and I was pretty sure I could hear her breathing on the extension, so I hedged. "Nana wanted my opinion on a piece of art but needed to change our appointment." I didn't like to mislead them, but give Aunt Martha a potential mystery to solve and there was no holding her back. And Nana wouldn't appreciate her help. The pair could scarcely say three civil words to each other.

"Oh, well, I'm glad she got hold of you," Mom went on. "Aunt Martha mentioned you were watching a movie with Nate last night?" Her voice upticked in that can-I-order-the-wedding-invitations-and-start-knitting-booties way of hers.

"I'm afraid I need to go now, Mom, or I'll be late for work." Discussing the men in my life with my mother was not for the faint of heart—and definitely not something to undertake on an empty stomach.

By the time I'd made the fifteen-minute drive across town to FBI headquarters, I'd come up with a plan that would justify my *happening* to be in the neighborhood of the MAC around lunchtime and, better yet, a plan that gave me a reason to happen to have what I hoped would prove to be Gladys's missing Degas on me. An art restorer and acquaintance, Nicki Phelps, had a studio two blocks away and had a nifty piece of equipment that could quickly test the paint to tell me if it was even the right vintage for a genuine Degas.

But first I needed to backstop my alter ego's identity in case Nate's brother or his forger friend decided to look into my background.

My supervisor, Maxwell Benton, motioned me into his office the moment I reached the second-floor bullpen where my cubicle was one among dozens, flanked on one side by windows and the other by a long row of filing cabinets.

"What's up?" I asked him.

In his late forties and completely gray, Benton always reminded me of the actor Richard Gere, except he rarely sported the actor's easy smile. Today was no exception. He handed me a folder the instant I stepped into his office.

"What's this?"

"A copy of the list of financial records recovered from the drug dealer's safe. It includes several payments made in paintings instead of cash. I need you to track down where they came from and if they were real."

I scanned the list. The artists to whom the

paintings were attributed were new to me, with the exception of one. "Will do." I filled him in on last night's escapade at the bar. "With a bit of luck, we might connect with a forger who can give us a lead."

"Sounds good. Okay, get to work."

Tanner intercepted me as I reached my cubicle. "Everything okay?"

"Sure." I filled him in on Benton's request, then turned to my desk but sensed Tanner's gaze was still zeroed in on me. Peeling off my coat, I glanced his way once more. "Was there something else?"

He searched my eyes, apparently hesitant to say whatever was on his mind.

A sanity check after yesterday's bomb scare? Something about the case? An inquisition about Nate? My stomach somersaulted. Oh man, with the way it was tumbling around lately, maybe I should've taken my uncle up on that offer of free antacid samples from the Tums factory.

Tanner just said, "No, that was all," and returned to his own cubicle.

I let out a breath. My heart was actually racing. Ridiculous. I shook it off and turned my attention to the file Benton had given me. In most art-crime investigations, tracking down leads was as fruitless as searching for something recognizable in the paint spatters of a Jackson Pollock. In this case, the paintings listed in the log were all of moderate value. Nothing worth more than twenty-five thousand dollars. Nothing that would be too difficult to fence. And nothing that would attract a lot of media attention if stolen.

After a morning of computer searches and phone calls, I concluded none of the paintings had been reported stolen, which meant I didn't have anything on which to build a case against the drug dealer.

I headed downtown to get the Degas tested before my appointment with Nana. The weather was sunny, so I parked my car in the lot next to the athletic club, a ten-story, century-old building on Washington Avenue near Eads Bridge, and then walked the two blocks to Nicki's studio with the Degas safely tucked in a tote bag under my arm.

The studio was housed in a loft apartment in a converted garment factory building with a brick exterior that still had the tiny lion heads whose open mouths had at one time spewed steam from the clothes presses. I loved the nostalgic feel of the place, a perfect backdrop for Nicki's work.

She ushered me into a sunny room and pointed to an empty easel. "Set the piece here."

As I carefully unwrapped the alleged Degas, Nicki retrieved an electronic gadget I called her "art gun."

"The ballerinas certainly exude the spirit of Degas." She examined the back of the painting.

"The mahogany base was a common one for him. Did you find the image in the catalogue raisonné?" Nicki asked, referring to the official catalog of Degas's work.

"Yes. According to the write up, it was sold to a dealer in France in 1887. A colleague in France is seeing if he can trace what happened to it after that."

Nicki sighed. "If the painting's owner was Jewish, it was likely confiscated by the Nazis. The vast number of paintings lost during the war made for a perfect breeding ground for forgers in the decades that followed." She fiddled with the controls on her art gun and pointed it at the painting.

The electronic device could identify chemicals in oil paint, which would enable Nicki to deduce the pigments used.

"There's lots of mercury in it," Nicki said. "That was common in vermillion, a popular pigment used by Impressionist painters to create the brilliant scarlet."

"Is there any titanium white?" Since the pigment wasn't available before the 1900s, I knew that would be a certain giveaway. It was the discovery of that particular pigment in one of the master forger Beltrachi's pieces that led to his downfall. Of course, smart forgers, Beltrachi included, knew to avoid it, but that hadn't stopped him from unwittingly using a pigment containing it.

Nicki studied the readout of chemicals appearing on the gun's small screen. "No titanium white, but there isn't any arsenic either."

"What does that mean?"

"Arsenic and copper were the main components of emerald green. But arsenic was banned in the 1960s."

"So if you're not seeing any trace of it, the pigment unlikely predates the '60s."

"Exactly." She shifted the gun's aim to another section of the painting. "The concentrations of a couple of other chemicals are not typical to pre-1900s art either." She turned off the gun. "I'd say you're looking at a forgery."

My heart sank. I'd suspected as much, but if it turned out to be Gladys's missing painting, she wouldn't be happy to learn it was a fake. Or that Nana had lassoed me into the investigation. And I didn't even want to contemplate how Nana might react. Probably fume that I had no business questioning its authenticity. No one wanted to find out their prized painting was worthless.

Thanking Nicki, I wrapped the painting and hooked the tote over my shoulder a lot less carefully than I had for the walk over. The wind had picked up and tunneled down the street. I pressed the crosswalk button to escape the shadow of the buildings. Raised voices drew my attention to a couple emerging from a Ford

Bronco half a block down the other side of the street. The man fed a coin into the parking meter, ranting all the while, then opened the passenger door, rooted around inside for a second, and returned to the meter as the woman stormed off.

The crosswalk signal turned to WALK and some guy in a dark hoodie charged past me, sending me tumbling into the street.

5

"Hey, watch where you're going!" I shouted after the guy who'd knocked me to my knees. As I pushed to my feet, I glanced down at my suddenly lighter bag and back up in time to see Hoodie Guy hit the opposite sidewalk at a sprint, my painting under his arm.

"Stop, thief!" I shouted, racing after him.

He veered toward the Bronco. Or more precisely, the set of keys dangling from the passenger door's lock. He grabbed them and raced around to the driver's side.

"You picked the wrong person to pickpocket today, buddy." I vaulted off the bumper, over the hood, and dove onto his back, knocking the painting out of his hand.

"Are you crazy?" He swung around like a wild man, trying to shake me loose.

Tires screeched. The guy jumped back, slamming my back into the side of the Bronco, driving the breath from my lungs.

My grip loosened, and the guy took off on foot. I snatched up the painting before someone ran over it.

A white-haired lady jumped from a vehicle three cars back and pointed to an alley between two buildings. "He went that way!"

I took off to the sound of St. Louis PD cruisers squealing up from every direction. Wow, everyone and their grandmother must've called 911 the second I shouted "thief."

"Serena Jones, stop this instant!"

Nana? Since there was still no sign of my suspect, I skidded to a stop and returned to the street. Nana glowered at me from beside the white-haired lady who'd tipped me off.

I forced a smile. "Fancy meeting you here."

"This wasn't in the plan," Nana fumed for my ears only.

"I appreciate the invitation," I said cheerily, since the plan had been that we bump into each other and she invites me to join them for lunch. "I'll join you as soon as I can get away."

Gladys beamed at me. "That would be wonderful. You were wonderful out there. I'm glad you're okay. You are wonder—"

"Okay, okay," Nana shushed, fluttering her hand toward an approaching officer. "Let her finish her job so we can park."

I winked at Gladys, happy that at least Nana's

friend had been impressed by the takedown, even if my would-be mugger did get away.

An old schoolmate, Matt Speers, sauntered up to me in his spotless police uniform and dark shades, shaking his head. Amusement teased the corners of his lips as he pulled off his sunglasses. "Mind telling me what you were doing taking down a car thief in the middle of the street? He's not in your jurisdiction until he crosses the Mississippi."

I folded my arms and feigned indignation. "You could show a little gratitude. I saved you guys a lot of hassle."

"For your information, stunt woman wannabe, you grabbed him too soon. We can't charge him with stealing a car when he didn't even get the door open."

I laughed. "Are you telling me that was a bait car?" It explained how all the cruisers had gotten here so quickly.

"Uh, *yeah*. Nice swan dive off the bumper, by the way," he added with a smirk.

Oh great. "Don't even think of submitting that to funniest cop videos," I said mock-sternly. With a bait car, the cops would leave a vehicle unlocked with the keys "accidentally" dropped on the seat, or outside the door, or in this case, in the door lock. Then wait and watch. Since the car was equipped with cameras and the technology to remotely disable and lock it, a thief would soon find himself in custody. Or if the cops were having a really good day, the thief might first lead them to a chop shop, and a whole lot of people would find themselves in custody. "If it makes you feel better, if you catch him you can still charge him with theft. He stole a painting from my tote bag before he tried to steal the car."

Matt pulled out a notebook and pen. "That helps. What's it worth?"

"Not much. Listen, could we finish the interview later? I'm late for an appointment."

"Not much as in, under five thousand?"

I chuckled. "As in, less than fifty."

He dropped his hand holding the notebook and shot me an exasperated look. "And you figured that was worth pulling the I-can-fly stunt, why?"

"The painting is evidence in an investigation."

"Did *he* know that?"

Did he? I stared at Matt for a full three seconds, probably looking as whacked out as the women in Picasso's portraits who have two eyes gongoozling out one side of their faces. If I hadn't been side-tracked by Nana's appearance, it would've been one of the first questions I'd have asked myself. Except . . .

I shook my head. The Degas was a fake. The drug dealer had to know that and wouldn't go to the trouble of hiring a punk to get it back. Not to mention, no one knew I was bringing it to Nicki's.

The clock tower struck twelve, wailing *you're late, you're late, you're late* with each gong.

"I'm sorry. I've got to run. But please let me know if you get any leads on the mugger."

"Fine, go!"

I jogged back to the Missouri Athletic Club and found Nana and Gladys waiting for me in the luxurious sitting area to the left of the main entrance. The club's interior always made me think of old money with its richly paneled walls, ornate fixtures, and numerous paintings. Or maybe it was just the lingering smell from the cigar parlor.

"Serena, we're so glad you could join us," Nana crooned in the sweetest voice I'd ever heard her use with me.

The club boasted four restaurants, a ballroom, a barbershop, numerous private meeting rooms, a reading room, a billiard parlor, a rooftop deck, and eighty guest rooms, in addition to the full-service athletic facilities. I'd visited many times, as my grandmother's guest, to attend events in the ballroom or to eat. Yet somehow the place always made me feel as if I were walking on glass, as if one wrong step or word would result in a serious faux pas. Or maybe that was just the Nana-effect.

Gladys pressed her clasped hands to her chest with an eager "Yes, I can't wait to hear more about your work."

Nana's expression soured.

It would've been funny if it didn't remind me how many times she'd reiterated her opinion that my job was far too unladylike. Kind of ironic that she wanted to exploit it now.

And to get to eat at the MAC was a nice bonus. The food was fantastic. The club members—from company CEOs and bankers and lawyers to politicians and sports figures—wouldn't tolerate anything less.

The maître d' led us to a round table in the center of the room.

My gaze skipped over the nearby tables, and I did a double take. *Aunt Martha?*

She tootled her fingers as if she'd been expecting me.

I slanted a glance at Nana, but she hadn't seemed to notice her. How did Aunt Martha know I'd be here? I didn't tell Mom where or when I was meeting Nana.

It could be a coincidence. It wasn't unheard of for Martha to share lunch at the MAC with a member friend. Then again, it also wasn't beneath her to tail Nana all morning if she'd overheard me say I was meeting her and had guessed it might be concerning something interesting like an art theft.

Nana's clucking tongue cut through my thoughts. "Serena, sit. It's poor manners to stand there staring at others."

I sank into the closest seat and scarcely contained a groan at the sight of all the forks and spoons. Nana had spent countless Sunday dinners drilling the art of proper eating into my brother and me—a skill I could begrudgingly admit to appreciating now, considering the circles I sometimes needed to circulate in while investigating art crimes. But somehow, around Nana I always seemed to forget everything I'd learned.

Hopefully she'd be too preoccupied with the discussion to notice—I snuck a sideways glance at Aunt Martha—*to notice a lot of things.*

We ordered the daily specials, then Gladys asked about the man I'd apprehended. "You're so brave," she gushed. "The work must be very satisfying."

"It can be. It would be very satisfying to be able to help you recover your Degas."

Gladys shot Nana a flustered look.

What did I say wrong?

"It's a Dali, not a Degas," Nana hissed.

"But you said—"

"I certainly know the difference between a surrealist and an impressionist," she interjected.

My heart raced as if I were still eight instead of twenty-eight and not smart enough to know correcting Nana was taboo. "Of course." At least this meant the forgery in my tote bag *wasn't* Gladys's. I returned my attention to her. "I'm surprised you wouldn't ask for your son's help, though."

"Oh no. If he heard about"—she glanced around and lowered her voice—"*you know* . . . he'd be more determined than ever to put me in a home."

I wanted to argue, but I didn't know Pete all that well. "Very well, then the first thing we need to do is arrange a time for me to visit your house."

"I suppose we could go after lun—" Gladys's gaze lifted, and she let out a choked squawk.

"Hi, Mom." A male voice that could only be Pete Hoffemeier's sounded from behind me. "I saw you and Mrs. Jones walking in as I wrapped up a call and thought I'd join you for lunch, if that's okay."

Gladys's face lost some of its color.

"Of course it's okay," Nana jumped in.

Gladys pasted on a cheery expression. "Yes, and look who else we ran into outside. Stella's granddaughter, Serena."

I turned in my chair. "Hey, Pete, good to see you again." He was in his late thirties, not as tall as I remembered, maybe five eleven, and his dark hair had thinned quite a bit since I last saw him. He was dressed in the usual patrolman's uniform of a blue shirt and navy slacks and a gun belt weighted down with a good ten pounds of weapons, cuffs, and gadgets. Not typical attire for the MAC.

"Good to see you too. I heard you were the one who foiled our bait-car apprehension out there."

I shrugged. "Someone's gotta give you guys fresh fodder to fuel your FBI rants."

Laughing, Pete plunked down in the chair next to mine, then motioned to the waitress. "Could you add a steak sandwich to the order for this table?" He watched the waitress fill his water glass, then returned his attention to me. "So this little luncheon is the appointment you had to rush off to?"

My spidey senses went on high alert. Matt was the only one I'd told about my appointment. And he wouldn't have volunteered the information unless Pete had specifically asked about me. And there was only one reason why Pete would.

He didn't want me talking to his mother.

"My annual fundraiser for the art program at the drop-in center is coming up," Nana said when I failed to respond to Pete's question.

I nodded mutely at her explanation. After all, suspecting my grandmother's best friend's son of stealing said friend's missing Dali painting would not win me any brownie points here.

"She teaches a class at the center," Gladys added, apparently feeling the need to explain what the fundraiser had to do with me.

"That's great," Pete said, although his tone didn't match his words.

Gladys must've noticed, because she rushed on with, "Pete buys and sells real estate when he's not working."

"Really?" I said in my that's-fascinating voice. "How's that going?"

He traced lines through the condensation clinging to his glass of water. "It has its ups and downs."

Downs, huh? Struggling to recover from a financial hit would be a strong motive to develop sticky fingers. He'd certainly have had easy access to his mother's painting.

"He's too modest," Gladys protested. "He's a whiz at it. His father, God rest his soul, got him started doing it for his twenty-first birthday. He's done so well he could quit the police force if he wanted to." She patted Pete's hand and beamed at him. "But he enjoys serving the community."

Okay, so maybe his monetary motive wasn't as strong as I'd thought. His mother clearly didn't suspect him.

A plain, dark-haired woman materialized at Pete's side. "Well, isn't this cozy?"

"Hey, Tasha, good to see you." Pete stood and gave the woman a peck on the cheek. "Can you join us?"

A girlfriend?

"Not today. I'm meeting a friend." She rounded the table and leaned down to press a kiss to Gladys's cheek. "Hi, Mom."

Ah, his sister. Yes, side by side, the family resemblance was obvious—the close-set eyes, the flat cheeks, the slender nose. Like her mother she also wore expensive jewelry and designer clothes, although they weren't as flattering as one might expect. Then again, what did I know? I dressed for taking down bad guys, not picking up bad boys.

"You know Mrs. Jones," Gladys said to her

66

daughter by way of introduction. "This is her granddaughter, Serena."

Tasha limply shook my hand, her gaze bouncing from me to Pete.

"We're not together," Pete said. "She's FBI. It'd never work." He winked at me, which earned me a peculiar second look from Tasha.

"Is Lucas with you?" Gladys asked, then turned to me. "Lucas is her husband."

Okay, so scratch the picking-up-bad-boys remark.

"No, I'm meeting a friend." She waved across the room to another woman and headed off.

Our food arrived, and as the conversation waned, I started getting antsy. I could hardly bring up the stolen painting with Pete at the table when Gladys had made it clear she didn't want him to know. And I was sure I could feel Aunt Martha's gaze on us.

"Have you heard I specialize in art crime?" The question tumbled out of my mouth in a moment of recklessness, just to see how Pete would respond.

Gladys choked on her food. Nana shot me a scowl.

Pete seemed unfazed. "Yeah, you were called out to that Westmoreland burglary back in February, weren't you?"

"That's right. I—"

A man strode up to the table and slapped Pete on the back. "Hey, Pete, is that you? It's been a long time."

What was this, Grand Central Station? At this rate, I should have said I needed to get back to work and made arrangements to visit Gladys later. Once I had the full story on the missing painting, I'd have a better sense whether Pete's business dealings merited a closer look.

I flicked a glance at Pete's friend, and scarcely muffled my surprised squawk. What was Nate's brother doing here?

His head cocked inquisitively. "Do I know you?"

"No, I don't think so." Remembering to breathe, I redirected my gaze to my plate and prayed he wouldn't recognize me from last night.

He pulled up a chair between Pete and me.

"Excuse me, I need to use the ladies' room," I mumbled to Nana and Gladys, rising from my chair.

"You manage to sell that albatross yet?" Randy asked Pete.

My step faltered. Was he talking about Pete's real estate holdings? I stooped to tie my shoe, to stall long enough to catch Pete's response.

He made a face that I took to mean *no*.

Hmm, the plot thickens. Being saddled with an expensive piece of unsalable real estate could've conceivably left him in a financial pickle.

Across the room, Tasha also seemed to be more interested in the men's discussion than whatever her friend was saying.

Pete changed the subject, and I made a quick

visit to the ladies' room for appearance's sake. When I emerged, Aunt Martha was standing in the hall, chatting with Nate's brother.

I shrank back, debating the wisdom of passing them to return to the table.

"I imagine Nate's mentioned Serena," Aunt Martha said to him in a conspiratorial do-tell tone.

"Serena? No. Only Sara. The woman he was with last night."

"Last night? But—" She whirled toward the ladies' room door. "Oh, there's Serena now. Are you sure she's not who you saw him with?"

I froze. *Please don't recognize me as Sara.*

6

Randy grinned as our eyes met across the hallway outside the ladies' lounge on the second floor of the MAC. "We meet again." He extended his hand, and my breath lodged in my throat.

Was he talking about last night? Or back at the table?

"Your Aunt Martha tells me you're a friend of my brother, Nate."

"Ah—" I forced the lump from my throat. "Yes."

His grin widened as his fingers closed around mine. "He's been holding out on me."

Aunt Martha beamed at me, apparently forgetting that her favorite pick for me had been out with *another* woman last night. "Randy didn't realize we were related."

Randy's thumb lingered over an abrasion on the side of my hand that I must've gotten during the takedown. "You and Nate dating?"

"Just friends."

Aunt Martha rolled her eyes. "Only because she's as gun-shy as your brother."

I shot her the evil eye. She made it sound like I was afraid of commitment, when I was just being practical. What kind of guy wanted to put up with the hours I kept?

Randy chuckled, and I couldn't help but wonder if, unlike me, Nate really was gun-shy. And why.

Movement at the dining room's entrance seemed to catch Randy's eye, and he excused himself.

"What are you doing here? Following me?" I asked Aunt Martha, realizing too late that if I was wrong and her luncheon date had been entirely innocent, her antenna would shoot up now. After all, I wouldn't be worried about being spied on if I wasn't up to something I didn't want her to know about.

"Pfft." She waved off the accusation. "I was here before you." Only she didn't meet my gaze, and her hand was fluttering again. "You know if you keep taking every chap's interest for granted, one day you're going to find they've all gone shopping elsewhere."

Oh yeah, she was definitely deflecting. That was

70

my mother's line, not my happily single-all-her-life Aunt Martha's line.

"Okay, so you were following Nana to find out why she wanted to see me?"

"Nonsense! Your mum already told me that. She wanted your opinion on some art."

I searched her eyes, certain she was playing me. And not minding, really. But Nana would be livid if I spilled anything about Gladys's misfortune to Aunt Martha. "So you'll be heading home now?"

"Not yet. I wanted to nip to a friend's first." She gave me a hug. "I won't keep you from your lunch date any longer. Wouldn't want to get you in your grandmother's bad books."

By the time I returned to the table, Pete was gone.

Nana clapped her knife and fork on her plate a tad too deliberately. "What kept you so long?"

"Sorry, couldn't be helped. Pete gone back to work?"

"Yes," Gladys chirped, appearing much more at ease than she had before I left. "He said to tell you bye."

"Well, then, what do you say we head to your house so I can get the full story on your missing painting?" I tucked my tote bag sporting the Degas under my arm. "I just need to stop by headquarters to drop this off and then I'll meet you there."

• • •

Gladys lived in the affluent Central West End, northeast of Forest Park—the neighborhood at one time or another of such famous families as the Johnsons of Johnson & Johnson, Tennessee Williams, and poet T. S. Eliot. Gladys's home was built just before the World's Fair of 1904, if I remembered correctly. It had been an opulent place in the colonial revival style, but it fell into disrepair following the Great Depression and cost the Hoffemeiers a fortune to return to its old glory when they bought it for a steal in the early 1950s.

When I pulled into the driveway, my foot almost slipped from the brake at the sight of an unexpected couple—Nate and Aunt Martha— emerging from the house next to Gladys's. My car jolted to a stop behind Nana's BMW as my internal radar went on hyperalert. And . . . what was that wooden contraption Nate was carrying?

A spinning wheel?

Curiosity warred with the certainty that it was no coincidence the *friend* Aunt Martha *happened* to be visiting this afternoon was Gladys's next-door neighbor. Except she usually asked me straight out about my cases *before* she started snooping.

I spared a quick glance at Gladys's front window to make sure she wasn't watching for me, then scooted across the driveway. "What's with the spinning wheel?"

Nate stumbled down a step, then caught himself. "Don't ask me. I'm just the hired muscle."

"Ooh, isn't it wonderful?" Aunt Martha raved. "I overheard Ida at the hairdresser's complaining about having to dust this old thing, so I told her I knew someone who could make good use of it. You know Theresa down the hall from you? She's been spinning cat fur for years using a little hand spinner. She's going to love this."

"Who's Ida?"

"The Kresges' housekeeper." Aunt Martha motioned to a woman standing in the home's doorway. "Ida, this is the great-niece I was telling you about who works for the FBI."

The slim, gray-haired fifty-something-year-old nodded. "I imagine you're here to investigate Mrs. Hoffemeier's missing Dali painting? Ruby told me Gladys's friend had an in with the FBI."

Okay, I had no idea who Ruby was either, but if the neighbors' housekeeper already knew about the theft, how did Gladys expect to keep the news from her son?

"Oh my," Aunt Martha exclaimed, not fooling me for a second with her feigned surprise. "Was that the painting your grandmother—"

"We'd better not keep you," Nate said, slamming the hatch on his old Land Rover, the spinning wheel now stowed in back.

I tossed him a silent thank-you and spun back toward Gladys's driveway.

Nana and Gladys chose that moment to meander around the side of the house, apparently having been strolling in the garden. A tall man in a well-tailored, three-piece gray suit, carrying a small cardboard box under his arm, accompanied them.

"Guess that answers my question," Aunt Martha said. "I thought that looked like Stella's BMW in the driveway." To her friend, she muttered, "Can you imagine why anyone in their right mind would spend so much on a car?" This from the woman who drove a powder-blue clunker that was older than I was.

The man in the suit kissed Gladys's cheek, said something I couldn't make out, then strode past me to a Bentley parked at the curb. He looked to be fortyish, half Gladys's age, and wore a wedding band.

"My son-in-law," Gladys said in response to the curious look that must've crossed my face. "Tasha asked him to stop by to pick up a tureen she needs to borrow for their dinner party."

Or the family tag-teamed each other to keep an eye on their mother and the FBI agent that kept popping into her life.

"Hello, Stella," Aunt Martha oozed in Nana's direction. "It's been too long."

Yeah, we could thank Mom's strategic timing of the obligatory monthly mother-in-law invitation for that, considering Nana was not one of Aunt

74

Martha's favorite people. Mom never complained in my hearing about her mother-in-law's slights, but I suspected listening to Aunt Martha on top of it, harassing her about putting up with the woman, was more than she could handle.

"You should come to dinner tomorrow," Aunt Martha went on in a saccharine voice.

Oh, I really didn't like the sound of this. Now that she knew about the stolen painting, she'd clearly decided to sidestep me and go straight to the source for leads.

"I'm cooking shepherd's pie. One of your favorites, isn't it?"

I'm not sure if it was shock at the unprecedented friendly invitation or the pressure of so many pairs of eyes on her, but Nana accepted.

"Wonderful. We'll see you then. You too, Serena."

I forced a smile, mentally debating whether it'd be better to go and mitigate potential damage or to stay as far away as I could get.

Gladys led Nana and me to the front door. A middle-aged Latino woman greeted us, wearing the kind of dress-and-apron getup I hadn't seen since *Brady Bunch* reruns. "I set the tea in the drawing room, ma'am," she said.

"Thank you, Ruby."

Ah, so that cleared up the who's-Ruby mystery.

The foyer was massive, with high ceilings, Italian slate floors, dark, intricately carved moldings, and a stained-glass window that cast a colorful light show on the wall.

"The drawing room is this way." Gladys led us to a formal room to the right of the foyer. The floors looked as if they'd been recently updated to a warm oak, but the marble fireplace, flanked by built-in bookshelves edged in the same ornate moldings that finished the windows, was exquisite and definitely original.

"Wasn't the housekeeper implicated in that Westmoreland theft you investigated a few months back?" Nana asked conversationally.

Gladys gasped. "You can't be suggesting my Ruby would . . ." Her voice cut out as if she couldn't even bear to put it into words. "She's been with me for twenty years."

Nana, who had no illusions of the loyalty of the help, turned my way, her eyes widening ever so slightly as if to say, *I wouldn't cross her off the suspect list.*

I walked to the fireplace to scrutinize the Salvador Dali water-paint-on-paper forgery that hung above it. "This is very good." The jerkiness of the signature gave it away, but why would Gladys scrutinize the signature of something that had hung on her wall for years? "I'm not surprised you didn't notice the switch."

"Who knows how much longer it would have hung there undetected if I hadn't brought in that appraiser?"

76

"Why did you bring him in?"

"Oh, uh," Gladys spluttered, her gaze bouncing from Nana to the painting and back to me. "Uh, with Dali's work becoming more valuable these days, I thought it might be worth listing it on the insurance policy."

"It isn't already listed on your policy?" The disbelief in Nana's voice practically made the teacups rattle. "Dali's work is selling at auction for over a hundred million."

Gladys blanched, apparently just coming to terms with the magnitude of her loss. "It was only a few hundred dollars when we first bought it."

"Do you still have the sales record?" I asked.

"Yes." She handed me a file folder. "But the insurance company limits payment to a maximum of five hundred dollars for art that hasn't been specifically appraised and listed. And that's my deductible."

I reviewed the invoice. Her husband had bought the piece from a respectable dealer forty years ago, making the likelihood that it was a fake from the start slim. "Do you have any idea when the switch could have happened?"

"Oh yes, it couldn't have been more than a month ago."

"How can you be so sure?"

"Because my painting had a mar in the corner. I'd been explaining as much to the appraiser when I realized this one didn't have it. You see, Peter

77

took a Magic Marker to it as a child. But we caught him before he made more than a small mark, and we managed to shift the painting in the frame so no one would see it. But when I shifted it to show the appraiser . . . the mark wasn't there."

"But you'd seen the mark a month ago?"

"That's right. Squirrels got into the chimney. My son tried to smoke them out, but only succeeded in smoking us out, so he called a pest control service."

My mind flashed to the man outside my office at the drop-in center last night, and I glanced at Nana. "Who knew you were coming to see me last night?"

"Don't interrupt Gladys when she's speaking," Nana scolded.

I bristled. "The man you tripped over at the drop-in center last night said he was from pest control."

Nana's eyes widened. "Oh." Her gaze shifted to Gladys. "I was here when I called you at work, and when you said you couldn't come, I decided to meet you at the center."

"So Gladys knew. Anyone else?"

"The exterminator didn't do it," Gladys piped up. "I was explaining how I knew it was still here when he left. You see, the painting went askew from all the young man's banging. I remember needing to shift it in the frame after he left to hide the mark again."

"I'm surprised someone went to all the trouble of painting a forgery," Nana chimed in, "when they could've simply replaced it with a print."

"No prints were ever made of this piece. My husband was picky that way. He didn't want something a thousand other people might one day have a poster of, hanging on their walls."

"And it never left the premises?"

"No."

"Then the thief must've taken a picture to give the forger and then returned a second time to make the switch, unless . . . Have you been on an extended vacation in the past month?"

"No, I'm never out of the house more than a few hours. I usually go to my sister's in early September, but my arthritis has been acting up too much. I haven't been away at all."

"Did your pest control service make a second call?"

"No, he cleaned out the squirrel's hoard of nuts, put some kind of guard on the top of the chimney, and I haven't had any more problems."

So if he photographed the painting, he would've needed an accomplice to make the switch. "Who else has been in this room in the last four weeks?"

"Well, your grandmother. The appraiser. My housekeeper. My daughter, Tasha, and her husband, Lucas. And of course, my Peter."

Ruby brought in a plate of cookies, which prompted Gladys to pour the tea.

"Ruby," Gladys called after the departing woman, "do you remember if anyone else has been over since the squirrel incident?"

Something in the flick of Ruby's gaze suggested she'd thought of someone. "No, ma'am. Not other than your children."

"Do you recall the exterminator's name?" I asked Gladys.

"You'd have to ask Pete. No, wait." Gladys plopped down the teapot. "You can't ask him, because then he'll wonder why you're asking. Oh dear, maybe we should just forget about this."

"Gladys," my grandmother said in her listen-to-reason voice, "my granddaughter is not going to forget about this. You've had a very valuable painting stolen."

Gladys stirred her tea a tad too vigorously. "It probably wasn't valuable. Not with that Magic-Marker mark on it. The appraiser said that could reduce the value significantly."

Nana's snort came out as a refined, ladylike tsk. "He said that because insurance companies don't want to pay you more than they have to, but who knows how high it could've gone at auction?"

Gladys twisted her wedding band. "I wish Frank were still alive. He'd know what to do."

Nana patted her hand. "You're doing the right thing now. Serena will find your painting."

My heart should've soared at Nana's surprising

confidence, but all I could think about was how disappointed she'd be if I failed. As it was, I had to do some pretty fancy talking just to convince her to let me take the forgery into evidence in the hopes of finding a clue as to the forger. And so I could compare it to the forgeries we'd recovered from the drug bust, but I didn't tell her that part.

Her housekeeper returned to collect the tea tray as Nana and I rose to leave. "I remembered there was another gentleman who visited," she said to Gladys. "The one you hoped might buy Pete's property, remember?"

Gladys spluttered again, her face going red this time. "No, no, he came before the exterminator. Remember? Mr. Fuhrman was the one who heard the squirrel in the chimney."

Fuhrman? "The real estate mogul?" I jotted down the name, the whole scenario sounding even more suspicious, given the men's connection.

"He's an old family friend," Gladys said quickly—too quickly.

Had Pete asked her for the plug? Or had it been her idea?

An uneasy feeling settled in my gut. If Pete's side business wasn't doing as well as Gladys seemed to want me to believe, her fears of being pushed from her home could stem from something even scarier—a fear that her son was her thief.

7

Back at headquarters, I sent out an email alert about Gladys's missing Dali to my art-crime contact list—basically anyone the thief might try to sell the work to—art galleries, dealers, auction houses, law enforcement contacts, and even criminals.

Next, I ran cursory background checks on Gladys's children and housekeeper. The housekeeper's credit history was spotty, but she didn't have any liens against her. She'd been at the same address for the past twenty years—the same length of time she'd been with Gladys. She'd also had a couple of side jobs through the years. Never married and had a lead foot if her speeding tickets were any indication.

Gladys's daughter, Tasha, didn't have any red marks against her. She'd gone to the top private schools, joined a sorority in her college years, married as soon as she graduated at twenty-two. Taught piano lessons from her home. Her husband, Lucas, was a different story. He'd had a DUI at nineteen and spent a weekend in jail. He'd gone through more than twenty employers by the time he graduated with a masters in business, and another three before he landed in the CFO job at his current bank. He was questioned in connection with a possession charge during a raid at a local bar, but it didn't look as if anything came of it. Six years ago, a woman had filed a paternity suit against him. I did a deeper search but couldn't find any information on the outcome.

Could mean someone paid her off. Or that it was still unresolved. If Lucas was getting himself into trouble sowing his wild oats, it could be motivation to secretly sell one of mother-in-law-dearest's expensive paintings.

Gladys's son, Pete, had a clean criminal record and a good credit history. So whatever real estate albatross Randy had been referring to earlier hadn't affected his daily transactions. At least not yet. Pete hadn't missed a single payment on his mortgage, utilities, or credit card.

Stretching out the kinks in my neck, I decided to wait on pumping Pete for the name of the exterminator he'd hired to catch Gladys's squirrel. Despite Ted's appearance at the drop-in center, it seemed like a stretch to suppose he knew why Nana wanted to see me and had followed her. Besides, he couldn't have switched the paintings without an accomplice. An accomplice that I had a bad feeling had to be someone Gladys trusted too much.

My cell phone rang, and a fuzzy image of my mugger appeared on the screen.

"This your guy?" Matt Speers, my friend on the St. Louis PD, asked.

"Yes, where'd you get the pic?"

"Pulled the image off the security footage of the coffee shop across the street from your art expert. According to the time stamp, he was already in the shop before you went into the building across the road."

"So he wasn't following me. That's good. Saves me worrying about one more thing."

"Yeah, figured you'd be happy about that. We didn't manage to ID him. The barista said he wasn't a regular, but that it's not the first time someone's been mugged coming out of the artist's place."

"No? Did you look up the report on the other mugging?"

"No report was filed. According to the clerk, the victim said the joke was on his mugger, because he'd just found out the painting was a forgery."

"Really? Sounds a little too coincidental, wouldn't you say?"

"How well do you know that expert you were visiting? You think she could be pulling a scam? Telling people their genuine paintings are fakes, then alerting a mugger to take them off their hands."

I shook my head, not that Matt could see me. I didn't want to believe it. Zoe, my good friend, not to mention the head of security at Forest Park Art Museum, had highly recommended Nicki. "I watched the readout for the paint elements come up on the screen. My painting was definitely a forgery."

"You sure she didn't scan it over a nearby palette on the sly when your attention was diverted?"

"Wow, you're devious. I'm glad you're on our side."

He chuckled. "I've seen it all."

"Okay, I think I'll get a second opinion to be on the safe side." Zoe was in the middle of planning her wedding, and as her maid of honor—*somewhat* delinquent though I was—I could vouch for how distracted she'd been lately. And I certainly hadn't been watching for any sleight of hand on Nicki's part. I tidied my desk and then snatched up my bag so I could go down to evidence to retrieve the Degas one more time.

Tanner rounded the corner of my cubicle as I turned from my desk and caught me before I ran into him. "Whoa, you get a lead already?"

"Lead?"

"You know . . . another day, another *Dali*." He turned his cell phone screen my way. "Got your email alert."

"*Cute*. No lead. I was heading out to get a second opinion on the Degas. My friend with the St. Louis PD thinks the expert I took it to might've lied about its authenticity."

Tanner's cheek muscle twitched, a sure sign he didn't like what he was hearing.

"What? You know something I should?"

"Nah, I hoped to pull you in on a surveillance run. But if you need—"

"It's fine. This can wait until Monday. How can I help?"

"How's a sunset cruise sound to you?"

"Ooh, sounds like my kind of surveillance."

"Perfect. I figured having a 'date' to photograph would give me a good excuse to get my targets on film without raising suspicions."

I glanced down at my standard FBI-wear—charcoal-gray slacks and blazer, white blouse. "I guess I should get changed."

"Good plan. If I pick you up at your apartment in an hour, that give you enough time?"

I rolled my eyes.

He backed away, hands raised in surrender. "Hey, what do I know? I thought sometimes women want to do their nails or—"

"Is something wrong with my nails?" I needled, studying my splayed fingers. Okay, they could use a little TLC. Nail polish wasn't really my thing.

Tanner shook his head. "I'll see you in an hour."

Back at my apartment, I slid into a classic black cocktail dress, sheer pantyhose, and black pumps—because if Tanner was noticing fingernails, I sure didn't want him seeing my toes. I added a swipe of gloss to my lips and a touch of glittery shadow to my eyelids and glanced at the digital clock next to my bed. Still had fifteen minutes to figure out what to do with my hair. I undid my ponytail and experimented with a couple of updos, trying to decide which Tanner would prefer.

I dropped my hair like a hot potato. What was I doing? It wasn't as if this was a real date. I snatched up my favorite hair product, spritzed it on, and scrunched my blond waves into the kind of rumpled disarray men seemed to find appealing, if magazine ads were anything to go by.

My thoughts drifted to the one and only river cruise I'd ever been on. I'd been sixteen, the boy seventeen, and it had all seemed so astronomically romantic—the music, the gentle sway of the boat, the breathtaking colors splashing across the water and sky as the sun slipped below the horizon.

Laughter filtered through my apartment wall. Laughter that sounded a lot like Aunt Martha's. I glanced out my back window and spotted her powder-blue car in the parking lot. How had I missed it? Sometimes I wondered why she begged me to take over her apartment lease. She seemed to spend more time here than at my parents'. Chances were she was visiting friends other than me, but just in case, I grabbed my wrap, stuffed my Glock and wallet into a nicer purse, and snuck out my kitchen door that opened onto a metal staircase on the side of the building.

Tanner pulled up just as I reached the bottom stair. His appreciative whistle filled the air.

I rolled my eyes.

He shifted into park and reached for his door handle, but I waved him off and let myself in the passenger side. No point risking hanging around a second longer than necessary. Aunt Martha wasn't like Mom, trying to marry me off to every guy who asked me out. But who knew what she might say to Mom if she saw me like this?

"Uh . . ."

Wow, rendering Tanner speechless was a first. Because I looked so hot and he wasn't used to seeing me this way? I hid a smile. Wait . . . what was with the funny expression?

I twisted to check the sides and back of my dress. "Did I forget to take the price tag off? What?"

"Um"—Tanner glanced at his watch, and a look of pain flickered over his face—"nothing. Really." He rammed his truck into reverse and squealed out of the driveway. "You look amazing."

Ri-i-i-ght. That was totally convincing.

"We've got to get on the boat before six in case my target's contact doesn't stick around for dinner."

I laughed. "What's he going to do to get away? Jump overboard?"

Tanner's hand jerked the stick shift, grinding the gears. I'd never seen him so flustered over a stakeout. He was practically squirming in his seat. At the next intersection, he suddenly turned into Forest Park. "Why are you going this way? We'll miss the boat for sure."

As if he'd simultaneously turned a corner in settling whatever had him so antsy, he stopped squirming and that familiar bantering gleam returned to his eye. "I'm pretty sure they'll hold our boat until we arrive."

"Don't count on it."

He pulled up alongside the Boathouse restaurant in the middle of Forest Park.

"Why are you stopping here?" The Boathouse offered casual indoor and patio dining overlooking Post-Dispatch Lake, as well as . . . *paddleboat rentals*. "No way. I'm not dressed for this. You said you were taking me on a sunset cruise!"

"It is." He pointed to a sign advertising sunset cruises, complete with a deluxe picnic supper and rental of a two-person *paddleboat* to chug around the rivers in Forest Park. An instant later he materialized outside my truck door in his cream-colored chinos and navy blue windbreaker, a DSLR camera slung over his shoulder.

"You're serious?" I said as he opened my door.

"C'mon, it'll be fun."

"Fun? Look at me. I can't go in a paddleboat like this."

Grinning wickedly, he looked his fill. "I'm sorry. Back at headquarters, when you asked about changing, I assumed you meant into something more casual. Then it was too late to do anything about it. But trust me, it'll be fine." He caught my hand and helped me out. "I'll be the envy of every guy in the place."

I grabbed my wrap from the seat. "*Fine,* but I'm not paddling."

Laughter rumbled through his chest. "Wouldn't dream of making you." Tanner led me through the gate and gave his name to the man in charge of the boats. The outside patio was packed with dinner patrons.

I clutched his arm and leaned in close as I pretended to pick a stone from my shoe. I lowered my voice. "Your target here yet?" I asked, ignoring the appealing woodsy scent that wafted from his warm skin.

"One of them." He half turned his head, and his lips brushed my cheek.

I jerked back, and Tanner gave me a sardonic look before adding, "Nine o'clock."

I focused on making a casual visual sweep of the area, not reacting as my gaze noted the well-dressed Russian with neatly trimmed salt-and-pepper hair, mustache, and beard.

"Don't think you won't pay for this wardrobe malfunction," I said under my breath to Tanner, then turned to smile at the boatman who'd just secured a picnic basket aboard our paddleboat.

"Never doubted it for a second."

The boatman handed us each a life jacket. "Your boat is ready."

Tanner nodded, then patted my hand still clutching his arm. "Shall we?"

Tanner stepped into the boat first, then extended his hand to help me.

"Wait!" I toed off my shoes and, turning away from him, discreetly shimmied off my pantyhose.

"Uh . . . what are you doing?"

"Do you have any idea how much these things cost?" I carefully stuffed them into my clutch, but one look at my toes convinced me to slip the shoes back on. "Guaranteed those babies would've run the second I sat down, and they were my last decent pair."

He erupted in a fresh bout of laughter. But as I stepped over the side of the boat, his gaze snagged on my bare legs and his laughter abruptly stopped.

I tugged my wrap tighter around my shoulders against a sudden shiver that didn't have much to do with the breeze dancing off the water.

"You going to be warm enough?" Tanner asked, steering the boat away from the dock.

"I'm good." If I ignored the unnerving feeling that I'd just stepped into Édouard Manet's *Boating* painting. The only thing missing was a boater hat for Tanner. I lifted the camera from around his neck and aimed it his way. "I don't see how you plan to pretend to take pictures of me and get your target in your sights when I'm sitting right beside you."

He steered left, bringing the boat behind a small island.

"Wait," I whispered and pretended to focus on him when I was really zooming in on his target at the patio table. I snapped half a dozen pictures as Tanner grinned crazily. "Got it." I lowered the camera to my lap and brought the pictures back up on the viewing screen for him to see.

"Wow, talk about handsome, huh?" Tanner said, and I did a double take of the target, who reminded me of Alan Rickman as the bad guy in *Die Hard.* "Not him, silly," Tanner said, jostling my shoulder. "Me."

"Hah," I said. "Just paddle."

In truth, Tanner had the warmest brown eyes and a killer dimple that made most girls go weak in the knees.

Good thing I wasn't most girls.

"Robert Downey Jr?"

"Huh?"

"My lookalike. You know, from"—he deepened his voice—"*The Avengers.*"

I smacked my hand to my forehead. "Of course! Anyone with two eyes could see it—you wish."

He shrugged good-naturedly, speeding the boat to the next island. "Target's contact is due in ten minutes, so that'll give us enough time to set up our picnic in the gazebo on the island. I figured from there, I can take pictures of you from all kinds of angles."

I shook my head. "You better not let my mother hear you talking like that."

He laughed.

Yeah, who was I kidding? Mom would totally miss the "for work" part and be so thrilled to hear I was out on a *date* that she wouldn't care what kind of pictures he was taking.

Tanner moored the boat to the island and climbed out. "Hand me the basket first, then I'll help you out."

My stomach grumbled as I handed him the basket and the delicious aroma of fried chicken swirled past. I scrambled out before Tanner had time to lower the basket. His hand swallowed mine, and he tugged me toward the gazebo.

"I hope we're going to get a chance to eat this supper," I said. "I'm starving."

Tanner pulled a blanket from the basket and, spreading it on the floor of the gazebo, squinted toward the Boathouse. "We can start eating. No sign of the target's contact yet."

I sank onto the blanket, my legs tucked under me as ladylike as I could manage in a cocktail dress, and helped Tanner pull out the food containers. In addition to fried chicken, there was potato salad, coleslaw, a fancy quinoa dish, warm rolls, and . . . "Mmm, brownies."

"Ordered those just for you."

"This sure beats the last surveillance we did."

"I don't know. What's not to like about a hot, stuffy car, bologna sandwiches, and cold coffee?"

"Hmm." I savored a bite of brownie. "At least I didn't have to wear a dress."

"You don't like wearing dresses?"

I shrugged.

"They look good on you."

"Is that a compliment?" I fanned my face as if I were going to faint.

Tanner rolled his eyes. "*Thank you* is the correct response, Jones."

He sprang up and started snapping pictures of me. "Stand by the tree over there and fling your hair around."

"Fling my hair around?"

"You know. Act like we're being silly imitating a professional photo shoot."

I glanced toward the Boathouse. Tanner's target stood and extended a hand to a hefty man in a pinstriped business suit. I sashayed to a better position for Tanner to focus on them while appearing to photograph me. "Who's the target?" I asked.

"A player in a case I'm working on," he said in his usual evasive way.

I flipped my hair off my shoulder and flung back my head like a prima donna model. "What would you think if you asked me about a case I was working on, and I gave you that kind of cagey answer?"

He stopped snapping pictures and shot me a confused look. Not surprising since he'd been my field-training agent. It'd probably never occurred to him that one day I might stop discussing my cases with him. "I'm sorry." He resumed snapping. "It's been so ingrained in me to not discuss cases outside the office that I answer like that without thinking."

"So who is he?"

"A player in a case I'm working on," he repeated, amusement in his voice this time.

I stuck out my tongue at him.

"No, I'm sorry. It really is a sensitive case." He circled around me, taking photos from every angle, probably to check out the rest of the patrons in the area, some of whom were no doubt his target's bodyguards. "Okay, I think I have plenty of shots. We can finish the picnic now."

We tucked into the chicken and salads as Tanner regaled me with outrageous stories about some of the stakeouts he'd been on. I was having so much fun that, when my cell phone rang, I ignored it.

"Aren't you going to answer that?" Tanner asked.

"It can go to voice mail."

"What if it's important?"

Clearly, the idea of ignoring a phone call was a foreign concept to Tanner.

I retrieved my phone from my purse and glanced at the name on the screen. "Hey, Nate, what's up?"

Tanner's expression soured.

I grinned and winked at him before turning away and lowering the phone's volume so he wouldn't overhear.

"Randy wants to meet us in an hour to introduce us to the forger he found. Will that work for you?"

"One sec." I covered the phone and turned to Tanner. "Are we just about done here?"

Tanner squinted in the direction of his target. "Might look suspicious if we leave before sunset."

"I kind of need to use the bathroom anyway."

Tanner started tossing dishes into the basket. "I can take you home. Wouldn't want your mother to accuse me of messing up your social life."

I gave him an exasperated look. Ever since the blustery February day Tanner found Nate peering in my kitchen window and mistook him for a stalker, just the mention of Nate's name seemed to get under Tanner's skin.

"I can be ready in about forty-five minutes," I said to Nate and clicked off.

"Big date?" Tanner stuffed the blanket into the basket.

I shrugged. "You know what they say about all work and no play . . ." After all, I couldn't tell him I was going undercover with Nate. He'd have a conniption. Not to mention that if he figured out I'd already fooled him with my Sara Thompson

96

imitation, he might assume Nate and I had had a good laugh over it, and nothing could be further from the truth. Then again, considering he was way less forthcoming about his own cases, I shouldn't feel guilty about keeping one from him.

"I don't know." He put the basket in the boat then offered me a hand. "I thought this was fun. Didn't you?" He jostled the boat and I lost my balance.

"Ahh!" Cold water soaked my foot as the mucky bottom ate my shoe.

Tanner's gaze shot to the restaurant's patio patrons looking our way. "Shh." He hauled me back on shore.

"My shoe!"

He fished my pump out of the muck as I wrung the water from the hem of my dress. "I'm sorry." He rinsed the shoe clean, then knelt at my feet and slipped it back on my foot.

I couldn't help but giggle at the fairytale ending to our *date*.

A few minutes later, we neared the shore in the paddleboat and I glanced toward his target, still sitting on the patio. "Are you sure you're okay to leave?"

He tossed the rope to the boatman on the dock, then hopped out and reached for my hand. "Your wish is my command." He gallantly brought my hand to his lips as he drew me out of the boat.

My heart skipped a beat. "You're an idiot," I said, trying to tug my hand away.

He pressed his palm to his chest. "You wound me."

"Don't tempt me." I bit down on a grin. "Let me slip into the restroom. Might counter anyone's suspicions about why we came in before the sunset."

Clapping heels rushed up behind me, and a "Serena!" squeal practically ruptured my eardrum.

Oh no. I glanced at Tanner, whose gaze jumped to his target. Could we have been any more conspicuous?

8

My cousin squeezed my arm and herded me into the Boathouse's restroom. "You've been holding out on us!" She backed up, clasping my hands and spreading my arms as she admired my dress. "Look at you. Who's the guy? Your mother was just over yesterday lamenting that the closest thing you've had to a date is watching movies with your super. Who is Bradley Cooper–hot, by the way."

Pretty sure half the restaurant could hear, I shushed her with, "He's a colleague. It's not a date."

"Ha! You tell yourself whatever you need to, girl, but I saw the way he looked at you."

I mentally rolled my eyes. Yes, Tanner could be

really good at role-playing when he needed to be. This was *so* not good. April was a motormouth, and if I admitted I was on an undercover op, she'd go out and blab it to her date and who knew who might overhear. But if I let her think this was really a date, she'd tell my aunt, who'd tell my mom, who'd have wedding invitations ordered by Friday. If she didn't have a stroke first over the fact that he was in law enforcement. "Okay, yes, it's a date, but please don't tell your mother. Or mine. I'd like . . . time."

"Yee," she squealed. "Of course, of course. I understand." She squeezed my arm again. "I'm so happy for you." She twirled out of the bathroom like the giddy teen she was, and I was pretty sure the phone lines to my parents' house would be humming tonight.

I flushed a toilet without using it and emerged from the restroom to find Tanner grinning at me over April's head as she hugged his middle.

He extricated himself from her arms, said something I couldn't hear, then strode my way and splayed his hand across the middle of my back as if he was my boyfriend.

"Sorry about April," I whispered as warmth spread through me. Tanner was a little *too* good at role-playing sometimes.

"It's all good." His hand moved up to give my neck a squeeze. *"Honeybunch."*

I smacked him.

His chuckle resonated through me as we turned onto the walkway. It meandered through a colorful courtyard decorated with a variety of plants and sculptures, and he took his time twining me through it en route to his truck, even though we were already out of sight of his target.

We drove to my place in silence, and the instant Tanner pulled alongside my building next to my metal staircase, I flung open the door before he got it into his head to walk me to my apartment and . . . hang around until Nate arrived. "Thanks, it was fun!"

I scurried up the stairs with a wave and launched through my kitchen door before registering it wasn't locked.

"There you are." Aunt Martha sat at my kitchen table with Harold purring on her lap, a steaming cup of tea on her place mat. "Ooh, look at you. Were you on a date?" Her gaze slid down my dress to the damp hem and then slanted to the stove's digital clock. "I guess it didn't go well."

"A small surveillance mishap. And I'm afraid I'm heading right back out again."

"Righto, I just stopped by because I thought you might want to hear what I found out about Gladys's missing painting."

I blinked. "*You* have information for *me?*" I'd assumed she'd come to grill me.

Aunt Martha grinned. "I'm not just another pretty face."

100

A knock at the hall door interrupted us before she could start. I hurried across the kitchen to the entrance and peeked out the peephole. Nate. I opened the door.

"Whoa," he said. "I mean, wow! You look stunning, but it's Sara—"

I gave my head a sideways jerk toward the kitchen to alert him to Aunt Martha's presence.

Oblivious, he went on. "—who's supposed to show up at the meeting."

"I'll be sure to tell *her*," I interjected and jerked my head more urgently in Aunt Martha's direction.

She trundled to the doorway with Harold nuzzled against her neck. "Did Randy tell you he ran into Serena and me at the MAC today?"

Nate's gaze zipped back to mine, looking a tad panicked. "Did he recognize you?" he whispered.

"I introduced them. He took quite a shine to her too." Aunt Martha went on in that singsong, the-early-bird-gets-the-worm voice, clearly trying to provoke Nate to stake his claim or risk losing it to his brother, when all Nate cared about was whether I'd blown my cover.

Aunt Martha shook her head. "Sometimes men are thicker than cheese," she muttered into Harold's fur.

"You free tonight?" Nate suddenly asked, as if he didn't already have plans with my alter ego.

I glanced at Aunt Martha.

"I'm not staying," she blurted. "Goodness! Who am I to stand in the way of a real date? Go. Go!" She made a shooing motion with her hands as if she expected me to leave on the spot. Except I needed at least five minutes of privacy to bring the actual woman Nate wanted to take out, back to life.

"Oh, I thought I'd lost this." Aunt Martha caught up the poncho I'd hooked on the closet's doorknob when I got home last night.

I mentally inventoried my wardrobe for an alternative hippy-like option and, recalling none, I blurted, "Could I borrow it?"

"Of course. You can keep it, if you'd like."

I shrugged noncommittally. "I just thought it might be fun to try it out."

"Good save," Nate whispered.

I stood, holding open the door, expecting Aunt Martha to leave. Instead, she dug around in her purse, then victoriously held out a note.

"What's this?"

"What I've learned so far about your suspects."

"My sus—" Taking the list that cataloged more than half my suspects—namely, Gladys's children and housekeeper—I pressed my lips together.

"I know. I know," Aunt Martha went on. "You're not supposed to talk about it. That's why I grilled Ida and went from there." Aunt Martha tapped the paper. "For instance, did you know Pete has cash flow problems because he overextended himself on a real estate deal?"

"Yes, I did."

"Oh, well, what about Gladys's son-in-law? Did you know he bought a classic 1964 Shelby Mustang in mint condition?"

"He's CFO of the bank. I'm sure he can afford it."

"Do you know what they're worth?" Aunt Martha's voice rattled the windows. "If he had that kind of coin, why'd he cancel their cruise to the Caribbean? That's all his wife has complained about at the hairdresser's for the past month or more."

Aunt Martha went to a Central West End hairdresser for a wash and set every Friday, and I was beginning to think it was a prime location to plant a confidential informant. A hairdresser was privy to more secrets than a therapist.

Nate still stood at the door. "How much time do you need to get ready?"

"Oh dear," Aunt Martha fussed. "Don't let me hold you up." She grabbed the poncho, must've remembered my request to borrow it, and dropped it again, then bustled out.

Nate said good-bye to her, then stepped inside. "You might want to check over the poncho. Make sure she didn't plant a GPS tracker in it or something."

I chuckled.

"You laugh, but I wouldn't put it past her. She takes her sleuthing very seriously."

"I'm sure she doesn't own a GPS transmitter."

Nate's eyebrow lifted in a skeptical arch.

"Okay, come to think of it, Dad mentioned seeing her browsing an online spy shop last week." I checked the pockets. "They're empty. Where does Randy want to meet?"

"His apartment in Soulard."

"Yeah that fits." Soulard was historically the French district and one of the oldest St. Louis neighborhoods. "Randy looks like the type who'd want to live close to all those blues and jazz bars." My cell phone rang. I glanced at the screen. Matt Speers. "I need to take this. Have a seat on the couch, and I'll be ready to go in ten minutes." I hurried to the bedroom and put Matt on speaker-phone as I changed into my "Sara" getup.

"I took another look at the coffee shop's surveillance video. Your mugger talked to someone just before he left. I'm emailing you the picture now."

I snatched up my phone and shut off the speaker. "Hold on a sec." I thumbed in my email and opened the image. "Randy."

"You know him?"

"Yeah."

"I snapped that from the screen with my phone, but I'll download the clip and send it to you. This guy and your mugger talked for over a minute and both left around the same time."

"Thanks, Matt. I appreciate you going the extra mile on this for me."

"Hey, you can show your appreciation by babysitting the little terror."

"Uh . . ." My mind whirled with questions about Randy. Did he know the guy who mugged me? Did he see him do it? Did he tell him to do it? Was that why he came into the MAC? Looking for another opportunity?

Matt laughed. "*Little Terror* is a pet name. The munchkin's not that bad. But"—his voice sobered—"Tracey's last pregnancy got really dicey toward the end, so I'm trying to give her all the breaks I can, and I've kind of maxed out all the family members."

"Um . . ." I dragged my mind back to the conversation and strained to focus on what Matt was saying. "Sure. I can babysit. Just let me know when," I said and clicked off. How hard could it be to take care of one pint-sized kid for an evening? If I ran into trouble, I could always call Mom. Witnessing my ineptitude might cool her jets on the whole get-Serena-married crusade. Then again, if he was a little cherub, it would only fuel her enthusiasm.

Ack. I had more important things to worry about at the moment. I turned the corner and came face to face with one of them—Nate.

105

Was his brother in cahoots with the drug dealers?

"I think I should drive tonight." I opened my clutch to grab my wallet and keys, and my pantyhose tumbled out.

Nate's eyeballs popped and a tiny frown tugged at the corners of his lips.

I snatched up the pantyhose and tossed them into the hall closet. "I didn't want them to run," I explained.

"Right."

Okay, that didn't sound as if he believed me, and I didn't want to contemplate what he might be imagining pantyhose in my purse meant. I was pretty sure he didn't know I'd been out with Tanner. Not that it was really a date, anyway. Not that Nate would care if it had been. Or maybe he would. My heart tumbled around my chest. Maybe I wanted him to care. Oh man, I didn't want to analyze that right now.

Nate pulled his keys from his pocket. "I'd better drive. Don't want Randy looking too closely at your car."

"Right." But as much as I trusted Nate, I wasn't sure we could trust his brother. And if push came to shove, I had no idea which way Nate's loyalties would fall.

We let ourselves out my kitchen door, and the clang of a heavy footfall on the bottom step made me jump. "Tanner, what are you doing back here?"

His head cocked, and I remembered that I didn't

look like Serena with my floppy hat, hippy poncho, leather boots to the knees, and dark hair extensions. His gaze raked over my outfit and then settled on my face. A twitch at the corner of his lips was the closest he came to acknowledging whatever he thought of my performance. At least he didn't seem mad over my not coming clean when he happened upon us last night. "I guess this answers my question about whether you knew your super was seeing another woman."

"What brought you back?"

He held up my wrap. "You forgot this in my truck." He motioned to my outfit. "Another undercover op?"

"Benton knows about it," I blurted, suddenly feeling like a rookie who needed to call down the authority of her boss to prove she hadn't gone rogue.

That telltale muscle in Tanner's cheek flicked, as if that didn't make him feel any better. Probably made him more annoyed I'd left him out of the loop. He threw a squinty glance Nate's way. "You got backup?"

Clearly, he didn't think Nate fit the bill. And with what I'd just learned about his brother, he might be right. "You volunteering?" I asked.

"What do I need to know?"

Tanner tailed us across town and pulled to the curb half a block shy of Randy's apartment.

I adjusted the earpiece we'd stopped at headquarters to retrieve. "You hear me okay?" I asked as we headed up the sidewalk to the building's front door.

"Loud and clear."

"What on earth?" Nate veered toward the alley. "Hey!" he shouted and disappeared behind the building.

"What's going on?" Tanner asked.

I raced to the corner of the building. "Someone's getting beat up."

The attacker shoved the victim at Nate and bolted straight into me. I caught him by the arm, but before I could crank it behind his back and shove him up against the side of the building, he yanked my blasted poncho over my face and drove *me* into the brick wall.

"Ser-e—" Tanner choked off my name. Hopefully before Randy caught it.

The next thing I knew, Tanner and Nate were jostling each other out of the way to help me up from the ground.

"Go! I'm fine. Get the bad guy!"

Tanner sprinted down the alley after him.

Nate hesitated half a second. "You sure you're okay?"

"Yes, go help Tanner. I'll see to Randy."

Randy pushed to his feet and swayed.

I dashed to his side and caught his arm to steady him. "Who was that? Why'd he jump you?"

"Just a punk." Randy peeled my hand off his arm and momentarily stared at it before releasing it.

I stuffed it under my poncho. Had he felt the abrasion on my hand? In the exact same spot as he'd noticed *Serena's* this afternoon?

He pressed the back of his shirt cuff to his cut lip. "Sorry. I don't think I'm up to introducing you to anyone tonight."

No kidding. In addition to the cut lip, he had a swollen eye, and judging from the way he cradled his middle, bruised ribs, maybe worse. But considering he'd been chatting with my mugger mere hours ago, I doubted the attack was as random as he seemed to want me to believe.

"Let me help you up to your apartment."

His eyes narrowed. "Didn't you have a British accent before?"

I forced a chuckle, hoping he couldn't see the heat climbing to my cheeks in the deepening darkness. "I play up the accent for Nate because he's fond of it."

Nate and Tanner thankfully chose that moment to round the corner. Except . . .

"He got away?" I asked.

"Sorry," Nate said.

Tanner's snort suggested he doubted the sentiment.

"Who's he?" Randy hitched his chin toward Tanner.

Nate and I exchanged a panicked glance. A good FBI agent would have a plausible answer on the spot. *Crud!*

"Calhoun." Tanner extended his hand to Randy. What was he doing?

"I'm a private investigator."

I choked down my gasp and, conjuring up an accusing glare, played along. "Did my husband hire you?"

Nate's hand fisted at his side. "I'm sorry, Sara. I don't know how he found us."

Not as sorry as Tanner was going to be if his *admission* changed Randy's mind about introducing us to his forger friend. "Whatever my husband's paying you," I said to Tanner in my most desperate-sounding voice, "I'll double it for your silence."

"And how are you going to get your hands on that kind of money?"

I glanced back at Randy, the link to my potential meal ticket. "Do you think your friend can help me?"

Randy headed to the front of his building. "With a PI breathing down your neck? Not a chance."

"Take her home," Nate whispered to Tanner. "I'll talk to him." He disappeared into the building behind his brother.

"I don't trust him," Tanner said, steering me toward his SUV. "We had his brother's attacker cornered, and Nate let him slip past him."

"He's not an agent, Tanner." I slid into the passenger seat. "He hasn't been trained to take down suspects."

Tanner shut the door with a tad more force than necessary. "Why do you trust him?"

"What makes you think I do?"

He snorted and started his car.

I filled him in on Randy's chat with my mugger and his coincidental visit to the MAC at lunchtime. "I have my suspicions of Randy, and I'm not at all sure who Nate would side with if he had to make a choice."

"Maybe he's ratted you out from the beginning. You thought of that?"

I muffled a gulp. I'd discussed the forgery case with Nate last night. It'd been his idea to go to the bar where we ran into his brother. But I couldn't imagine him ratting me out.

Protecting his brother if he learned Randy was up to no good? Yes.

Helping Randy do something bad? No.

Although his brother clearly had no qualms. My Sara alter ego had told him how I planned to dupe my soon-to-be-ex-husband with the forgery, and he hadn't so much as batted an eye.

"You do know his brother is no saint?" Tanner said. "He got his first DUI at seventeen and half a dozen speeding tickets before he was twenty."

"You know this how?"

"I asked the office to run a background check

during the drive to his place. The system has extensive information on him, even interviews with friends."

That sounded as if they had an employment check on file. Like the one they did on me when I applied to the FBI.

"People can change."

"But has he?"

"He must have, or Nate would've steered me away from him as quick as he could. If my brother was buttering his bread from the wrong side, I sure wouldn't introduce him to an FBI agent. Would you?"

"Depends on my motives."

Okay, I did not want to hash this out a second longer because I suspected Tanner's motives at the moment didn't have a thing to do with wanting to help me make contact with local forgers.

Tanner parked at the foot of my exterior stairs. The sky was moonless, and aside from a patch of light here and there from the odd window, the area was cloaked in dark shadows.

"That's weird. I'm sure I turned on the outside light before I left."

"Maybe the bulb burned out."

"Nate changed it last week."

Tanner jumped out of the truck right behind me. "I'll walk you up."

I climbed the steps without arguing and then rummaged through my purse for my house key.

Tanner, at six foot four, easily examined the negligent bulb. A moment later, light splashed over the landing.

"Loose connection?" I asked, fitting my key into the lock. The lock that seemed a lot more hacked up than I ever remembered it being.

"No, someone unscrewed your bulb."

I whirled around to scan the driveway, treetops, and rooftops. "I think someone tried to pick the lock too."

Tanner whipped out the gun he'd had tucked in a waistband holster as I grabbed mine from my purse. I lived in a good neighborhood. Not the kind where bad guys hung out in bushes, waiting for an opportunity. Trouble was, that fact made it more likely my visitor had chosen me for a reason.

Tanner examined the nearby window. "Looks like someone tried to pry open the window too. Let me go in first. Make sure they didn't get in."

I sucked in a sudden breath. "Oh no! Harold." What if the intruder hurt him? Or kicked him out? He could be huddled under a bush somewhere, scared and lost. *Oh, please, God, let Harold be okay.*

"Hey, relax, Serena. I'm sure he's fine."

I blinked rapidly, nodding. This was crazy. I hadn't even thought I was much of a cat person, but the little guy had really gotten to me.

Tanner took my key and unlocked the door.

He was SWAT and used to going first in situations like this, so who was I to mess up routine? I mentally ran through suspects in my current cases. None of them seemed the type to come looking for more trouble.

Tanner crept through the kitchen, checked the broom closet and every corner, then disappeared around the corner. I padded across the kitchen and positioned myself at the opening to the entranceway—a wide hall that stretched to my right into the living room and ahead of me to the two bedrooms and bathroom.

"All clear there," Tanner whispered, emerging from the living room. Next he cleared the bathroom and my bedroom, then chucked his chin toward the spare room. "Do you usually keep the door closed?"

I crept closer. "No."

Tanner slowly pushed it open, scanned the room by the scant illumination of the streetlight outside the window, then inched inside. "Owwwww!"

Gun first, I whipped around the corner of the door.

Tanner's gaze swung to my gun. "It's the cat! The cat!" He dove for cover as Harold's yowl arced the room, followed by a soft thud on the other side of the bed.

I lowered my gun a cat's whisker. "Take it easy.

I wouldn't have shot you," I said, fighting to control the jitter in my voice.

Tanner sprang up and slapped on the light. "You could've fooled me."

My hands were shaking, giving away how totally freaked I'd been, but I went for cool as a cucumber. "Hey, you would've been thanking me if that had been a bad guy."

Tanner shook his head. "A bad guy would've been easier to deal with. Your crazy cat thinks he's a kamikaze."

I shoved my gun into my waistband and consoled Harold. "It's okay, boy. You did good."

"Did good? He almost took my eyes out!"

"Sure, but if you'd been a bad guy, we'd be cracking open a tin of tuna and singing his praises."

Harold mewed a "yeah."

"Okay, okay, *Serene*-uh." Tanner squinted up at the ceiling—probably praying for patience.

The man was maddening. *Tell me he wouldn't have been freaking out if I'd gone into the room first and he'd heard me scream.*

"Well, the good news is," he said, "it doesn't look like your prowler got inside. Any ideas who it could be?"

"Not really."

He holstered his gun and headed toward the living room. "A suspect from the art theft profiled in this afternoon's email blast? The timing would fit."

"I haven't narrowed in on anyone yet."

"Could be taking preemptive measures."

Hmm, I didn't like the sound of that.

A knock sounded at the hall door. I hurried to answer it, grateful for the distraction. I flipped on the rest of the lights as I went and peered out the peephole. "It's my neighbor, Mr. Sutton." I yanked it open.

"Serena, what's wrong? I thought I heard a scream."

"Yes, sorry about that. Everything's fine."

He shook his head, deep furrows creasing his brow. "I don't think so." He held out a napkin. "This note was tacked to your door."

"Note?" The only thing I could see on it was the Boathouse restaurant logo.

"May I?" Tanner opened the napkin and groaned.

"Written by a real slangwhanger," Mr. Sutton said. "That's an obnoxious writer. Maybe that can be tomorrow's word of the day."

"Thank you for bringing it to my attention," I said, easing the door closed before I turned to Tanner and the note. "Do I want to know what it says?"

Tanner sighed. "I shouldn't have brought you in on this case. I don't know who he thinks we are. Probably doesn't realize we're agents."

"What does it say?"

"'Watch where you step or next time you might lose more than a shoe.'"

I crossed my arms over my midriff to fight the sudden wave of wooziness. "Clever play on words."

"These men don't play."

9

Loud pounding jerked me from my sleep. I squinted at the morning light streaming through the window, then at my digital clock blinking a time that didn't make sense. The electricity must've been off.

The pounding started again, accompanied by the peal of my cell phone.

"I'm coming. I'm coming," I called, dragging on my robe, then snatching up my phone. "Hey, Zoe, hold on a second. I got a crazy person pounding down my door." Reaching for the dead bolt, I glanced out the peephole. Terri, Zoe's bridesmaid. *Uh-oh.* "What time is it?" I said into the phone as I yanked open the door.

Zoe jockeyed around Terri and burst into the apartment, her chestnut-brown hair almost as wild as her eyes. "Ten minutes to our appointment at the bridal shop!"

Oops. I clicked off my phone. "I overslept."

"Yeah, and last Saturday you got called out of town. And the week before that was something else. Trust me, you haven't begun to see what this *crazy person* will do if you're not dressed in five minutes."

I laughed, thinking she was teasing, until her eyes flared. "Hey, I'm the one who introduced you to Jax, remember? That should compensate for being a delinquent maid of honor, don't you think?"

"There's a statute of limitations on how many times you can play that card." Zoe blew a hank of hair from her face and handed over a steaming cup of coffee. "Here, this'll wake you up. Now go get ready."

"Feed Harold for me, will you?" I dashed to my bedroom and pulled on jeans and a T-shirt, moved to the bathroom and brushed my teeth, spritzed and scrunched my hair, then dashed back to the living room. "Okay, I'm ready."

Terri glanced up from her phone. "How do you do that? It takes me an hour to look that good." She swiped her thumb across her phone screen. "No way! You'll never believe what Phil does for a living."

"Who's Phil?" I asked.

Zoe herded us out the door. "He's her latest prospect on that Catch Me a Fish dating site she's always on."

"Hey, you'd be on it too if Serena hadn't set you up with Jax."

"No, it drove me crazy. None of the guys could write a complete sentence, let alone spell." Zoe clicked her remote to unlock the doors of her new car—a treat to herself after the art museum recognized her skill as head of security with a raise following our recovery of their stolen Monet.

I glanced around, looking for any sign last night's note-writing *visitor* was keeping tabs on me.

"You've got to find her a man, Serena."

"Nah, I think Phil might be the one," Terri said from the backseat. "He can write and spell. Even reads. He's a prison librarian."

"O-kay," Zoe said, sounding a little weirded out. "That's different."

"Yeah," I joked. "Never saw that job on those aptitude tests they made us do in high school."

Zoe injected optimism into her voice. "At least you wouldn't have to worry about a pretty girl at his work catching his eye." She handed me a piece of paper and then sped out of the parking lot.

"What's this?"

"The list of bridal shops we're going to visit."

"We're going to more than one?"

She gave me a longsuffering look. "I want you guys to have the most perfect bridesmaids dresses."

"I'm sure all the shops carry pretty much the same dresses." Shiny pink taffeta with poufy sleeves and an even poufier balloon-like skirt that crunched when you moved. I'd been to enough weddings to know.

"Oh no, we have to check out all the possibilities before we choose," Terri said.

"You'll have to be patient with Serena," Zoe explained. "She doesn't like to shop."

Terri gasped. "Get out! You've got to be kidding me."

"Don't mind her," Zoe said to me. "She secretly worries about anyone who doesn't like to shop."

"Why do you keep looking at the side mirror?" Terri asked.

Zoe glanced across the seat at me, her fingers tightening around the steering wheel. "Please tell me a psycho guy isn't following us."

I slanted another quick glance at the side mirror. The silver Escalade that had picked up our tail the second we'd pulled out of the driveway turned onto a side street. "A psycho guy isn't following us."

She looked at me as if she wanted to believe me but didn't.

"Relax. This wedding planning has you way too tense." My phone rang before she could grill me further.

"Have you seen your super yet? What did his brother have to say?" Tanner asked the instant I hit Connect.

"Haven't seen Nate yet. I gave up waiting at midnight, and I had to hurry out this morning before I could catch up to him."

"Okay, keep your eyes open for trouble."

"Always."

A couple of bridal shops later, I was almost wishing for trouble. Catching bad guys, I could cope with. Catching Zoe's eclectic vision for our dresses, not so much. "What kind of dress are you looking for?" I asked Zoe as we walked out of the second shop without trying on a single dress.

"I'll know it when I see it." She dragged us across the street to the Bridezmaidz Boutique that offered dresses that were to traditional gowns what avant-garde art is to classical.

"If you give us a hint, we could help you be on the lookout for it," I said.

Zoe stopped in front of the store's massive window and gasped at the Mondrian-style dress on the mannequin. "This is it!"

Terri paled. "Squares aren't terribly slimming," she whispered.

Hmm, that went double for giant colored squares outlined in black on a white background, but . . . "All the art buffs will think it's pretty cool," I offered. "It could be worse. Think Picasso!"

Zoe scrutinized Terri's figure. Where I was tallish, slim, and fair haired, Terri was dark, petite, and plump—and yeah, Mondrian's squares were not going to work for her.

I pulled open the shop door and lifted my voice encouragingly. "Maybe we can find something else artsy inside that will suit both of us."

Zoe had always been uber chic when it came to fashion, and since her wedding reception would be held at the art gallery where she worked, it made total sense to go with an artsy kind of dress. I pulled a teal number off the rack. It had an asymmetrical hemline reminiscent of cubism.

"Ooh, I like," Zoe gushed.

Terri looked up from her smartphone, on which she'd been thumbing another message on the Kettle of Fish dating site or whatever she'd called it. "Do they have it in a pastel color? I look better in pastels."

"Hey, maybe we can go with different colors," I suggested. "That would look artistic. The guys could wear bow ties and cummerbunds to match."

"That's a great idea." Zoe handed me a skin-skimming yellow gown and Terri a soft pink, A-skirt style. "Here, try these."

There was no mirror in the actual changing room. So I quickly slipped into the gown and stepped out in front of the three-way mirrors.

"Oh, it's gorgeous," Zoe gushed.

I let out a strangled squawk and looked at her as if she had banana antennas coming out of her head. "Yeah, if you want me to look like a piece of fruit in one of Cézanne's still lifes." What was it about getting engaged that suddenly made a woman's taste in dresses so . . . so . . . so . . . ?

"Too many Cinderella movies," a guy behind me said.

Wait, did I ask that question out loud? My gaze shifted to the reflection in the mirror of a guy reclining on one of the upholstered chairs behind me. Billy? I spun around to face him. "What are you doing here?"

"I've been helping my buddy do deliveries for his dad's furniture store across the street. And when I spotted you coming in here as we got back, I decided to see what you were up to. Figured I could use a laugh."

Zoe swatted him.

Billy was Zoe's cousin and my first crush—and first kiss, if you count a New Millennium's Eve kiss at twelve years old when my worst fear was that the world would end with my never having been kissed. By the time I was old enough to date four years later, I was also old enough to clue in that Billy was a Casanova that any girl would have had to be an idiot to go out with. And apparently, every girl in his grade at school, three years ahead of me, was certifiable.

Terri emerged from her dressing room in her pink number, looking like a grapefruit. It was unbelievable how poorly the dresses' artistic promises translated on the canvas of our real-world figures.

"Going for a tropical theme," Billy deadpanned.

I muffled a laugh since Zoe did not look amused.

Terri's gaze flitted to Billy, and she audibly

gasped. "Why can't guys on the dating site look like him?" she whispered.

Billy was ex-military and looked as if he'd just walked off the cover of *GI Quarterly*. Add in his magnetic smile, and every shopper in the place was looking his way.

"Go," Zoe ordered.

He stood and backed away from the viewing area, hands raised in surrender. "I was just trying to help."

Zoe shooed us back to the dressing rooms and delivered a parade of artsy-type dresses. The ones that suited Terri hung on me, although the clerk reassured Zoe a nip here and a tuck there would do the trick.

"I'm sure it'll be fine," I said feebly. To be honest, I was ready to wave the white flag and give the nod to Terri's adored mauve chiffon number, reminiscent of the French Impressionists. It did absolutely nothing for me, but one day in an unflattering dress—and in a bazillion photographs forever—seemed less torturous than shopping a second longer.

"No, the style doesn't suit," Zoe concluded. "Let's try the next shop."

"How about we take a break and look at flowers?" I suggested. "My assistant's parents own the flower shop up the block."

"Since when do you have an assistant?"

"At the drop-in center, for my art class." I

slipped back into the dressing room to escape the cubist number.

A few minutes later, we meandered out of the shop, and Terri, as ready as I was for a dress-shopping reprieve, said, "We might as well check out the flower shop Serena suggested while we're so close."

Two doors down from the flower shop was a pawnshop with a vintage '70s dress in the window, complete with the daisy trim around the neckline. "That would be kind of cool," I said. "I wouldn't mind looking in here for a minute."

"It's your day off," Zoe said.

"What's that got to do with her wanting to go to a pawnshop?" Terri asked.

"Because half the stuff in there was probably stolen and fenced."

I chuckled. "I wasn't thinking of scouting for any cases, honest."

"Well, Jax and I have already picked out our wedding bands, so I'm good." Zoe tugged me toward the flower shop. A bell above the door jingled as Terri pulled it open, but a familiar voice snagged my attention. I glanced back in time to see Tasha blowing a kiss to the man climbing out of her car in front of the pawnshop. A man who wasn't her husband.

He turned, and my breath hitched. Ted the exterminator. I tapped Zoe's arm. "You go ahead. I want to check out one thing."

"You're going to abandon us?"

"Of course not. I'll just be a few minutes." By the time I turned back to the pawnshop, Tasha was speeding away, and Ted had disappeared. *I don't like this.* Ted's appearance at the drop-in center during Nana's visit was looking more suspicious by the second. Tasha was a married woman. She shouldn't be blowing kisses at another man. Nana was not going to be happy if Gladys's thief turned out to be her own daughter and her . . . her . . . whatever Ted was to her.

I peered through the pawnshop window but saw no sign of Ted. I scanned the street, the nearby shops, and the windows of the apartments above the shops. I'd turned away for mere seconds. For him to disappear so quickly, he had to have gone into the pawnshop.

I slipped inside and smiled at the clerk, who looked like an extra out of a low-budget mafia movie. "Can you tell Ted I need to talk to him?" I said.

"Who?"

Right, Ted wouldn't have given me his real name if he was spying on my conversation with Nana. "The guy who just came in here."

The clerk hesitated half a beat and then looked around. "You see anyone else in here?"

I motioned to the door behind the cash desk. "In the back."

"There's no one back there."

"Look, I saw him come in less than a minute ago. Blond, shaggy hair, has kind of a nasally southern drawl."

The clerk frowned and shook his head.

I rounded the desk. "Mind if I look?"

He stepped back, blocking the door. "Yeah, I'm not allowed to let anyone in there." The twitch in his eye confirmed he was hiding something, although, this being a pawnshop, it wasn't necessarily Ted.

Maybe he had taken off somewhere else when I'd turned to speak to Zoe and Terri. I debated flashing my badge, but I suspected he was too savvy to give consent. Not to mention, I'd kept Zoe waiting long enough. "Thanks anyway." I headed out.

Zoe waved me over the second I opened the flower shop door. "What do you think of this arrangement for the church?" She showed me a picture.

"Very nice."

Lisa, my assistant from the drop-in center, hurried over to me. "Did you hear?"

"Hear what?"

"Tyrone pulled his painting from the gala's fundraising auction."

My heart sank. Tyrone was our most talented artist. "Why?"

"He came by the drop-in center after school yesterday and spouted nonsense about not wanting to be a charity case and took it home with him. Didn't even want to leave it hanging at the center for the open house."

"Maybe I should pay him a visit. See if I can change his mind."

"You can try. He sure didn't want to listen to me."

"Please tell me talking to Tyrone can wait," Zoe said. "We still haven't picked out a dress."

"Of course, I'm all yours until five o'clock." Then I had to hightail it over to Mom and Dad's for dinner before Aunt Martha's dislike of Nana overpowered her curiosity about the theft, and things got out of hand.

Terri groaned.

"What's wrong?" Zoe and I said in unison.

Terri swiped her fingers across her cell-phone screen, then slapped the phone against her leg. "My date just canceled. We seemed to be getting along so well too. I don't know what I said."

Zoe gave her a sideways hug. "Maybe Serena can find you a guy. She's good at it."

Terri's eyes brightened. "The guy from the bridal shop?" she asked hopefully.

"You don't want him," Zoe said. "Trust me. He's my cousin. A nice enough guy. But a player."

A little of the light in Terri's eyes dimmed.

"Come on." Zoe beckoned her back outside. "More dress shopping will make you feel better."

I slipped ahead of them to take another peek in the pawnshop window, hoping to catch a glimpse of Ted.

The window exploded with a burst of gunfire.

10

I spun away from the pawnshop window and made a dive for Zoe and Terri, taking them to the ground with me.

Bullets ripped through the car beside us and whizzed over our heads, as if we'd landed in the middle of a Barnaby Furnas painting. Screams filled the air.

The gunfire ended with a squeal of tires.

I surged to my feet, gun drawn, and hunched behind a car for what little cover it gave, but the gunman's car disappeared around the first corner before I could so much as make out the model. The hair on the back of my neck prickled. I scanned the sidewalks, the street. Deserted.

This had all the marks of a gang hit, but—I glanced at the pawnshop's shattered window, at my friends still splayed on the sidewalk—who was the target?

Ignoring my stampeding heart, I holstered my weapon and turned back to Terri and Zoe. "You two okay?"

Zoe sat up, visibly shaken, and swiped glass

fragments out of her hair. "Of course we're not okay! We just got shot at."

She must've sensed from my rigid stance that I'd gone into FBI mode, because her expression morphed from panicked anger to something akin to horror. "Please tell me those guys weren't aiming at you."

Terri gasped. "They could've been gunning for you?" She army-crawled toward the aerated car at the curb and huddled next to the tire, hugging her legs with shaky arms.

"No, of course not," I said, not knowing if it was a lie. My hands fisted, my nails biting into my palms. What if she'd been killed because of me?

"Are you sure?" Zoe pressed.

Sirens filled the air.

Movement inside the pawnshop caught my attention, and at the sight of the clerk nervously emerging from behind the counter, I expelled a breath. "Ninety-nine percent sure."

"Why on earth would you work a job that makes you enemies like that?" Terri asked.

My mind flashed to the note Mr. Sutton had found taped to my door last night, but for Terri's sake, I shrugged nonchalantly. "Adrenaline junkie, I guess."

I'd become so used to faking courage since starting the job that somewhere along the line, I actually began to embody the trait, if not quite feel it.

Zoe must've sensed what I was trying to do because she forced out a chuckle. "More like she adores the hot agent who trained her."

I rolled my eyes.

Terri's lips trembled into a semblance of a smile. "Does he have a friend?"

I stared at her, at a loss for words. We'd just been shot at and she was still fishing for a date. Seriously? My phone rang.

"See," Zoe said. "That's probably him now. He has this sixth sense about when she's in trouble."

I glanced at Tanner's name on my screen and got a shiver. Okay, this was too weird. I clicked on the phone as police cruisers surrounded the scene.

"Please tell me you're okay," Tanner said, sounding worried.

Zoe smiled smugly and mouthed, *What did I tell you?*

Ignoring her, I turned and lowered my voice, last night's warning ricocheting around my brain. "Why wouldn't I be okay?"

"I hear sirens."

"Oh, that. I was kind of in the wrong place at the wrong time."

Tanner let out a strangled sound.

"What's wrong? Why did you call?"

Police cars swerved to block both ends of the street.

"I got a note like yours."

I didn't think my heart could pound any harder,

but I was wrong. I scanned the street again as the police waved back the curiosity-seekers who'd emerged from hiding. But there was no sign of the lowlifes Tanner photographed at the Boathouse. "What did the note say?"

"Back off or the girlfriend dies."

"But you don't have a girlfriend."

Silence.

Okay, maybe I just couldn't hear him over the sudden roar in my ears. "They think *I'm* your—"

"Girlfriend. Yeah."

"But were you working on your case today?"

"No."

"Then it's probably just a coincidence."

"Or proof they're serious."

A police officer came out of the pawnshop and waved in a couple of waiting paramedics. The officer taking down Zoe's and Terri's statements glanced my way. A third officer cordoned off the scene with police tape.

"Okay, what do you want me to tell the police?"

"Nothing about the notes. The last thing I need is a bunch of detectives interfering."

The paramedics wheeled a victim out of the pawnshop on a gurney.

Lucas? When did he go in there? "Uh," I said to Tanner, "a suspect in my Dali case was hit. This might not be what you think."

"The note was pretty clear. And I'm not working *your* case."

"You did last night. When you followed us to Randy's."

The paramedics loaded Gladys's son-in-law into the ambulance. Awfully coincidental that he happened to be in the very pawnshop his wife had dropped her apparent lover off at less than—I glanced at my watch—forty minutes ago. Was he following Tasha?

"Tanner, I've got to go. I'll call you later." I disconnected before he could protest and hurried toward the ambulance.

An officer caught me by the arm. "Where do you think you're going? We need to ask you some questions."

"I'm Serena Jones, St. Louis FBI." I showed him my badge. "I need to talk to the victim."

"The victim is unconscious, so how about you talk to me first?"

A news crew careened to a stop at the end of the street, and a cameraman and a reporter poured out of the doors.

"Can we talk inside?" The last thing Mom needed was to see her daughter in the middle of a shooting spree. Not to mention whoever sent Tanner the note.

The officer motioned me into the pawnshop ahead of him.

"I won't be long," I called back to Zoe and Terri, who were now huddled at the edge of the tape, watching my exchange with the officer.

133

The same clerk I'd met earlier was talking to another officer inside. There was still no sign of Ted.

I told the officer who I was and what I'd seen, which wasn't much. "I have no idea who was behind the shooting or what motivated it. I didn't even know my suspect was in this shop until I saw the paramedics wheel him out."

"So you don't think the shooting is connected to your investigation involving the victim?"

"I can't imagine how. It's an art burglary. The only reason he's a suspect is he's a relative of the theft victim and has unfettered access to the house. But I'd like to question the clerk about his visit, if I may."

"Sure, go ahead." The officer signaled to the one interviewing the clerk, then headed toward the evidence-recovery team, photographing the bullets and glass spatter at the front of the store.

"Oh, officer," I called after him. "Was there anyone else in the store?"

"No. But a second employee was supposed to be in today. I sent an officer out to locate him."

"What was his name?"

"Ted something." The officer glanced at his notepad. "Vale. Ted Vale."

I bit down on a grin. "Thanks." I turned to the clerk. "Special Agent Serena Jones." I showed him my badge. "Want to start by telling me why you lied about Ted?"

The clerk held up his hands in surrender. "Hey, you didn't tell me you were an agent then. Ted came in, said his ex-girlfriend was stalking him and was outside and that if she came in, to tell her he didn't work here."

"So why didn't he return to work after I left?"

"We weren't busy, so I said he might as well take the day off."

"What about the victim? Did you know him?"

"Sure, he's a regular."

"What did he want?"

"To buy back the jewelry he'd pawned a couple of months ago. But he was out of luck. We sold it." The clerk reached below the counter and set a gold pocket watch on the display case. "So he was about to buy this back when that maniac started shooting."

The watch had *Lucas Watson—for 25 years of service* inscribed on the back. Lucas wasn't old enough to have worked anywhere that long, so the watch had likely been his father's or maybe his grandfather's. I whipped out my phone and called Nana. "Quick question. Do you know if Gladys's son-in-law's parents are still alive?"

"Both dead. He has a sister still living."

"Okay, thanks."

"Do you have a lead?" Nana asked.

"I'm not sure. Maybe." In my experience, most people didn't peddle a pocket watch if they'd lifted a million-dollar painting. But a couple of months ago, he could've had a forger to pay before making the score.

I found Zoe and Terri waiting for me outside, both still looking shaky. "Do you mind if we cut our shopping trip short?" I asked.

"That's fine with me," Zoe said. Getting shot at had evidently killed her enthusiasm. That and the fear of being within twenty feet of me.

"I wasn't the target," I repeated as Zoe dropped me off at my apartment.

"You tell yourself whatever you need to. Just please make sure it's true before you are standing beside me on my wedding day."

Yeah, Tanner was already on that, so I saluted, and she drove off. I went straight to my car and drove to the hospital. The staff directed me to the waiting room for surgical patients.

Pete and another officer, both in uniform, emerged from the room, looking somber.

"How is he?" I asked, ignoring for the moment my suspicions about his connection to the Dali theft.

Pete didn't seem surprised to see me there. Had Gladys told him about my investigation after all? Or maybe he'd heard that I'd been caught in the shooting spree too. "He's still in surgery." Pete exchanged glances with his fellow officer. "My mom and sister are in there."

When I stepped in, they were pacing. "How are you holding up?" I asked.

"Oh, Serena," Gladys said. "How nice of you to come by. I guess you heard Tasha's husband got caught in the middle of some gang shooting. We don't know what on earth he was doing in the pawnshop. Saw something in the window that caught his eye, I imagine."

Tasha's almost-imperceptible snort suggested she had other ideas.

"How bad is it?"

"Shards of glass embedded in his skin. I figure he passed out at the sight of his blood," Tasha chimed in. "He's always been kind of squeamish. The doctor says he'll be fine once they remove all the fragments."

"Were you aware he frequented that particular pawnshop?" I asked.

She cut short a sudden intake of breath and shot her mother a quick glance. "I could use a cup of coffee. Mom, you want us to get you anything?"

"Oh, I'll come along."

"No, no," Tasha protested. "One of us needs to stay here in case the doctor returns, and I really need to get out of this room for a few minutes."

"Oh yes, of course. Bring me back a tea, then."

Tasha steered me out of the room, toward the elevator.

"Mind if we take the stairs?" I asked.

Tasha swerved toward the stairs door, and I had to almost jog to keep up with her. The instant the door closed behind us, she blurted, "Yeah, I knew.

137

I saw him go to the pawnshop a couple of months ago. He'd been slinking around, acting cagey for a while, so I decided to follow him." She stomped down the stairs, gripping the stair rail in a stranglehold. "The lowlife pawned my jewelry! Can you believe that? I bought it back, but of course, it didn't help me, because I couldn't wear it without him figuring out I was onto his deception."

"Why didn't you confront him?"

Her step faltered. "I don't know. I guess I was afraid he'd just up and disappear with the rest of our money."

"How long have you been seeing Ted?"

She blushed. "My husband makes phone calls and clandestine trips at all hours. I'm sure he's cheating on me again. He's already had one woman file a paternity suit against him. For all I know, that's who he's still skulking around with." She lowered her voice. "I wouldn't be surprised if he stole Mom's painting to build their little love nest. I mean, if he'd hock his wife's jewels behind her back . . ."

"You know about the missing painting?" Had Gladys changed her mind about keeping the theft from her children?

"The housekeeper told me after your grandmother got Mom so worked up the other day. That's why I asked Ted to follow your grandmother, to see if he could find out what she was going to do."

"And how long have you been seeing him?"

She let out a resigned sigh. "A couple of months. I met him in that pawnshop I'd spied Lucas in. Ted works there."

"I see."

"But you know what? I'm not sure Lucas is smart enough to pull off such an elaborate ruse. He's impulsive, you know? He gets himself into trouble and then looks for a quick fix, like hocking my jewelry." Tasha yanked open the door that exited to the coffee-shop level. "No, the more I think about it, the more I think Mom's so upset because, deep down, she's afraid Pete made the switch." Tasha picked up a tray and, leaning closer to me, lowered her voice. "Of course, talking your grandmother out of doing what she's set her mind to is like talking to a brick wall . . . at least that's what the housekeeper said."

I refrained from commenting. Tasha was doing a good job of talking, and the way I saw it, the more she tried to fill in all the blanks, the closer we were likely to get to the real truth.

Tasha added a couple of plastic-wrapped muffins to her tray and ordered a tea and a coffee. "And you know, Pete would know where to find a forger, right? And a fence. I bet he knows all kinds of bad guys who could help him make a quick buck on a stolen painting. You want a coffee?"

"He always seemed honest to me," I said, declining the coffee offer.

139

Tasha shook her head. "Desperation makes you do desperate things. Mom has already bailed him out of financial hot water a couple of times, but she doesn't have a lot of liquid assets anymore. That old house costs a fortune to keep up. And the taxes." She rolled her eyes skyward. "*Woowee.* Ridiculous. I keep telling her she should move. But she and Daddy lived there for forty-five years, and she can't stand the thought of leaving it for something more affordable."

Okay, Tasha had thrown just about every name into the suspect pool except her own. Which edged her closer to the top of my list.

▌▌

I climbed my exterior stairs and examined the door and window for signs of forced entry or booby traps. Nothing.

Erring on the side of caution, I jogged back down and rounded the building to go in through the front. I stopped by Nate's apartment first to find out what his brother had to say after we left yesterday. He wasn't home. I wandered around the building looking for him, figured he must be doing repairs in one of the apartments. He was always here on Saturdays.

But today he wasn't. *Strange.*

Okay, I'd put off entering my place as long as I

could. No note on the door. That was a good sign. I walked closer. No evidence of tampering on the lock or around the frame. I tapped the door with my knuckles. "Harold? You okay in there?" I pressed my ear to the door. "Harold?"

"Meow!"

Good, no toxic gases inside primed to take me out. I unlocked the door and scooped up Harold. "Good boy," I cooed, nuzzling him against my chest until my heart stopped knocking around inside and Harold started clamoring to be released.

"Okay, okay, I guess the shooting rattled me." The police interrogation hadn't helped. "Sure, an FBI agent should've had the presence of mind to get a description of the guys shooting at her and the vehicle they were driving. Because hey, we're not like sane people who duck the second they hear gunfire!"

Harold paused long enough from his face-cleaning regimen to give me a Grumpy Cat frown.

"What? I'm a little rattled. Okay?"

One thing was for certain: I'd better get unrattled before tonight's dinner. I changed into an old T-shirt and jeans and pulled out my paints. Painting always calmed my mind. I was currently working on a still life of a bowl of fruit. Never mind that I'd eaten two pieces from the bowl—the banana and an orange—since starting it over a week ago.

It was a good thing I didn't intend to let Aunt

Martha wangle information about the Dali theft out of Nana tonight, because I sure didn't want to give a rundown on my prime suspects. Not with Gladys's kids and Tasha's probable lover topping the list.

A blob of paint smeared the banana skin, making it look rotten, along with my painting skills. Ugh. This wasn't working. I was getting tenser instead of relaxed!

I shook out my arms, willing my muscles to become as flaccid as Dali's dripping clocks, and suddenly inspiration struck. I could paint a *surrealistic* bowl of fruit. The image of Ramaz Razmadze's scowl-faced apple chomping into a slice of another apple came to mind.

Hmm, something less . . . cannibalistic would be better. Something cheerful. I tried transforming the banana's bruise into a tuxedo so I could paint him dancing with a pear, but he came out looking more like a disgruntled zucchini.

Oh, forget this. I jabbed my brush into the paint thinner.

A pithy Scott Adams quote I'd once seen on an art poster came to mind—*Creativity is allowing yourself to make mistakes. Art is knowing which to keep.* Well, this was definitely *not* a keeper.

I finished cleaning the brush and opted for a hot shower instead, since I hadn't had time for one this morning. I brought my iPod into the bathroom and cranked up the volume to drown out the thoughts of what Nana would think about the direction of my investigation. And I locked the bathroom door. I'd seen *Psycho*.

I turned on the water and waited for it to get to the right temperature. Okay, now visions of Norman Bates slashing my shower curtain were plaguing my mind. Suddenly the loud music didn't seem like such a smart call. I flicked off the iPod.

A shower didn't seem like a great idea either. I put the plug in the tub and switched the water to the tub spout. A nice, quiet bath—that's what I needed.

I dutifully arrived at my parents' house at a quarter to six. Early enough to help calm down Mom before Dad arrived with Nana, but not so early that Aunt Martha would have time to grill me about my progress on the case. My parents still lived in the same modest, 1940s two-story I grew up in in University City, just west of St. Louis. The street had been loud and full of bikes and skateboards when I was a kid, but my generation had grown up and moved out, leaving behind a quieter street with more flowerbeds and lawn ornaments than ever would've survived my childhood.

I pulled into my parents' empty driveway just as their neighbor, Mrs. Peterson, burst out her door, chasing after a half-dressed tyke. She scooped him into her arms and smacked a big kiss on his cheek, then scolded him for running out. Only it sounded more like a playful game than that he was in trouble. No wonder Mom had grandkids on the brain. Half the neighbors were entertaining them these days.

Those flowerbeds' days were seriously numbered.

I let myself inside. "Hey, where's Aunt Martha's car?"

"She finally listened to your father and sent it to the shop to have that pinging noise checked," Mom said from the dining room off the entrance.

How Dad had distinguished a *ping* from the *pongs* and *plufts* it'd been making for years was a mystery to me.

I dropped my coat onto the hook by the door and joined Mom in the dining room. I knew we were in trouble when she didn't even lift her head as she circled the table, polishing and laying out silverware. "Everything okay?" I whispered so Aunt Martha, who sounded as if she were leading a marching band of pot bangers in the kitchen, wouldn't hear me.

Mom spun around, slicing the air with the last fork in her hand. "I don't know what's gotten into her. She's been baking and cooking all day, going on and on about how much your grandmother is going to love the meal. Malgucci even delivered fresh beef from his brother's butcher shop."

Malgucci was either Aunt Martha's newest male

friend or her pet project. I wasn't sure which. His selfless donation of one of his kidneys to save Mrs. Burke's life seemed to convince Aunt Martha he was a reformed man, despite his mob ties.

Mom gasped. "You don't think she's planning to poison your grandmother, do you?"

I laughed. Then abruptly clamped my mouth shut at Mom's frown. She was serious.

"Aunt Martha despises your grandmother. For a wedding gift, she gave me a tiny 'Stella' doll and a package of pins."

I couldn't help it. I laughed again.

Mom pulled a stack of her best china plates from the hutch and handed them to me. "Martha can't stand your grandmother's pretentiousness, but that's just the way Stella is. I figure why fret over what I can't change."

"But be honest. Did you ever poke a pin or two in the doll?"

Mom grinned. "The whole package. The first day of our honeymoon, when she called our hotel room and kept your father talking for close to an hour."

"No way!"

"Yes way. I hid in the bathroom and vented on that ridiculous doll so I wouldn't be tempted to say anything negative to my new husband about his mother."

I gaped. Wow, my mom was pretty amazing. I think I'd have read Dad the riot act. Or worse, blown up long before the wedding day and forced him to choose who he really wanted to spend the rest of his life with. "Did Dad know about the doll?"

She nodded. "After he hung up the phone, he came looking for me and saw it, pins and all."

"What did he do?"

"Apologized. Tossed the doll in the dustbin. And whisked me out of the hotel." Mom got a far-off look, and a serene smile slid to her lips. "We *sightseed* our way around the western states, never staying at any hotel more than one night."

"Sightseed?"

"Sightsaw?"

She wrinkled her nose, and I had to agree it didn't sound any better.

"You know what I mean," she went on. "And we unplugged the phone the minute we checked in each night."

Ha. My dad, the romantic.

Mom lifted a crystal tumbler from the cupboard and seemed to lose herself in watching the light dance off the decorative pattern. "I decided that week if his mother wanted to spend the rest of her life finding fault with me, that was her choice, but I wasn't going to ruin another minute of my life fretting over her opinion of me. Or give her more ammunition. She'd raised the man of my dreams, and for that, I could never thank her enough."

Tears clogged my throat.

The doorbell rang.

"Did you invite more people to dinner?" I asked, quickly finishing setting out the plates.

"Oh no." Mom hurried to the front window. "You don't think Aunt Martha invited Malgucci?" She peeked past the curtain. "It's Tanner."

My heart jumped. What was he doing here? He'd given me the green light to come. Said he was sure no drive-by shooters would serve up appetizers before the meal. Had he changed his mind? He should've called. Now he was going to get Aunt Martha speculating and Mom worrying and . . .

I strode to the door and swallowed hard, forcing calm, cool, and collected into my voice. "Hey, Tanner, what's up?"

Tanner rested his forearm on the edge of the doorframe and leaned into it ever so casually. "Is that a trick question?"

"No, what are you doing here?"

"Your father invited me for dinner."

For a nanosecond, I suspected he'd made up the invitation as an excuse to play watchdog for drive-by shooters, until a whisper of uneasiness snuck into his eyes as he shifted his attention to Mom. "He didn't tell you?"

"No worries," Mom exclaimed, cheerily waving away his concern. "You're always welcome." Once upon a time, Tanner had been a star pupil in my father's second-year economics class, and they'd gotten reacquainted when Tanner was assigned as my field-training agent. I'd still been living at home at the time, and Mom had invited him in for dinner when he'd followed me home so I could change before a surveillance stint. He'd won Mom over with his assurances that he'd always have my back. My dad had just been excited to have a guest who understood his economic words of wisdom.

In Dad's mind, everything about the world and human nature could be compared to the stock market, so having someone at dinner versed in the lingo made his day. And he'd made a point of inviting Tanner back at every opportunity. Sometimes it drove me a little crazy. Tonight . . . I was grateful for the reinforcements.

Stepping inside, Tanner swept his arm from behind his back and offered Mom a colorful bouquet. "These are for you."

Mom blushed. "Oh my, you didn't need to do that." She beamed up at me with her he's-a-keeper eyes, before bustling off to the kitchen in search of a vase.

"I hope you know what you're in for," I whispered in his ear.

Tanner glanced at Dad's car pulling into the driveway with Nana. "Your dad mentioned something about needing an impartial referee."

"Hah." I stepped out to hold open the screen door since Nana had decided she needed to use a walker to get around tonight. "You are so not going to think this is worth a free meal."

Nana hobbled inside, muttering about the uncomfortable ride in Dad's *little* car. Dad's disinterest in status symbols had never ceased to be a disappointment to her. While the streets named after prestigious universities gave Mom and Dad's neighborhood an air of respectability, it wasn't prestigious enough for Nana's only child. She'd wanted Dad hobnobbing with the upper class. But Dad hated pretense. He'd just wanted to live in a nice neighborhood with a good school and to be within walking distance of his job at Wash U.

At the sight of Tanner, Nana paused in the doorway, straightening to her full five-foot-eight, straight-as-an-arrow height. "Who is this young man?"

"My colleague Tanner Calhoun."

He stuck out his hand. "Pleased to meet you, ma'am."

Nana's jaw tightened, her gaze shifting to mine, telepathing *Why is your colleague joining us for dinner?*

Apparently, Dad could read her mind too, because he climbed the stoop behind Nana and said, "I invited him to join us."

Nana's demeanor warmed considerably at the news, no doubt assuming that, as requested, I hadn't shared any information about Gladys's missing painting after all. But I had a bad feeling that keeping Aunt Martha from saying anything about the case wouldn't be easy.

Aunt Martha bustled into the dining room, carrying a large pan of shepherd's pie between her giant oven mitts.

The kind of oblong cake version of meatloaf with mashed potatoes squashed on top had been one of my more favorite meals as a kid . . . when Mom stuck to mixing vegetables like peas and corn with the beef, not . . . brussels sprouts.

"Sit, sit. Dinner's ready." Aunt Martha's gaze skittered across each of us, and when she spotted Tanner, she frowned.

"I seem to be back in her bad books," he whispered close to my ear.

"No accounting for taste," I said with a shrug. The truth was, Aunt Martha was secretly, or maybe not so secretly, rooting for Nate to be my beau. He'd been her apartment superintendent for several years before she convinced me to take over her place. A scheme that I now suspected was designed to throw Nate and me into each other's paths.

Not that Dad's impromptu invitation meant Dad was rooting for Tanner. At least . . . I didn't think so.

Dad said grace and then launched into a discussion with Tanner about last week's market dip.

Nana spooned a bird-sized portion of shepherd's pie onto her plate, then proceeded to study it as she sipped her water. Mom scooped up a big helping and began shoveling it into her mouth, no doubt to keep from saying anything she'd regret if Nana got around to voicing whatever she was thinking.

"It smells delicious," I said to Aunt Martha, who rewarded me with a beaming smile.

"How are plans for the drop-in center fundraiser coming along?" Aunt Martha asked, directing the question to Nana.

Tanner must've heard my sudden intake of breath because he shot me a concerned glance.

I knew Aunt Martha too well. The question was a ploy to get around to talking about art— Gladys's art.

"Quite well, thank you for asking." Nana picked up her fork and held it in precisely the right way as she nudged a minute sample of the food onto the tines.

I readjusted my cavewoman hold on my fork and shot Aunt Martha an ixnay-on-where-I-know-you're-going-with-this glare.

She ignored it. "I'm delighted you've decided to include a few of the youths' pieces in the silent auction. Will that charming Tyrone's be one of them?" She patted her napkin to her lips, the picture of innocence. "I met him last month when I filled in for Serena's assistant. Such an accomplished chap. I'm thinking of buying one of his pieces."

Nana deflected the question to me with a shift of her gaze.

"Oh. Um, that was the plan," I said vaguely, still hoping I could convince Tyrone to change his mind about pulling his piece.

"Will you purchase a new piece for yourself, Stella? I couldn't help but overhear, when you called looking for Serena yesterday, that you'd wanted her advice on some art."

"Perhaps." Nana's interest in the food on her plate intensified.

I tapped my foot against Tanner's leg and with a head twitch in Aunt Martha's direction, signaled I could use some help.

The serving spoon he'd just filled with seconds paused in midair. "The meal is delicious, Martha. How do you get such a nice flavor in the meat?"

"HP Sauce," Aunt Martha said and returned her attention to Nana.

I widened my eyes at Tanner to induce him to say more, but he shrugged and mouthed *I tried,* then tucked into his seconds.

"The housekeeper who works next door to your friend Gladys," Aunt Martha chattered on, "said your friend had an expensive painting nicked."

Nana's fork clattered against her plate. "Why am I not surprised? Can never trust the help to mind their own business." She looked to Dad.

"Remember the trouble I had with that busybody housekeeper I had to let go after your father died?"

"That's it!" Aunt Martha exclaimed, and all our gazes snapped to her.

"What's it?" Mom asked.

"The housekeeper. Her name was Horvak, wasn't it?" Aunt Martha asked Nana and then turned to me. "I told you the name sounded familiar. Eight months. Eight months I've been racking my brain, trying to remember where I'd heard it before."

My mouth went dry. Petra—the woman who'd orchestrated the Forest Park Art Museum heist—was a Horvak. A Horvak who'd claimed to know who killed my grandfather. A claim I hadn't been able to substantiate since a sniper took her out to save the man she'd kidnapped.

At Nana's yes to Aunt Martha's question, my own questions piled up in my mind, but I couldn't push a single one past my thickening throat. I didn't remember much about Nana and Granddad's housekeeper. Only that Nana had fired her soon after Granddad's death. I'd assumed it was because Nana put the house up for sale, but apparently it had been something the housekeeper had said . . . or knew.

Inexplicably, my attention shifted to Nana's hands deftly cutting the meat on her plate. They were pale and bony and bedecked with gold rings

153

studded with gemstones. I gasped, a memory of the night Granddad died flitting through my mind. I'd been ten years old, staying over to paint with Granddad while Nana went out to a church event. When we'd heard a car pull in the driveway, Granddad had scooted me back to my room through the secret passage, saying Nana would have his hide if she saw he'd let me stay up so late. Except I didn't because I heard strange noises and got scared. I remembered seeing a pinpoint of light seeping through the paneled wall, and when I stuck my eye to it, I saw a hand returning a book to the shelf.

My breath stalled in my throat. It couldn't have been Nana's. She wasn't a murderer.

I forced my attention from Nana's hands to Tanner. After hitting nothing but dead ends trying to substantiate Petra Horvak's claim, Tanner had convinced me the woman's assertion had been nothing more than a well-researched ploy to buy herself time to get away.

Now . . . a hint of doubt shadowed his gaze as it shifted to Nana. "What was your housekeeper's first name?"

I was still holding my breath and got a tad lightheaded. Her housekeeper couldn't have been Petra. She was too young. And Horvak had been Petra's married name, so it couldn't have been her mother.

Nana shot Tanner an indignant look. "Why on

earth should you care about the name of my former housekeeper?"

"Her name was Lucille," my father said in a tone that warned us not to answer Nana's question, which was fine by me. The only other female Horvak with a familial connection to Petra was her ex-husband's deceased mother, and her name was Irina.

I imagined Dad didn't want us to upset Nana by bringing up Granddad's unsolved murder. Not that I'd ever seen her get terribly emotional over anything. She had the British stiff-upper-lip stereotype down to an art.

Aunt Martha drew a breath as if she was about to launch into another question, but Tanner spoke up first.

"I brought a special treat to go with our after-dinner tea."

"You did?" I interjected. Tanner was actually more of a coffee man, but he knew the surest way to my parents' hearts was to embrace their British roots.

He flashed me a wink that I didn't like the looks of, then pushed away from the table and began picking up dishes. "Some stunning photos of Serena I thought you'd like. I'll just help you clear the table and then maybe we can plug my thumb drive into the computer."

"Oh, we can view them on the new TV," Mom said, jumping up to join him in clearing the table.

"Brilliant idea," Aunt Martha chimed in, not sounding put out by having her interrogation thwarted, which I couldn't help but think should worry me. "I'll put the kettle on and bring the plate of biscuits I fixed into the living room."

Dad carried a dining room chair to the living room and shifted the sofa chairs so everyone would have a good view of the TV. Nana joined him without comment, probably as relieved as I was to escape Aunt Martha's probing.

By the time Mom, Aunt Martha, and I joined them with the tea and cookies, Tanner had the first picture up on the TV.

Mom gasped. "You look so happy, Serena. Ward, doesn't she look happy?" Mom said to Dad as if it were a rare sight. She beamed at Tanner.

Great, now my parents thought we were dating. "I was help—"

Tanner nudged my elbow and gave me the evil eye.

I shot back an imploring look. Couldn't he see what they were thinking?

He just shrugged.

Men.

"Is that at the paddleboats?" Aunt Martha asked as Tanner advanced to the next picture—pictures, I'd noticed, that didn't include his suspects in the background.

He chuckled. "I forgot to specify which sunset cruise I was treating her to."

156

"And he didn't give me time to change."

"Hey, can I help it if I wanted to show you off like you were?"

Mom giggled. "She's never been the type to dress up much."

Oh, Tanner had no idea the fire he was playing with. Mom was bound to get on the phone to my aunts the second we were out of the house, and the next thing we'd know, April would be twittering about seeing us at the Boathouse and telling how Tanner looked at me and who knows what other nonsense.

Tanner advanced through a couple more pictures. How many did the man take without his suspects?

"You have a nice smile," Nana offered.

Really? Too much teeth showing, in my opinion. She must be trying to refrain from pointing out how windblown my hair had gotten.

Tanner flicked to the next one. One of him. And an *ahhh* went up around the room. Well, except from Aunt Martha.

Tanner really was a hunk, with those warm brown eyes laughing at the camera and that adorable dimple denting his cheek. He flicked quickly to the next picture.

"So these were taken *last* night?" Aunt Martha quizzed. "On your date that ended before seven, with a wet frock?"

"Yes, that was my fault," Tanner admitted.

Aunt Martha waved off his implied apology. "Worked out for the best. Nate took her out after that."

Ooh, Aunt Martha, that was harsh.

Mom frowned, her happy bubble burst.

Dad squeezed her hand and looked at Tanner. "You know what I say when it comes to investing—when there's blood in the streets, that's the time to buy. Even if it's your own."

A chill skittered down my spine. Dad didn't sound as if he was talking about investing, which meant all these dinner invitations to Tanner . . . Huh, Dad was slyer than I thought.

"Oh, look at that." Aunt Martha pointed to the TV screen. "Isn't that Tyrone, the chap from the drop-in center? What's he doing in the bushes?"

12

After church on Sunday, I shared a quiet lunch with Harold—tuna fish sandwiches, minus the bread, were his special Sunday treat—then stared at the painting I'd planned to continue working on. I tried to take a complete mental break from my cases on Sundays. After all, God must've known what He was talking about when He said we needed rest. More than once, a breakthrough had come on Monday morning thanks to a "sudden" insightful thought about a lead, and, yes,

I suspected they were God's little rewards for resisting the temptation to work. But today, I couldn't get that image of Tyrone at the Boathouse out of my head. He'd looked as if he were hiding in the bushes.

But why?

Was he spying on someone? On me?

I'd never broadcast the fact that I was an FBI agent to my class at the drop-in center, but that didn't mean he couldn't have found out. He'd always struck me as a pretty good kid. Sure, he shared the bad-boy, swaggering attitude of his hero artist Basquiat, but I suspected that was more a front against his peers who relegated any art, other than graffiti, to sissy's play. Then again, I couldn't ignore the fact that his neighborhood was a hotbed of crime. His brothers had been arrested more than once on charges ranging from petty theft to possession.

Harold twined around my legs, purring.

I picked him up and scratched behind his ears. "Talking to Tyrone isn't really working a case. He doesn't have anything to do with my cases. It's more concern for his well-being, and acting on that would be a good thing to do on a Sunday, right?"

Harold dug his head deeper into my palm.

"Yeah, yeah, I know, your vote is for my petting you all afternoon." I set him down on his favorite chair. "Maybe when I get back, we can find Nate and watch the movie I borrowed from my colleague. And you'll get all the fuss you want. Deal?"

Harold's whiskers twitched as if he'd have to give it some thought.

I traded my painting smock for a Wash U sweatshirt over my jeans and tugged on my sneakers. "I'll be back soon."

I took the exterior stairs down and couldn't help but hear the raised voices coming from Nate's apartment below mine. I hadn't seen him since I left him with his brother Friday night, which was not like him, considering he had to know I'd be anxious to hear what the attack was about, let alone whether his brother had seen through our masquerade.

I stepped past the open window, still within earshot but outside their view.

"Honest like you?" Randy hissed, his tone so caustic my ears burned. "I should've known you'd never stoop to helping a woman dupe her husband, no matter what her sob story. You could've told me the truth. It's not like I don't know what you *really are,*" he spat out.

My heart pounded. I never should have agreed to continue the charade after Nate and I ran into his brother. It was my fault Randy was mad at him. It was surprising Randy ever bought into Nate's story in the first place. Sure, Nate would help a woman in distress, but not by cheating her supposed husband out of his wealth.

"Does Serena know?" Randy went on.

"Of course not," Nate said so quietly I scarcely made out his words. "So you're not going to help us?"

Know what? What did Nate figure out that he hadn't bothered to share with me?

"I'd never be welcome there again if they knew I talked to an FBI agent. You know that. It's not like they're criminals. The people buying the paintings from them know they're copies. My friends aren't trying to pass the pieces off as anything else."

"Maybe not, but they have to know some of their clients are," Nate said.

"Try making a living painting and then see if you're still so quick to judge."

Was Randy still trying to make a living with his art—one way or the other? Would Nate cover for him if he knew he was eyeball-deep in one of my cases?

It looked as if I'd need to put surveillance on Randy, question him about my mugger.

Someone touched my shoulder and, reflexively, I jerked up my fist and pivoted, ready to take the person out.

Tanner yanked back his hand as if he'd touched fire. "Easy. I come in peace."

I dropped my defensive stance. "Sorry, you surprised me."

"No kidding. Have time to talk?"

Nate's voice drifted through the window.

I prodded Tanner up the stairs. "Yeah, sure. Come on up. What's going on?"

"I was looking through the other photos I took at the Boathouse and noticed your student Tyrone in a few of them."

As I unlocked the door, Randy's angry voice snagged my attention once more. "Are you going to tell her?"

I hurriedly let Tanner in as I strained to make out Nate's response. It was too quiet. Reluctantly, I shut the door. "You want to put the photos on my computer?"

Tanner pulled a flash drive from his pocket. "Yeah, that would be good."

My laptop sat on the coffee table. I opened it and tapped in my password. "Go ahead."

As Tanner pulled up the photos, my gaze strayed to the door. My neck prickled, and I glanced back to find Tanner scrutinizing me.

"What's going on?" he asked.

"What do you mean?"

He cocked his head with a look that said he wasn't falling for the deflection.

I wrapped my arms around my waist to mask an involuntary shiver. "I'd just been on my way to pay Tyrone a visit."

"Perfect." His eyes narrowed. "But what's bothering you?"

I let out a soft huff. "I overheard Randy and

Nate arguing. Randy seemed concerned about whether Nate planned to tell me something. At least, I assume I'm the *her* they were talking about. As far as I know, I'm the only female FBI agent Nate knows."

"What did he say?"

"I missed that part, but"—at the sound of a car door, I hurried to the window and edged open the curtains. Randy was leaving—"I'm sure Nate'll fill me in as soon as he can."

Tanner shook his head. "I wouldn't be so sure. There's something shady about him."

I burst into laughter. "Nate? You've got to be kidding me. They don't come any cleaner."

"Time will tell." Tanner motioned me to take a look at the photos he'd pulled up on my laptop. "What do you see?" Tanner asked.

"Tyrone seems to be very interested in the guy in the black polo shirt. Do you know who he is?"

"Yeah, Adrik Avilov. He and this guy"—Tanner pointed to a second bouncer-type dude sporting the same black polo shirt, sitting at a table on the other side of his target—"are Dmitri's body-guards."

"Dmitri's your target?"

"Yeah, Russian mob."

My heart thundered, but I managed to maintain a neutral expression. "What would a young black kid from St. Louis's North End want with a Russian mobster?"

163

"I was hoping you could tell me."

"I haven't got a clue."

"I'd like to ask him, but I suspect he'd be more forthcoming with you."

"For sure."

"You said you were heading out when I arrived. You still game to do it now?"

"No problem. I'll use the pretense of having heard he pulled his art out of the auction."

Tanner's cell phone rang. "Excuse me a second."

I nodded, then wandered to the window. Nate should've come up by now. He had to know I'd be anxious to hear what his brother had to say to him. At the sight of Nate heading toward the back parking lot, my gut kicked. I glanced at Tanner, who'd pulled out his notepad and was jotting down information. I slipped outside. I wasn't ready to buy into Tanner's suspicions of Nate, but considering the surveillance video of my mugger had picked up Nate's brother, I was a tad disturbed he seemed to be leaving again without touching base.

"Hey," I called after him.

He glanced over his shoulder. "Oh, hi." He stopped and turned. "I figured you'd be at your folks' today."

Hmm, a reasonable assumption if he couldn't see my car parked next to his in the lot. "What did your brother have to say?"

164

"He doesn't want to help us anymore. Says it'll hurt his reputation."

"You told him I was FBI?"

"No." His forehead crinkled. "I thought you must've when he met you at the MAC. He recognized you as Serena when you dropped the British accent after he was attacked."

"But I never told him I was FBI."

"Your aunt, then?"

"Maybe. He tell you anything else I should know?"

"Afraid not." Nate was still standing at the corner of the building, making no move to bridge the gap between us. Tanner's *There's something shady about him* whispered through my thoughts.

I descended the steps, expecting him to meet me halfway.

He didn't.

I paused on the bottom step. "Randy tell you why he was beat up?"

I'd never noticed Nate's Adam's apple before It wasn't particularly prominent, but it bobbed at my question. "He says he was in the wrong place at the wrong time."

"You believe him?"

Nate shrugged. "I want to, but my brother's teetered on the edge of the law before. I'm afraid he could've gotten himself in too deep with the wrong kind of company."

"What kind of company?" Tanner interjected

from behind and above me. He'd stepped out onto the landing.

Nate's gaze lifted to his, and an emotion I couldn't decipher flickered in his eyes. "I suspect you already know that."

Tanner's slight nod acknowledged Nate's astuteness. He jogged down the steps. "SWAT's been called out. I've got to go." He leaned close and added in a whisper, "Be careful if you pay Tyrone a visit. I don't have to tell you what could happen if Dmitri's men think you're nosing into their business."

"I'll be careful."

"I better go too," Nate said, his light tone sounding forced. He waved, then turned and headed for his truck.

Not like himself at all. Not a good sign. Not at all.

Traffic was light between my place west of Forest Park and the North End where Tyrone lived. Many residents of St. Louis never ventured north of Delmar Boulevard for fear of landing in a scary neighborhood. Tyrone's would fall into that category. The houses were mostly old, brick two-stories with scarcely enough room to walk between them. And the number with boarded windows scattered throughout the neighborhood didn't help its reputation. But at this time of day, the wide, tree-lined streets were pretty empty.

I wasn't sure where exactly Tyrone lived, but I knew Charlenae, one of the drop-in center volunteers, would, so I parked in front of her house. That and I figured my car would be safer there. Her husband was a two-hundred-fifty-pound construction worker. Any sane person would think twice before messing with a car parked in front of his house.

Charlenae was sitting on her front stoop with a glass of lemonade. "Hey, girl, what brings you here?" she called out as I climbed from my car.

"I wanted to talk to Tyrone. He lives on this street, right?"

"Just past the next intersection." She motioned up the street. "The one with the chain-link fence, two houses in from the corner."

"Thanks. Okay if I leave my car here?"

Charlenae's lips twitched into a smile. "Yeah, we'll make sure no one messes with it. Got time for a lemonade first?"

"That'd be great."

"Be right back."

As Charlenae slipped inside, I made myself comfortable on the stoop and watched Tyrone's place. A wiry old man came out of the house, carrying a large paint canvas and propped it in the backseat of an old burgundy sedan parked at the curb. Apparently, Aunt Martha wasn't the only art enthusiast buying Tyrone's paintings. Good for

167

him. The car cruised past, and I made a mental note of the license plate number for no particular reason, except that the driver might be why Tyrone was at the Boathouse Friday night.

Charlenae returned and handed me a tall glass of lemonade. "Hey, isn't that your auntie?" She pointed toward Tyrone's.

Dad's car—she must've borrowed it—was parked on the side street, and Aunt Martha approached Tyrone's yard, carrying what looked like a plate of baked goods.

"Yes." I should've known she'd be as curious as I was about why he was skulking around the Boathouse Friday night.

Aunt Martha detoured across the street toward a couple of tough-looking kids in faded jeans and black, skull-monogrammed T-shirts, cigarettes hanging from their mouths.

Charlenae laughed. "Do you think she's going to lecture them on the hazards of smoking?"

Aunt Martha fanned away one of the kid's cigarette smoke, as if that was exactly what she was doing.

The kid grabbed Aunt Martha's plate and the other reached for her purse.

"Hey!" I shouted. I passed Charlenae my lemonade. "Excuse me." I raced to the sidewalk.

But Aunt Martha spun away so fast her purse strap ripped from the kid's fingers, and the heavy bag caught him up the side of the head on its way back around. A rear elbow jab took the air out of the plate-holding kid.

I stopped dead in the middle of the street and blinked. Whoa, where did my Aunt Martha learn moves like that? She was like a female version of a Jackie Chan spy movie star.

She relieved the kid of the plate as he doubled over. "You need to learn some manners, young man."

The kids looked my way, their eyes widening, and took off.

Okay, I didn't think I looked that scary.

"Everything okay?" Charlenae's husband, all two hundred and fifty hulking pounds of him, said from behind me.

"Ah, yes. Looks like between you and my Wonder Woman aunt, they figured they'd hunt for an easier mark." I turned back in time to see Aunt Martha dart inside Tyrone's house, no doubt thinking I might stop her if she gave me a chance to catch up.

I mentally debated the merits of letting her talk to Tyrone alone versus joining her. Waiting won out. I needed to ask him about his visit to the Boathouse, and the last thing I wanted to do was raise Aunt Martha's curiosity about a case involving a Russian mob boss.

I casually leaned against Dad's car to wait her out.

She reappeared fifteen minutes later, minus a

plate of cookies but up a painting. "Serena dear. What are you doing here?"

"Waiting to ask you the same question." I pushed off the car and took hold of the paper-wrapped painting to free her hands to search her purse for her key.

"Why, I stopped by to convince Tyrone not to pull his painting from the fundraising auction. I sweetened the request by buying one of his pieces myself. I think they'll be worth a pretty penny someday."

"That was nice of you."

She shrugged. "I do what I can."

"That was an impressive judo routine you pulled on the boys who tried to steal your cookies and purse."

She laughed. "Catches them off guard every time. Brash young men don't expect an old woman to know how to defend herself."

"Where'd you learn how to do that?"

"Oh, here and there." She opened the back hatch and relieved me of the painting. "I wasn't always old, you know."

"You're hardly old. Seventy is the new fifty, they say."

"Look who's being nice now." She winked and opened her car door. "See you later."

I stared after her car. Aunt Martha never let an opportunity to grill me on my current cases pass. Something had to be up. And considering we had a psycho Russian in the picture, I didn't like not knowing what she was up to.

Tyrone galloped out of his house and pulled up short at the sight of me standing at the bottom of his stoop. "You can save your breath. Your aunt already talked me into resubmitting my piece for the auction."

"I'm glad to hear it. Mind if I ask why you pulled it in the first place?"

He shrugged and became acutely fascinated with his jacket's zipper.

"Were your classmates razzing you about it?"

His gaze bobbed up. "Yeah, that's it. But they're just jealous 'cause they can't paint as good."

"Hmm, you are gifted, but remember pride goes before a fall."

He ducked his head and mumbled something that sounded like "don't I know it."

"Hey," I said conversationally, "I happened to notice you at the Boathouse last night."

A panicked look flickered across his eyes. He lifted his hoodie. "I got to go. I've got friends waiting for me."

"I won't keep you. I was just wondering what brought you to my part of town. Did you come with someone?"

"Yeah, that's right," he said, once again seeming to latch on to the excuse I offered.

"I couldn't help but notice that you seemed to

pay particular attention to a burly guy in a black polo shirt. He a friend of yours?"

"I don't know what you're talking about. I wasn't paying attention to no one. I mind my own business."

Hmm, in this neighborhood, it was no doubt an essential survival tactic. Not that I believed him where Dmitri's bodyguard was concerned. But—I glanced around—the middle of Tyrone's street wasn't exactly a safe place to press the matter. "I understand that," I said, "but I want you to know that if you ever need my help, all you have to do is ask. You can trust me."

"I don't trust nobody." His voice cracked on the last word.

My heart squeezed, because he sounded as if he'd learned from hard experience it wasn't smart to trust anyone. "I'm sorry to hear that."

"What good is sorry? I got nothing to say." He stormed off.

Uh-huh, that went about as well as the last bath I'd attempted to give Harold. I headed back to my car and was struck by a thought. What if Tyrone's mention of not trusting anyone was more significant than it seemed? Had he seen Dmitri's guys do something shady?

Might explain why Tyrone had followed them. Except if Tyrone didn't plan on cooperating with law enforcement, what did he intend to do with whatever he learned?

· · ·

As I drove back to my apartment, I mentally itemized all the things I needed to do—question Ted and Lucas about Gladys's painting, question Randy about his conversation with my mugger—then again, maybe I should get that second opinion on the authenticity of the painting he tried to steal first. I still needed to take a closer look at Pete's financials too. Oh, and run the plate of the guy I saw driving away from Tyrone's.

He was probably a friend of the family, wanting to encourage the boy in his artistic pursuits. Like Aunt Martha. I drove another block, noting the boarded-up windows in too many of the brick two-stories and imagined what else "friends of the family" might do with Tyrone's paintings. I eased my foot off the gas.

It's Sunday, I reminded myself and pressed my foot down again.

It was no good. It'd only take a minute to look up the plate, and the wondering would drive me crazy all night if I didn't. I pulled over to the curb and buzzed the radio room to ask them to look up the plate on NCIC.

"The car belongs to Truman Capone," the operator reported a couple of minutes later and rattled off the address, which was a few blocks away. "His record is clean."

Aside from the unfortunate last name.

"No outstanding warrants."

173

"Thanks." I texted Tanner the info and details of my conversation with Tyrone. I figured I could afford to leave paying Capone a visit until tomorrow to give myself time to research his background and come up with a decent cover story for showing up on his doorstep. Didn't want to burn my bridges with Tyrone if the customer happened to not take kindly to an FBI agent poking around, asking questions, and gave Tyrone grief for it.

And I did promise Harold a movie . . . if Nate had returned from wherever he'd been off to. I pulled back onto the street, our earlier stilted conversation replaying in my mind.

"Call Aunt Martha," I said to my smartphone.

She picked up on the second ring. "I wondered how long it would take you to figure out what I was up to."

Okay, whatever it was, I had a feeling I wouldn't like it. I bit back my question about Nate's relationship with his brother and instead mumbled an "Uh-huh" that sounded as if I knew what she was talking about.

"Did you check out the guy who drove away from Tyrone's place with one of his paintings?"

I slowed the car. "Ye-e-es. His record is clean."

"Huh. Not what I expected. I figured he was some scoundrel using Tyrone's talent to his own selfish ends."

I'd had the same thought, but . . . I still wasn't

following what Aunt Martha thought I'd figured out about *her* actions.

"I mean, I'd gone there intending to buy one of his paintings anyway," she went on, "to encourage him and all."

"Hmm . . ." I interjected, hoping she'd get around to talking about what I still wasn't getting.

"It would be an unbelievable coincidence if they were a match. But he has painted lots of copies of famous paintings. Impressive copies. And he sure got his knickers in a knot when I asked him about the one he sold to the guy in the car."

Whoa. I swerved into my apartment's driveway. "You think *Tyrone* forged Gladys's painting?"

"Don't you? Why else would we test the paint? Do you have another forgery case you're working on?"

Test the paint? *Of course.* To see if it matched the paint used in the Dali. Aunt Martha really was brilliant sometimes.

"Not that it's illegal for him to sell a copy he's made, as long as the buyer knows, right? I hate to see him get into trouble. With the right encouragement, he could have such a bright future."

"Yes, um, while I have you on the phone." I parked next to Nate's truck. He was back. *Perfect.* "What can you tell me about Nate's relationship with his brother?"

"Is Randy showing an interest?" Aunt Martha

175

asked, a giddy, mischievous tone creeping into her voice.

"No, nothing like that. Nate just seemed out of sorts after his brother's visit this afternoon, but he didn't want to talk about it."

"That's nothing new. Their parents died when Randy was still a teenager, and Nate, being six years older than him, has always been over-protective."

"Good to know. Thank you." I stopped by Nate's apartment before going up to mine to see if he wanted to join me for the movie we'd skipped Thursday night. And to cross one thing off my to-do list that was on a fuzzy line between work and personal for a Sunday . . . finding out what Randy knew, if anything, about my mugger and about whoever forged Gladys's painting.

Nate didn't respond to the knock. I tried again and cocked my ear to the door. No sound of a TV. Or a shower running. And it was too early for bed.

I knocked a third time. He wasn't the kind of guy who worked with ear buds hanging out of his ears, blasting music too loud for him to hear. And how long could anyone sit on a toilet? He must be fixing something around the building.

I strolled up and down the halls of all three floors and then around the perimeter, but there was no sign of him. His curtains were drawn. That was weird. I was sure they were open when I drove in a few minutes ago. Standing outside his window, I pulled out my cell phone and rang his number.

No response.

Concern warred with the niggling sense he was avoiding me. Was he embarrassed about his brother? Randy had flat out asked him if I *knew*. Whatever that was about. Did Nate know something he didn't want to have to tell me?

That was probably it.

But he'd come around. Do the right thing.

Except as I trudged upstairs to my apartment, Tanner's voice whispered through my thoughts.

There's something shady about him.

13

"Get away from me!" I screamed and with a colossal effort, flung the slithering, snake-like zucchini across the meadow. *Plunk.*

I jerked awake, tangled in my sheets on my bedroom floor. Harold leapt on top of me as if tumbling out of bed was a new game he wanted in on. I raked my fingers through my hair. *Wow, talk about a surrealist nightmare.* I definitely needed to get a new hobby that was more relaxing than painting—say, bomb defusing—because my fruit-and-veggie bowl seemed to want revenge for bad brushstrokes and poor color choices. I was still sweating from the vision of a giant zucchini slinking after me.

I squinted at my bedside clock. 7:00.

"What? How'd I sleep through the alarm?" I scrambled to my feet and raced to the shower. No time for my run this morning. Tanner had said he'd be here at seven thirty to accompany me to interviews.

An involuntary shiver rippled through my body. It was standard procedure to conduct interviews in pairs, but Dmitri's threats had no doubt motivated Tanner's offer, while I couldn't help but think I'd be a whole lot safer if Tanner weren't within five blocks of me.

Then again, he hadn't been around Saturday morning when the gunman opened fire on the pawnshop.

Twenty minutes later, dressed in my usual FBI fare of navy slacks and jacket with a white blouse, I searched my fridge for something quick to eat. I jerked open the crisper drawer and jumped at the sight of a cucumber that looked too much like a smaller version of the zucchini I'd been wrestling. I grabbed an apple and slammed the fridge shut.

Harold plunked himself in the middle of the kitchen floor and yowled.

"I guess you're hungry, too, huh?" I jiggled some kibbles into his dish and replenished his water bowl. "See you later," I said, adding a scratch behind his ears for good measure.

I glanced out my hall door, just to make sure my note writer hadn't paid me another visit. Mr. Sutton was coming up the hall with his daily newspaper in hand. "Today's word of the day is lachanophobia," he said.

"That wouldn't happen to be fear of zucchinis, would it? Because I'd have no trouble using that in a sentence today."

"Close. Fear of vegetables. Although botanically speaking, zucchini is a fruit."

Right, so I had a fruit phobia, which sounded even wimpier. "Well, have a good day. Hope it's lachanophobia-free," I said with a wave, which earned me a chuckle. He wouldn't be laughing if he'd heard the snorting noise the zucchini I'd tackled this morning had made. I mean, it wasn't as if I didn't eat my fair share of vegetables. Maybe I'd subconsciously superimposed Nana in the zucchini role. She'd always been a stickler for making us finish our vegetables. And I couldn't deny being anxious about how irritated she was with my nonexistent progress on Gladys's case.

I slid the dead bolt home and went out the kitchen door. Tanner's Bronco sat idling next to the bottom of the metal steps.

He reached across his front seat and pushed open the passenger door. "Guess what I found out about Peabody's Pawnshop?"

I climbed in and clicked on my seat belt. "Am I going to like it?"

He swung his arm over the back of the seat to reverse out of the driveway. "It might be good news."

"It's one of Dmitri's many holdings?"

He braked at the curb and looked at me as if I were mentally deficient.

"What? You said good news, so the way I see it, if Dmitri owns the pawnshop, he wouldn't shoot it up, not even to terrorize me. Don't you think?"

"Good point." He veered onto the street. "Then maybe it's not good news."

"Just tell me already."

"The pawnshop's connected to the drug dealer with the fake art. Seems a lot of his customers finance their habit by hocking their valuables there."

"And you thought this might be good news why?"

Tanner opened his mouth, but only a puff of air came out before he closed it again and shook his head. "Wishful thinking. Which way?"

I gave him directions to Gladys's son-in-law's place first. He'd been released from the hospital Saturday night, but if he was eager-beaver enough to return to work despite multiple lacerations, I figured we could still catch him before he left home.

Lucas was heading out his front door in a suit and tie, carrying a laptop bag, as we pulled into the driveway behind his Bentley. We exited the

Bronco, flashed our badges, and introduced ourselves.

"I remember you," he said. "You're the granddaughter of my mother-in-law's friend. Is this about Saturday's shooting? Because I already told the police everything I could remember."

"Can we go inside to talk?" I suggested.

He glanced at his watch. "Will this take long? I need to get to the bank for an eight o'clock meeting."

"It shouldn't." Frankly, I was surprised he was fit to return to work after all the glass the doctors had to extract from his skin two days ago.

He led us around the back of his house to a sun porch. "We can sit here. My wife's still in bed. This way we won't disturb her."

"Your wounds healing up okay?" I asked.

He cupped his hand over his upper arm. "Yes, had one nasty bleeder that was a bit of a concern. Ended up with thirty stitches all told."

"Why were you in the pawnshop?"

He gave the same story as the clerk about redeeming jewelry he'd hocked.

"I'm surprised a man in your position would have a cash flow problem."

He ducked his head. "I made some bad investments and needed temporary cash to meet the call options."

"The shop paid you enough on the jewelry to do that?"

He chuckled, his gaze darting away. "It helped." He swiped his hand over his mouth.

I glanced at Tanner to see if he noticed the telltale signs the man was lying.

Tanner nodded imperceptibly. "Why not ask your mother-in-law for help? Or get a short-term loan from your bank?"

"I didn't want my wife to know."

That would explain the furtive behavior his wife had complained about.

"What does any of this have to do with the shooting?"

"We're exploring motives," I said. "Would you mind if we review your investment statements to confirm your testimony?"

His face paled. "I don't see how that will help you catch the shooter."

The shooter wasn't my priority. I suspected that if we could convince a judge to sign a warrant to review Lucas's financial records, we'd find the extra cash he'd needed far exceeded the payoff for the jewelry, perhaps to the tune of a fenced Dali. Then again, when an option was called, the investor usually didn't have more than forty-eight hours to meet the obligation. Not enough time to commission a forgery to replace his mother-in-law's painting. Unless, of course, he had insider advance notice.

"Do you have any enemies?" Tanner interjected.

Lucas shifted in his chair. *Squirmed* might be

more accurate. "Uh, don't you coordinate with the police? I've already answered all these questions."

Tanner nodded, saying nothing, his gaze fixed on Lucas.

Lucas stared back, but after about ten seconds, he couldn't seem to handle the silence. "I've refused two or three loans to prospective borrowers at the bank over the past couple of months. That tends to get people riled."

"I noticed you were questioned in connection with a drug case several months ago. What was that about?" I asked.

Sweat beaded on his upper lip. "I was in the wrong place at the wrong time. The police thought I might've seen something helpful."

"Did you?"

He shrugged. "I guess." He glanced at his watch once more. "Are we done? I'm already late."

I looked to Tanner, who gave me a one-sided shoulder shrug.

"Yes," I said to Lucas, rising to shake his hand. "We'll be in touch if we have any more questions."

"What do you think?" Tanner asked as he climbed into the Bronco beside me.

"He has opportunity and motive for the Dali theft, and he looked real guilty."

"And nervous. Like maybe he's worried whoever shot at him will try again."

183

"You think he was the intended victim, then?" I asked.

Tanner backed out of the driveway and swerved onto the street. "I'd rather think it was him than you. After we finish interviewing your other suspect, I'll pay a visit to St. Louis PD and see what else they have on the shooter. Where to now?"

I read Ted's address from my notepad. "If he hasn't moved since the last time he renewed his driver's license," I added. "The pawnshop doesn't open until ten o'clock, so chances are good he'll still be home." I'd done a cursory background check last night after making the interview plans with Tanner. Ted had a clean record, but that didn't mean much considering he was dating a married woman and lied to me about his occupation. There was no such entity as Ted's Pest Control. He'd worked at the pawnshop for four years, and before that at The Arch. Not that I didn't appreciate the humor in his quip about pest control, considering Tasha had sent him to spy on Nana. At the time he said it, he'd probably counted on never seeing me again.

Ted lived on the ground floor of a three-story triplex that made Tyrone's neighborhood look good. Shredded screens hung from the windows. Hard-packed dirt dotted with weeds lined the covered front porch, which practically sat on the street. The porch sported a pair of foldout lawn chairs, the kind with wide netted bands criss-crossed to form the seat. Only, enough bands were missing that a small child would fall straight through. A thick layer of grime and a half dozen crushed beer cans covered the rusty TV tray propped between the chairs.

I gingerly stepped over a pile of bird droppings decorating the top step and avoided the equally decorated handrail altogether.

Tanner glanced up at the rafters, where cobwebs competed for space with birds' nests. "Nice."

Ted answered the door in his boxers. "What?"

We introduced ourselves and flashed our badges, but he betrayed no sign he recognized me from his spy run, despite having presumably recognized me outside the pawnshop. Unless his story about an ex-girlfriend stalker was legit and not meant to be about me. "We'd like to ask you a few questions."

He swung the door wide. "C'mon in. Is this about Saturday's shooting?"

"Yes, where were you at the time of the shooting?"

"On my way home."

"Can anyone verify that?"

He shrugged. "I took the bus. Swiped my Metro Pass in the fare box. Can they pull that record?"

"Perhaps." Not that it'd prove much since he could've exited the bus at the next stop.

"How would you describe your relationship with Tasha Watson?"

"She told you about us?"

I nodded.

He shrugged. "I help her forget her husband troubles now and again."

Tanner made a show of looking around Ted's dingy apartment. "So if her husband had died, you'd have been sitting pretty."

"Motive enough to kill her husband," I added.

Ted laughed. "Hardly. I'm a plaything to her. Not husband material. She wants a man she can show off at that club of hers, not one who strikes deals with the down and out." He tapped a cigarette out of the box that'd been lying on the couch beside him and clamped it between his lips as he went on a hunt for matches.

"The husband's life insurance could go a long way toward funding your transformation."

Ted's lips curved into a smile around his cigarette as he lit a match and touched the flame to its tip. He took a long draw, then blew the smoke out in a perfect ring. "Who says I want to be transformed?"

His bruised knuckles snagged my attention, reminding me of the attack on Randy. Tasha's brother knew Randy, which meant she likely did too. Maybe well enough to ask him to recommend a forger. Then again, if Randy had helped her, why ask her boyfriend to beat him up?

186

"How'd you get the bruised knuckles?" Tanner asked before I had the chance.

Ted glanced at the back of his hand as if noticing the bruises for the first time. He chucked his chin toward the phone, or rather the dent in the drywall beside it. "Lost my temper."

"Can you think of any reason someone might've shot up Peabody's Pawnshop?" I asked.

"Nope, management tries to steer clear of turf wars."

We asked him a few more questions before leaving, but Ted was a cool cucumber—a vegetable not unlike a zucchini—which might explain why I didn't trust him, given my new lachanophobia.

"What're you smiling about?" Tanner asked as we walked out to the car.

Was I? My lips stretched wider. *"Grilled* vegetables."

Tanner arched an eyebrow. "A new diet?"

"Ha! No, I could use a coffee. Maybe a donut." I usually wasn't a stress eater, which was a good thing, or I would need to go on a vegetable diet. "You think I got enough to convince a judge to give me a warrant on Lucas's financials?"

"You've got motive and opportunity. Throw in your disarming smile, and I don't see why he wouldn't."

Disarming?

A warm glow spread through my chest, but I

rolled my eyes. "The judge could be a *she,* you know."

Tanner nodded thoughtfully. "You're right." He flashed his lady-killer grin. "We might need *my* disarming smile."

14

Tanner dropped me back at headquarters so I could work on background checks and the search warrant for Lucas Watson's financials while Tanner called on his friend in the St. Louis PD to get the scoop on the shooting investigation.

Yvonne stopped by my desk. "So what did you think of the movie?"

"Oh, sorry, I've had a crazy few days. I haven't been able to find time to watch it with my friend."

A playful glint lit her eyes. "Tanner didn't seem too fond of the guy."

I shrugged. As a rookie, I'd learned that attempts to thwart speculation about the nature of my relationship with Tanner—thanks to him winding up at my parents' dinner table a time or two—only fueled people's imaginations.

Ron, an agent from the terrorism squad, stepped next to Yvonne. "Hey, Serena, I heard you were trying to sell tickets to a fundraising gala at the end of the week. I'd be interested, if you have one left."

"That's great." I pulled the ticket book from my purse. "Everyone's been so supportive this year. I appreciate it."

Yvonne laughed. "It's because you promised Ivan a dance if he bought one. So all the other guys think they'll get to dance with you too."

"Are you serious?" I looked to Ron, who turned an unbecoming shade of pink.

He shrugged. "What's a few dances for a good cause?"

Chuckling, I took his money and handed him his ticket. "Right."

Yvonne lowered her voice as he walked away. "I think the guys have a pool on who will score the most dances with you."

I rolled my eyes. "My mom will be in her glory."

I pulled together the search warrant request for Lucas Watson's financials and ran a more extensive background check on Truman Capone—the man who'd apparently bought one of Tyrone's paintings. He was a single, sixty-nine-year-old Caucasian with a spotty work history. He'd done stints selling souvenirs at Cardinals and Blues games, driving a trolley tour bus, and bussing tables on river cruises. It was the kind of work history that smacked of an alternate means of supplementing his income. Yet he had no criminal record and hadn't so much as collected food stamps.

I pulled up his driver's license photo on my computer screen one more time. It made sense that a guy like this would buy his paintings on the cheap. But how did he hear about Tyrone's talent?

"What's Capone on your radar for?"

I swiveled my desk chair to find my boss, Maxwell Benton, standing at the entrance to my cubicle.

"You know this guy?"

"Sure, hard name to forget." Benton grinned. "Capone's a fixture at the We're All Legit Flea Market."

"*We're All Legit* Flea Market?"

Benton chuckled. "I'm not convinced the moniker is always true."

"Which is why you frequent it?"

He shrugged, the twinkle in his eye suggesting he liked bargains as much as the next guy, but yeah, those FBI warnings on movies were there for a reason. *Pirates beware.* Benton was on the job. "Capone sketches portraits of people on the spot. He drew my daughter. The likeness is uncanny."

"That explains a few things." If nothing came of the warrant on Lucas's financials, maybe I'd just wait until the weekend to pay Capone a visit at the flea market. "He sell paintings at his booth too?"

"Some. He seems to do most of his business in portraits, though."

"Paintings he's done or ones by others?" Might explain why he picked up the painting from Tyrone.

"I assumed he'd done them. But I don't know. I never asked."

"Thanks." I shut down my computer so I could head to the courthouse to get the warrant signed.

"You never answered my question," Benton said. "Why the interest in Capone?"

"I saw him with one of my students' paintings. A gifted student. And I was concerned his motives might not be aboveboard."

Benton frowned. "I can't see it. He's always encouraging the kids who come up to the booth to try their hand at sketching a portrait. He seems like a really good guy."

"Good to know." I drove to the courthouse and got the warrant signed. The bank would have ten days to comply with the request for records and was bound by an additional nondisclosure request to not inform Lucas of the search. But considering he was the bank's CFO, I wasn't holding my breath that he wouldn't find out somehow.

As I returned to my car, I revisited Saturday night's dinner conversation at my parents' or, more specifically, Nana's mention of her busy-body housekeeper by the name of Horvak. It was too much of a coincidence for Petra Horvak, the mastermind behind the Monet heist, to claim she knew something about my grandfather's murder *and* to share the same last name as his housekeeper at the time.

Then again, housekeeper had been among the laundry list of jobs Petra had taken after her divorce. Maybe she met Nana's housekeeper precisely because they *did* share the same last name. And housekeepers talked. Gladys's and her neighbors' housekeepers were proof of that.

I returned to headquarters and ran a search on Lucille Horvak.

Nothing. Nothing. *Nothing.*

"Am I never going to catch a break?" I swiped the computer screen back to my blank desktop and stared at my hazy reflection. *Why can't I figure this out? Some detective. I can solve every crime except the one that matters most.*

Tanner telephoned. "Where are you?"

"Headquarters."

"Get over to Dinah's Diner. You're going to want to talk to Detective Richards. Burly guy, no hair, triple chin. Picture Robert Morley in *Around the World in Eighty Days.*"

I laughed. Tanner knew of my penchant for identifying people by their actor lookalikes very well, but I was surprised he was familiar with the sixty-year-old movie in which Morley played the governor of the Bank of England. I still remembered the night Granddad and I watched an old VHS recording of the movie. The movie was so long it filled two tapes.

"He worked an art theft like your grandmother's friend's," Tanner went on. "But he can only give you a few minutes while he grabs his lunch."

"Thanks for the tip. I'll head over now." Talking cases in a public place wasn't smart, but since it didn't sound as if I'd get another option anytime soon, I wasn't going to quibble.

I arrived at the '50s-style diner ten minutes later. It didn't look as if being overheard was going to be a problem. The place was deserted. I ordered a coffee and slid behind a steel-legged Formica table in the back corner.

As the waitress poured me a coffee, a man I presumed was Detective Richards, from his uncanny resemblance to Morley, strode into the restaurant.

"One of those for me too, Mabel," he said, hiking his belt up over his ample middle and striding my way. He looked to be in his midfifties, and I counted four chins. "You Jones?"

"Yes." I stood and shook his hand. "Thank you for taking time to meet with me."

The waitress set a mug of coffee in front of the chair opposite me. "Anything else, Charlie?"

"Yeah, bring me a slice of pie, will ya, honey?" He unbuttoned his brown herringbone sports jacket as if he knew it wouldn't be able to hold out against the dessert and plopped into his seat. "So Tanner says you're working a theft where the painting was replaced with a forgery too?"

"Yes, I was hoping we could compare notes."

He pulled a small, black notebook from his sports coat pocket, turned it to a page midway through the book, and pushed it across the table. "You're welcome to look all you want," he said, showing no interest in reviewing my notes. "It's pretty thin."

I jotted down the scant details he'd recorded about the missing piece—a Margaret Keane, who was best known for her large-eyed waifs, and a list of names, none of which matched my suspects' in Gladys's case. "What tipped the homeowner off to the forgery?"

Richards scarfed down half his coffee as if it wasn't hot enough to melt his hide. "The painter was cocky. Painted his initials—TC—into the splotches."

Huh, I'd have to take a closer look at the Dali, see if I could find anything comparable. *Wait a minute.* "TC, you said?"

"Yeah, I cross-referenced them to a database of known forgers, but nothing popped. You know any artists with those initials?"

"As a matter of fact, I do. Truman Capone. An older guy who sketches portraits at a booth in the flea market." Sounded as if paying Truman Capone a visit needed to be put back on today's to-do list. But even as fast as he worked, he'd need days to forge an oil painting. "Was the victim away from home for an extended time? Did you get a list of everyone who'd been in and out or who had unfettered access?"

"I know how to do my job." Richards's gaze rippled with impatience. "Tracking down a guy who wants to nab what passes for art these days, from people with more money than sense, isn't on the top of my priority list. Not when I got some creep terrorizing women, and—"

"Okay"—I raised my hand to stop his tirade—"I get the picture. And I appreciate your priorities." Although I suspected more mercenary reasons were also at play. To climb the ranks, detectives needed a high clearance rate on the crimes they were investigating. With no witness to the theft and no suspects, Richards had little incentive to spend time on the case.

Then again, a city the size of St. Louis has its own homicide detective unit, its own property crimes unit, its own robbery unit, and so on. And if Richards was investigating someone terrorizing women, it sounded as if he worked robberies, so how'd the art theft burglary—a property crime—land on his plate?

The waitress brought Richards his coconut cream pie, and he began shoveling it into his mouth. "If you ask me, the whole art market is one giant Ponzi scheme. But the truth is, the guy's house might as well have been Union Station for how many people he's had coming and going. He's getting the place ready to sell, so everyone from painters to real estate agents are parading through the place."

Real estate agents? As in, maybe Peter Hoffemeier? "Okay, thank you for your time." I returned the detective's notebook, dropped a couple of bucks on the table for the coffee I hadn't touched, and headed for the door. Apparently Gladys's son and Truman Capone both warranted a closer look.

15

By the time I got back to headquarters, Tanner was out on one of the SWAT team's weekly training exercises. In the rush to catch up with Detective Richards, I'd forgotten to ask Tanner what he'd learned about Saturday's shooter. That would have to wait now.

I called Zoe at her job as head of security of the Forest Park Art Museum. "Hey, I need a favor."

"Does this favor involve me being a bullet shield against drive-by shooters?"

"Ha. No."

"Good, because as grateful as Jax is to you for setting us up, he doesn't want me within a hundred yards of you until he's convinced Saturday's shooter wasn't aiming at you."

Hmm. He'd probably been jogging on the spot outside my apartment building this morning at my usual run time, itching to read me the riot act. I shuddered. Made fending off a vengeful, viper-like zucchini seem not so bad.

"Hey, I'm good with ordering from dial-a-dress-dot-com."

"In your dreams. What do you need?"

"Could you convince your chief art restorer to let me borrow the museum's electronic paint tester?"

"Shouldn't be a problem. I'd say we owe you."

I winced at the reminder of the investigation that resulted in Petra's death.

"Will you bring the painting here?"

"I'd prefer to borrow the tester. I have several paintings I need to test. Some are in evidence, and I'd rather not have to transport them."

"Fair enough. When do you want it?"

"I can be there in twenty minutes."

"Oh. As in, you want it now. Hold on a second." Zoe put me on hold.

While I was waiting, I jotted down a list of the paintings I wanted to test: Tyrone's that Aunt Martha bought, the forged Dali left at Gladys's, the supposedly forged Degas, the forged Renoir recovered from the drug bust, the forged Margaret Keane in evidence at St. Louis PD, and if possible, some of Truman Capone's pieces.

The line clicked back on. "No problem," Zoe said. "I'll have it in my office waiting for you."

"You sure you want to risk Jax's wrath by letting me get so close?"

"He might as well get used to my defiant streak now."

I laughed. Somehow I couldn't picture her facing Jax down on too many issues. Then again, she'd gone against the museum board's wishes last February and reported the thefts I wound up investigating.

I picked up the tester—without getting Zoe shot—then drove to my parents' house to test Tyrone's painting first.

I let myself in the door and did a double take at the sight of my mom in the middle of the living room floor, playing with my old Fisher-Price dollhouse. "Mom?" I eased the door shut so as not to startle her.

"Oh, Serena, look what I found when I was cleaning out the basement. You used to play with this for hours. I'm washing it up for my future grandchildren."

"Is there something I should know about Shawn?" Shawn was my brother who gallivanted around the world, planning and leading tour groups. A job that neatly left him free to enjoy a girl in every port without being tied to any and that left me as the de facto target of Mom's need to fill her empty nest with grandchildren.

She smiled knowingly, as if she were privy to some enormous secret I was keeping from her. Only I wasn't.

My heart kicked at the sight of the little toy girl

and her dog. "Where's Aunt Martha?" I asked quickly, before the Little People sucked me into their make-believe world along with Mom.

Mom put down the piece she'd been wiping and pushed to her feet. "She went out a couple of hours ago. Said not to hold dinner for her. Can you stay?"

I glanced at my watch. It was still two hours until suppertime. Far too long to hang around Mom when she was feeling nostalgic about my childhood toys. "Tonight's not a good night for me. I just need to run a test on the painting Aunt Martha bought last night. Do you know where she put it?"

"The den. Your father nearly had a conniption."

"Why? Which painting did she buy?" I strode to the den and gasped. It was one of Tyrone's Basquiat-like primitivist pieces with skull-like heads, massive mouths, and wild hair. "Oh." Dad was pretty open-minded when it came to art appreciation. After all, he was his father's son, but I didn't blame him for not wanting such an intense Neo-Expressionist piece gracing his private space.

I took it down from the wall and turned on the tester. This model kept a digital record I could download to my computer later, which was a good thing, considering how many different colors Tyrone had used in the piece. Cross-referencing the components to the readouts for the other paintings could prove to be a lot more work than I'd anticipated.

Mom bustled off to answer the phone while I did my thing. She returned a few seconds later with the cordless tucked under her ear and turned on the computer in the den. "I can tell you in a minute. She's always leaving her phone places, so she put an app on the computer so she could find it again."

"Aunt Martha lost her phone?" I asked.

Mom covered the phone's receiver with her palm. "No, Nate is wondering where she's gotten to. She was supposed to stop by twenty minutes ago, and she's not answering her phone."

"Maybe her car finally succumbed to all those *pings* and *pongs*."

"Yeah, because she's never late. That's why he's concerned." Mom squinted at the icons on the computer screen and clicked on one. "Loading it now," she said into the phone. "No, it's no problem. Hopefully, she's just stuck in traffic or lost track of time at the mall. But it doesn't hurt to check."

A map of St. Louis appeared and zoomed in to the north end. "That's weird. What's she doing over there?" Mom glanced up at me. "Did she say anything to you about going to the drop-in center?"

"That street's nowhere near the drop-in center." It was where Truman Capone lived! I snatched the phone from my mom. "Nate, this is Serena. Did Martha tell you what she was doing?"

"No, just said she'd be out and would bring me the book I wanted to borrow, before three. I think she was supposed to meet Malgucci at the bowling alley at three. What's wrong?"

"I don't know yet. Pray." I hung up and returned the tester to its case. "I'll go look for her," I said to Mom. "That's not the kind of neighborhood she should be walking around in on her own."

"Oh dear. Should I call the police?"

I am the police, more or less.

"The hospitals?"

"Let me go have a look first. Keep the phone lines open in case she calls, and phone me right away if she does." I raced out of the driveway and drove as fast as the streets clogged with students getting out of school would allow. I put in another call to Aunt Martha's phone.

"Hello," a young, high-pitched voice said.

"Hello?" I strived for a friendly lilt to avoid scaring her off. "Who is this?"

"Emma."

"Hi, Emma. I'm looking for the person who owns this phone, a gray-haired lady. Have you seen her?"

"No, the phone was in the bushes."

"Where was that?"

"Here."

"Where's here, honey?"

"I'm not supposed to talk to strangers." The phone clicked off.

I stepped on the gas and hit redial. The phone went to voice mail after five rings. I tried again as I turned on to the street the locate app had pinpointed. No sign of a kid with a phone, but . . . Aunt Martha's car was parked near the next corner. I didn't know how Aunt Martha found out who Capone was and where he lived, but I was sure he was the reason she was in the neighborhood.

I parked behind Aunt Martha's car and tried calling her phone one more time. Nothing. Capone's apartment building was a shabby three-story on the corner of Sunset and Emerson. A row of hedges edged the lot on the Emerson side. Bushes. The little girl had said she'd found Aunt Martha's phone in the bushes. I hurried across the street and examined the hedgerow. Branches were snapped where it appeared someone had crept through. I examined the ground. The dirt was packed hard, revealing no footprints. But a strand of gray hair clung to a branch.

Why would she sneak through the bush instead of going up to the front door?

I pushed aside branches and peeked through. The hedge edged a small parking lot behind Capone's building. His car was parked in the back corner. Knowing Aunt Martha, she'd probably seen him drive in and decided to spy on him to see what he brought up to his apartment. And her phone slipped from her pocket.

I walked around to the front of the building. There was no front door security so I let myself in and headed up to Capone's second-floor apartment.

I knocked. No answer.

"Aunt Martha, you in there?" I shouted, pounding louder.

Capone's neighbor—a blue-haired woman in oversized bifocals—poked her head out of her door.

"Hello. Did an older woman about this tall"— I held my hand at shoulder height—"go into Truman's apartment?"

"Someone came by about an hour ago."

"Did you see her leave again?"

"No. But I wasn't watching for her neither."

"Of course not. Thank you." The neighbor disappeared back into her apartment and I tried Capone's door. The knob turned easily in my hand. "Mr. Capone," I said, pushing open the door. "This is Serena Jones with the FBI. I'm looking for my Aunt Martha."

No response.

Aunt Martha's car was outside. She'd missed an appointment without calling. Not like her at all. And the neighbor had seen a woman go in Truman's apartment but not come out. Sounded exigent enough to warrant going in. I pulled my gun, stood to the side of the door, and toed it open. "I'm coming in, Mr. Capone."

I cleared the kitchen, the living room, the bathroom, and the bedroom. Then pausing outside a closed door, I pressed my back to the wall and inhaled a deep breath. I reached over and tested the knob. It turned easily.

The room was a studio. Canvases lined the walls. A huge, bare window offered a lackluster view of the back lot. An armchair sat facing it, along with an easel.

I edged along the wall to get a look around the chair and easel, but a shout over the grinding gears of a heavy truck yanked my gaze to the window. The truck—the kind that empties Dumpsters like the one in the back lot—was awkwardly trying to get around an illegally parked car.

The shout—which sounded like "Stop"—came again, and my gaze shot to the inside of the Dumpster. From this angle, I could see only half of the contents. I raced to the other end of the window, and a gray head bobbed into view. "Aunt Martha?"

The truck got around the car and headed for the Dumpster.

I flung open the window. "Wait! Stop!" The driver couldn't hear me. I spun on my heel, nearly knocking over the easel, and froze at the sight of Truman Capone.

16

Outside Capone's apartment building, Aunt Martha's screams punctuated the ominous grate of the garbage truck's gears. Capone sat in the armchair that had been half blocked from my view by the easel, staring at me with lifeless eyes. I tore my gaze away and raced out of the apartment, down the stairs, and out the back of the building.

The truck's rear bumper faced me. I ran toward the side of the truck, waving my arms like a wild woman as I screamed at the driver to stop.

The truck's tines slid home into the sides of the Dumpster, and the hydraulics started to lift.

I yanked open the driver's door. "Stop! There's a woman in the Dumpster."

The driver slammed it to a stop and lowered the bin back to the ground.

Fingers slid over the lip of the Dumpster. "Serena?" Aunt Martha's voice sounded hoarse.

The truck driver jumped onto one of the truck's tines and hoisted her out.

"Aunt Martha, are you okay? How'd you end up in there?"

"Thank you, young man," she said to the truck driver. "Could you see if you can find my mobile in there before you dump it? It must've fallen out of my pocket."

"Not in my job description, lady. Sorry." He climbed back into his truck.

I helped Aunt Martha out of his way. Her right ankle was swollen to double its size. "A little girl found your phone in the bush," I said. "But I didn't manage to find her before she made off with it."

"Oh goodness. If I'd known I dropped it earlier, I wouldn't have wasted so much time mucking about in there."

"Aunt Martha, what were you doing in there?" I repeated, pressing the backs of my fingers to my nostrils to block out her *eau de Dumpster* fragrance.

"Oh, my. What time is it? Nate's going to be wondering what happened to me."

I glanced at my watch. "Four thirty. He's the one who alerted me that you were missing. Hold on a second," I said once we were safely out of harm's way. I phoned 911 to request an ambulance and police.

"I don't need an ambulance," Aunt Martha fussed. "You know I hate hospitals. But the police might be a good idea. I saw a couple of dodgy-looking fellows loading expensive-looking paintings into the back of a white panel van. That's why I snuck through the hedge."

I moved upwind of her. "Did you get their plate number?"

"I tried. I couldn't see it from where I was so I crept over to take a look-see inside when they went back in the building, but they came back out so quickly, I had to duck behind the Dumpster."

"How'd you end up *inside* the Dumpster?"

"Oh, one of the men was drinking a cup of coffee and tossed the cup in the Dumpster before he drove away."

I fought not to roll my eyes, pretty sure I could guess what was coming. She watched entirely too much TV.

"So of course, I alley-ooped myself up and over the side to retrieve it for the DNA."

"What happened to it? Is it in your pocket?"

She grimaced. "Way too many people in this neighborhood drink coffee. There were too many cups to choose from."

"Promise me you won't ever do that again. You almost ended up in the city dump!" Could've wound up like Capone if the guys in the panel van had spotted her nosing around.

"Nonsense. I could've been out of there a long time ago if I'd known my phone wasn't lost. I just panicked when I heard the lorry, because I'd been so busy searching for the phone, I hadn't finished building the pile high enough to climb out. And by then my leg was hurting like the dickens." She leaned onto the hood of a nearby car and gave the leg a rub. "I don't think I'll be able to drive my car home."

I phoned Mom. "Aunt Martha twisted her ankle. But she'll be fine," I hurried to add, hoping it was true. "We'll be awhile yet, because the police will want to question her when they arrive."

"The police?" Mom's voice hit a new high.

"It's okay. Aunt Martha didn't do anything wrong. Can you let Nate know?"

"You're sure she's okay?"

"The ankle's a bit swollen." I bit my lip at the gross understatement, but Mom didn't need anything more to worry about.

"I suppose those men in the van could've just been picking up paintings they ordered from the artist who lives here," Aunt Martha said the instant I disconnected. She shrugged, the tiniest of grins tugging at her lips. "You know how my imagination gets the better of me sometimes."

"Actually, this time I think you might've been spot-on."

At the sound of approaching sirens, I guided her around to the front of the building. And debated what to say about Capone. She apparently hadn't made the connection that he was the man who'd already taken one of Tyrone's paintings. The man who twenty-four hours ago she'd imagined was up to no good. Which, considering his current state, was probably the right assumption.

"Why did you come here?"

"I was talking to Livvy about Tyrone's paintings. You know Livvy. She's the one who's always having garage sales down the street from your parents."

"Yes."

"Anyways, I remembered her raving about a vintage craft show she went to last fall, and I thought she might know who I should talk to about maybe getting Tyrone a booth there. She said I should talk to Truman Capone." Aunt Martha handed me a business card with Truman's name and address under the title *Art Made to Order*. "He has booths at all the fairs, and she thought he might be willing to share some space with Tyrone."

"You never made it up to his apartment?"

"I was in the dustbin, remember? I'd still like to talk to him before we leave."

I plucked a rotting piece of lettuce from Aunt Martha's hair. "I'm afraid that won't be possible." My skin suddenly felt clammy and my stomach queasy at the memory of Capone's vacant eyes, drooping jaw, colorless complexion. "He's dead."

"What? No! How?"

"I'm not sure." I helped Aunt Martha ease onto the apartment building's front stoop. "I found him at the same time I heard you screaming in the Dumpster, so I didn't have time to examine him."

A cruiser and ambulance pulled to the curb in front of us. I didn't recognize the female officer who hopped out. "You our 911 caller?" she asked. "I'm Officer Prescott."

I extended my hand. "Serena Jones, FBI. The deceased is a suspect in what is beginning to look like an art theft ring. I entered the premises because I believed my aunt was being held inside and found Truman Capone dead in his studio."

The officer glanced past me to Aunt Martha, who was still sitting on the stoop. "That your aunt?"

"Yes."

Officer Prescott discreetly blocked her nostrils with her hand. "Where did you find her?"

"In a Dumpster behind the building."

Her eyes widened.

"It was nothing sinister," Aunt Martha said, pushing to her feet, then changing her mind halfway up. "I wanted something out of it."

"Something?"

"It's a long story," I said.

Prescott returned her attention to me. "One I need to hear?"

"Possibly."

The EMTs brought a gurney to a halt behind her. "Where to?"

"Is the apartment secure?" Prescott asked me.

"I closed the door when I ran down to rescue my aunt, who I'd seen from Capone's window."

"Screaming like the dickens because a garbage truck was about to swallow me," Aunt Martha interjected.

"The apartment was clear," I added.

"Okay, wait here," Prescott said to the paramedics, "while I make sure it's still clear. Maybe check over this woman."

One of the paramedics cracked open an ice pack as the other palpated Aunt Martha's ankle.

"I'll be back in a few minutes," I whispered to Aunt Martha and hurried after Prescott. I caught up to her on the stairs, and she looked relieved to have backup.

We confirmed the apartment was clear and radioed the paramedics to come up. "This doesn't look like natural causes," Prescott said.

"You mean the bruises?" Capone had yellowing bruises on his arms and face. "They look like they are already a few days old, and the body's still warm."

She shook her head and pointed to three-inch-wide parallel lines on the area rug in front of the chair, formed by the carpet's pile being brushed the opposite direction as the rest of the carpet. "Looks like he was dragged to the chair and propped up. People who lose consciousness slump forward. They don't stay sitting like they're looking out the window."

The paramedics piled into the room, gear in tow.

"Disturb as little as possible," the officer cautioned them. "We may be looking at a crime scene." She pulled out her cell phone and snapped a picture of the carpet marks before the paramedics crossed them, then phoned in a request for an evidence team.

I visually canvassed the room. He'd been in the middle of painting a portrait of a young couple.

An eight-by-ten glossy similar to the canvas on the easel sat on the bench beside it.

"Can I borrow a pair of gloves?" I asked one of the paramedics. I slipped them on and leafed through the file folders propped in an open holder at the back of the bench. One folder contained portraits. Another landscapes. Another—my breath caught—photographs of paintings. Valuable paintings.

I thumbed through them, my pulse quickening at the sight of several I recognized from the walls of the Forest Park Art Museum. I came to a portrait of a large-eyed waif. A Margaret Keane. "Call Detective Richards," I said to Prescott. "I may have just found proof Capone was the forger in his art theft case." I pulled out my cell phone and started snapping pictures of the photographs, since chain of custody requirements wouldn't allow me easy access once the homicide detective arrived.

I reached the back of the folder without recognizing any others I knew were stolen. Of course, I'd have to track down every last one of them to be sure. The next file folder also contained photographs of paintings, but these were pre-1940s. My heart skipped at the sight of the Degas we'd recovered from the drug dealers. Capone's handiwork too?

I flipped through them faster, hopeful Gladys's Dali would be in here too.

It wasn't.

Then again, would someone with such a carefully devised plan be foolish enough to leave behind an incriminating photograph?

If I spooked the thief into thinking I was on to him, he may have come back to retrieve the photo to cover his tracks. I replayed this morning's interviews with Lucas and Ted in my mind. Lucas seemed the most likely suspect at this point, but was he capable of murder?

I went through the stack again, more methodically this time, and snapped a photograph of each. As the duplicate image of the bottom one appeared on my phone screen, my breath stalled. *Granddad's painting.*

17

I stumbled out the front of Truman Capone's apartment building, desperate for air. The sight of the photograph of Granddad's painting had hit me like a physical blow to the gut. That and the realization someone hired Capone to copy it.

Nate caught me by the arm as my foot missed a step.

"Nate? How—? What are you doing here?"

"Your mother called him and told him about my ankle," Aunt Martha said.

Except my mind was still on the photograph.

What it could mean. If the copy was made before the burglary that ended in Granddad's murder, who supplied the photo? Their housekeeper? Is that what Petra Horvak had meant when she'd taunted me about knowing who killed Granddad?

"So he had Randy drive him here, so he could drive my car home for me," Aunt Martha rambled on. "Wasn't that nice of him?"

"Huh? Oh yeah, nice." I stared at him in a bit of a daze, not sure what to think of his sudden helpfulness after he'd made himself so scarce all weekend. And finding that photo sure didn't make me want to take anything at face value.

"We spotted your aunt's car on the other street, where your mom said the phone had been," Nate explained. "When there was no sign of either of you there, we figured we'd find you with the police cruisers and ambulance. What's going on?"

"Truman Capone is gone." I bit my lip hard to stave off a rush of hot tears. Because so was my chance to ask Capone what he knew about Granddad's murder.

The name didn't seem to mean anything to Nate, but Randy lost a bit of color and took a step back. "What do you mean, *gone?*"

"I mean dead." At his flinch, my gaze narrowed. "You know him?"

"Sure. He's been around forever," Randy said quickly. "He's done portraits at the state fair since

I was a kid. Probably since our folks were kids. How'd he die? His heart finally give out?"

"Won't know until after the autopsy. The coroner's due any minute."

Randy backed up three more steps. "Well, I guess I'll get out of everyone's hair."

"Thanks for the lift," Nate said.

"Wait!" I ordered as Randy turned to leave.

He turned back, his expression guarded. "Yeah?"

"From what I saw in there, Capone was a master at copying others' work."

Aunt Martha gasped. "Do you think *he* painted the Dali?" Aunt Martha pressed a hand to her chest and shook her head. "Now I feel terrible for suspecting Tyrone."

Not wanting to make her feel worse, I opted to skip explaining Capone was the guy she'd seen leaving Tyrone's yesterday. Instead I said to Randy, "You ever hear rumors of Capone doing work for organized crime?" and then slanted Nate a glare that said, *Don't think I don't know you've been holding out on me.*

Randy laughed. "No way. The guy painted portraits of little kids. Everywhere he went, people lined up to have him draw them."

"People also hired him to paint copies of priceless paintings," I pointed out. Why else would he have folders full of photographs of them?

"There's nothing illegal about that."

"Was Capone the artist you'd planned to

introduce me to when I was posing as Sara?"

Randy's eyes darted back and forth as he clearly debated the safest answer. "Yeah," he said softly. "He was the first guy I'd thought of."

"You didn't think he'd have a problem with how *Sara*"—I punctuated the name with air quotes— "intended to use the finished product, then?"

"Who's Sara?" Aunt Martha blurted.

I sucked in a breath and counted to three. "I was," I said on the exhale. "I was undercover."

"Ooh, I wish I could've seen that."

"Answer Serena's question," Nate said to his brother with uncharacteristic impatience.

Randy shrugged. "I hadn't planned on telling Capone." Randy was attempting to play it cool, but he couldn't mask the sweat beading his upper lip.

I couldn't imagine a connection between the assault outside his apartment and his plan to introduce us to Capone, but I had a niggling sense it was all connected somehow. "Around twelve forty-five on Friday afternoon, you were in a coffee shop a block down from the Missouri Athletic Club."

"Could be. I drink a lot of coffee."

"I was mugged a few minutes later, and you'd spoken with the mugger minutes before he targeted me."

"What?" Aunt Martha squawked, grabbing my hand. "You never told us you were mugged!"

I patted her arm and disentangled myself from her grasp. "I wasn't hurt."

Nate's hands curled into fists as he glared at his brother.

Randy balked. Looked genuinely horrified, in fact. "I don't know what you're talking about. I didn't even know who you were before Martha introduced us at the MAC."

Or just didn't know I was a friend of your brother's? "Do you remember the guy you talked to in the coffee shop?"

"I talk to lots of people."

"It's true," Aunt Martha vouched. "He seems to strike up a conversation with everyone he meets."

I pulled out my phone and scrolled through my old messages to find the picture Matt sent me. I turned it toward Randy. "This guy."

Randy frowned, shook his head. "I don't know him."

The coroner arrived, and we moved out of the way of the building's front door.

"Can I go now?" Randy asked.

I looked to Nate, silently asking if he believed his brother. Nate had this uncanny sixth sense that seemed to tell him what I was thinking, but unfortunately he wasn't nearly as readable. Even with all my FBI training.

"We know where he lives if you have more questions for him," Nate said.

A police officer burst out the front door of the apartment building, and Randy skedaddled without waiting for further consent.

"You Jones?" the officer asked.

"That's right."

He motioned me inside. "They want you upstairs."

"I'll drive your aunt home," Nate said, offering Aunt Martha a hand.

"Hold on." The officer stepped toward them. "You the lady from the Dumpster?"

Nate's eyebrows shot up. "You were in a Dumpster?"

Aunt Martha giggled. "Long story."

"Well, I need you to tell me the whole thing," the officer said, letting the door slam shut behind me.

"Lord, please help her to stick to the facts," I murmured as I hurried up to Capone's apartment. Aunt Martha enjoyed spinning yarns far too much, possibly too much for her own good.

"Over here." Officer Prescott waved me over to an apartment across the hall from Capone's. "This is Miss Bradley."

The spectacled, blue-haired lady squinted up at me. "No, she was the one who came later. Made a racket with her pounding."

"We met earlier," I said to Prescott. "I thought it was my aunt she'd seen, but my aunt says she never made it upstairs."

218

"Miss Bradley saw someone enter Capone's apartment shortly after three."

"I know the time," the elderly woman said, "because my soap opera had just finished, and I went downstairs to collect my mail." She poked the officer's arm. "Tell her about the hood."

Prescott smiled at my widened eyes. "She said he or she wore a black, hooded sweatshirt."

"You couldn't tell if it was a man or woman?" I asked Miss Bradley. I thought she'd said a woman earlier, but maybe I'd assumed because I'd been so anxious to find my aunt.

"I only glimpsed the person from behind as I came up the stairs."

"Did you happen to see two men retrieving paintings from Capone's apartment some time after that?"

"You mean the boys he hired to set up his booth at the exhibition center?"

"I'm not sure. They were loading the paintings into a white panel van."

"That's them. Truman always uses the same guys. Um . . ." She looked at the ceiling as if it would help her tap into some buried memory. She snapped her fingers. "Oh, their names will come to me. Anyway, the flea market people let Truman keep his booth set up in a corner of their main building, so he only has to bring new supplies each weekend, but for the special events, he always hires those boys to set up for him."

Okay, so maybe we'd made a wrong assumption about the guys in the van. But they'd been in the apartment *after* the person in the hoodie.

Officer Prescott handed her a business card. "Give me a call if you think of their names." After Miss Bradley disappeared back into her apartment, Prescott turned to me. "Looks like we need to track down Capone's delivery boys."

"Yeah, the door to Capone's studio was closed when I went into the apartment, so it's conceivable the things they had to pick up were waiting for them by the door, and they didn't expect to see Capone."

"Conceivable, but unlikely."

"Hmm."

"Why was your aunt outside Capone's building?"

"Whoa, you can't think she killed him!"

"I can't dismiss her simply because she's your relation."

"Okay, yes, she came here to see Capone, but she never made it into the building." I explained Aunt Martha's interest in helping Tyrone make a go of his art. Was this why Prescott had summoned me up here? So her sidekick could grill Aunt Martha without me there to defend her? Thank goodness Nate had shown up.

Detective Richards strode out of Capone's apartment. "Jones, Prescott said you found evidence pertinent to the Keane theft?"

"Yes, I'll—"

A pair of EMTs guided a gurney holding a body bag out Capone's door. We waited as it passed, then I motioned Richards into the apartment and showed him the photograph of the Margaret Keane painting.

"Good catch," he said. "Irwin has located a ledger that might prove helpful in matching jobs to clients if we can figure out the guy's coding system."

"Irwin?" I asked.

A well-dressed Tom Selleck–type—tall, broad-shouldered, dark hair, and dark, bushy mustache—strode into the room with a leather-bound ledger under his arm. "You must be the agent who found the body."

"Yes, Serena Jones." I extended my hand.

"This is Detective Irwin. The homicide detective on the case," Richards said by way of introduction. "I've already filled him in on your interest in Capone."

"If it's all right with you," I said, matching his viselike grip, "I'd like to follow up on all the photographs of paintings. I think we may find other collectors have been unwitting victims and haven't realized it yet. One of them may be able to give us a lead on who was buying the forgeries from Capone and pulling the switches."

"I'm only interested in the people who had motive, means, and opportunity to kill him."

I dropped his hand. I'd hoped he'd be more

221

enthusiastic about my investigation. "May I?" I asked, pointing to the ledger.

He handed it over. The pages dated back more than thirty years and were yellowed with age. I thumbed through the most recent entries and found four in the weeks leading up to the Dali theft. The jobs had numbers I suspected would match those scratched on the back of each photograph. But without a numbered photograph of the Dali, there was no way of knowing if it was among the jobs listed. The customers were identified by an alphanumeric code. Several were repeat customers.

I thumbed back eighteen years to the weeks before my grandfather's murder. At the sight of a familiar number, I gasped.

"What is it?" Irwin asked.

"I have strong reason to believe that at least one of his customers murdered someone." I turned to the officer packing up the photos for processing back at the station. "May I?"

He looked to Detective Irwin, who nodded, then handed me the stack.

I found the photo of my grandfather's painting. The numbers matched the ledger entry. I moved the photograph to the top of the stack, my heart twisting at the memories that came flooding back. "See this?" I pointed to the matching entry in Capone's ledger. "The owner of this painting was murdered by the man who stole it."

"Here in St. Louis?"

"Yes, eighteen years ago."

He scrutinized me as if I didn't look old enough to know the city's *ancient* crime history. "How come you know so much about this painting? Is it famous? I don't recognize it."

I squared my chin. "The painting's owner was my grandfather."

"Oh, I see," Detective Irwin said, frowning. "Um, sorry for your loss."

Right, that was an afterthought if I ever heard one. What did he think? That a personal connection to the investigation would taint my perspective?

Irwin booted me off his crime scene with a "we'll keep you in the loop; thanks for calling," so I decided against telling him I'd snapped pics of the art photographs. I stepped out of the building and smiled at the evidence team loading boxes of them into the police van. What Irwin didn't know wouldn't get his nose out of joint.

I walked to the corner of the street where I'd parked my car and had the neck-prickling sensation I was being watched. I glanced over my shoulder. Detective Richards was heading toward me, but when our gazes met, he waved and turned toward a car at the curb.

I waited a moment to see if he actually climbed in it. He did.

I scanned my car inside and out before getting

in, but the churning in my stomach didn't abate. Of course, it was more likely nerves over the thought of telling Nana about the photo I'd found than the idea of someone following me. I might as well get it over with since Nate took care of driving Aunt Martha home.

Two streets later, a black Lexus that had cruised up behind me after I left Capone's was still on my tail. Then again, with everyone heading home for supper, traffic was tight. He could just be going the same direction. I pulled into the visitors' lot of Nana's condo just off King's Highway Boulevard, and the Lexus didn't even slow. *Good, glad I didn't waste time doing any evasive maneuvers.*

Nana lived in a full-security condo, so no one would be sneaking in after me anyway. "I'm here to visit Stella Jones. I'm her granddaughter," I said to the doorman. A doting granddaughter wouldn't have to tell him. I would come so often he'd recognize me on sight. I shoved aside the thought. Nothing would make me happier than to feel as if Nana would welcome my visits, but I suspected she ranked them up there with a house call from the dentist.

"You can go on up, Miss." The doorman tapped the elevator button for me.

"I prefer the stairs," I said with a practiced smile. Nana lived on the tenth floor and enjoyed a spectacular view of Forest Park. But the place felt more like a showplace than a home.

Nana opened the door the instant I knocked. "Serena, what a nice surprise. Have you brought news of the investigation?"

"Of a sort."

"That sounds cryptic. Come in. Would you like a spot of tea?"

"No thank you." I'd actually have liked nothing better, but getting through what I had to say would be hard enough without trying to balance a cup of tea while perched on Nana's pristine white sofa.

"Then come sit." Nana motioned me to her sitting room. It smelled like Chanel No. 5 and furniture polish—without a hint of the rich leather-and-sandalwood fragrance I fondly remembered from their home in Granddad's time. Or the deep, mellow tones of Frank Sinatra crooning in the background.

Nana wore a fashionable plum pantsuit with a floral blouse. She sat in the Queen Anne chair, her back ramrod straight, her legs crossed at the ankle.

I attempted to do the same, although the sofa's soft cushion made the posture thing a challenge. "I may have identified the person who painted the copy of Gladys's Dali."

"May have? You don't know?"

"Not definitively."

"I see. And do you think he made the switch?"

"No, I believe someone provided him with a photograph of the Dali and hired him to paint the copy, then made the switch himself at a later date."

"Someone who?"

"I'm still working on that."

"It sounds like you're doing a lot of supposition with nothing helpful to show for it. Can't you coerce this artist into giving you the name?"

"No, he's dead."

Nana's eyes narrowed. "Dead? So he'll be no help at all to us, then?"

I bristled at her utter lack of compassion. "We did find evidence he painted copies of at least two other stolen paintings. Evidence that may help us track down the thief."

"That's good, then."

I took a deep breath. I'd hedged long enough. "Have you heard of Truman Capone?"

"No, should I have?"

She'd answered quickly. Too quickly? No, if she recognized the name, something in her body language would've betrayed it. A twitch. A lip curl. Something.

"Capone had a file folder full of photographs of paintings we believe he copied. One of those photographs was of the Blacklock landscape stolen from your home the night Granddad was murdered."

Nana stiffened. "I see."

"According to his ledger, someone hired him to paint a copy."

Nana clasped the fine gold chain at her neck, trailing her fingers along it until they reached the lantern-shaped locket at her throat. She rubbed her thumb along the etching, her gaze drifting to the window.

"The ledger entry was dated a month before the robbery," I added softly.

She nodded, her gaze still fixed on something beyond the window.

I'd expected surprise. Anger even. I swallowed hard. I wouldn't blame her for being angry. If I hadn't begged to stay overnight so Granddad and I could finish my painting, he would've been out with Nana at their Bible study like they were every Wednesday.

"I trust this will *not* cause the police to reopen the investigation." Nana's features remained as hard as granite.

I blinked. "Excuse me? Don't you want Granddad's killer brought to justice?"

"Will the photograph of Gladys's Dali you found in this man's file help you locate the person who hired him?"

I reeled at her deliberate avoidance of my question. I'd been stupid to ask it. Why would she dignify it with an answer? "We didn't find a photograph of the Dali," I said.

"Then why are you involved? Surely this man's murder isn't an FBI matter. You should be working on Gladys's case."

I fought the urge to shrink back at her caustic tone. "I don't understand. I thought you'd be happy." For the past eighteen years, I'd spent half my waking hours dreaming of the day I'd bring Granddad's murderer to justice, for that reason. "I'm sure this will convince investigators to reopen Granddad's case."

Nana crossed her arms, not defiantly but as if to contain something building up inside her chest. "Then I hope you will ensure they don't."

"Why?" Was the prospect of an investigation so intolerable? I'd been ten at the time of the original investigation, so I didn't remember much about it. Her British stiff upper lip had remained firmly intact throughout, as I recalled.

Then again, in a murder investigation, the spouse is often the prime suspect until he or she alibis out. Maybe Nana's Bible study had finished too early to provide her with an ironclad alibi.

Nana shook her head. "Because picking at old scars only makes them worse." She stood, signaling the conversation was over. "Leave it alone."

18

Leave it alone? How could I leave it alone now? After finding a photograph of Granddad's painting in Capone's file?

Tears blurred my eyes as I drove out of Nana's parking lot. Stopping at the exit, I tightened my grip on the steering wheel. What did I think? That she would suddenly forgive me for begging Granddad to stay home with me? That she'd forget I was the reason he'd been in harm's way?

I slammed on my turn signal and blinked back the tears. It didn't change anything. Granddad deserved justice, whether Nana loathed the idea of another investigation or not.

A text alert chimed on my phone. Nate asking if I could give him a lift home from my parents' or if he should ask my dad. I tapped in that I'd be there in a few minutes.

The traffic blocking my exit began to move, exposing a black Lexus parked on the other side of the street. The same black Lexus that followed me from Capone's. And this time, it was close enough I could make out the license plate.

I bypassed the radio in case the driver was monitoring signals and phoned the FBI radio room for his info instead.

"The car is part of a fleet for a company called XYZ Inc.," the operator said.

"What kind of company?"

"Import/export."

"Is it under federal investigation?"

I heard more keyboard tapping. "Not that I have a record of."

"Okay, thank you."

Behind me, a horn beeped. Traffic had cleared, and I was blocking the guy's exit. I turned right onto the street, so the guy in the Lexus would have to pull a U-turn, and called Tanner. "Your case happen to be connected to XYZ Inc.?"

"Why?"

"One of their employees is tailing me."

"Where are you?" The urgency in his voice answered my other question. XYZ Inc. was definitely connected.

I squinted at the street names on the intersection I was approaching and shouted them out, then added, "He's three cars back."

"I'm at Malone's Grill five blocks down. Give me a second to pay my bill and—"

"I'm not picking you up. If this guy sees me with you, he might be more inclined to hurt me."

"Yeah, so drive by, I'll pick up his tail as you pass, and then you can work on losing him." He spoke to someone at his end of the line, and a moment later, the background noise changed as if he'd stepped outside. "Where did you pick up the tail?" he asked, the beep of a car door lock punctuating the question.

"As I left a murder scene thirty-five minutes ago. I stopped at my grandmother's house and he was still waiting for me when I came out."

"The Capone murder?" An uncharacteristic edge laced his voice. "The police van transporting the evidence just blew to smithereens."

"What?" The ledger, the photos . . . they were my only hope of tracking down Granddad's murderer. "Your guys are connected to Truman Capone?"

"I didn't think so, but you just put them at the scene."

I rolled my car past Tanner as he climbed into his SUV, and my heart tripped into double time at the panic on his face.

"Was anyone hurt in the explosion?"

"Two officers were seriously injured. The suspects hit the van with a couple of grenades as the officers were climbing in."

I studied my rearview mirror.

Tanner let a second car pass him after the Lexus, then pulled in behind it.

I coasted into the next intersection and cranked a hard left at a sudden break in traffic. "Why blow up the van? If they were worried about evidence incriminating them, why didn't they clear it out when they killed Capone?"

"Someone must've surprised them."

231

Horns honked at the Lexus as it cut off traffic to make the same left.

I grabbed the next right. "Capone's place was deserted when I got there. They could've hung back and waited for another chance if that were true."

"Maybe someone else killed Capone. Someone not connected to them. Where are you now?"

I named the street.

"Take the next left."

I did as he suggested and passed him at the next block. "So you think they showed up after hearing about the murder on the news?"

"I don't know. Maybe. And maybe the guys who blew up the van aren't connected to the ones on your tail."

"Yeah? And I suppose you think pigs can fly too?"

The Lexus suddenly accelerated and veered into oncoming traffic, passed the two cars behind me and then screeched back into my lane a hair before a honking cube van would've rearranged his windshield.

"What did you do?" I yelled at Tanner.

The bus in front of me slowed. I swerved around it using the turning lane.

The Lexus swerved into the oncoming lane and rammed me into the side of the bus. The airbags exploded, and the next thing I knew I was staring out the passenger window at a bus-sized image of the local news anchor's face.

Behind me, Tanner flipped on his siren and bubble light.

The Lexus sped off, clipping another car in the intersection.

The clipped car did a three sixty and plowed into my front end, bouncing me off the steering wheel of my now airbag-less car.

Tanner screeched to a stop beside me and yanked open my door. "You okay?"

"Yeah, go after that guy."

"I alerted the police. They'll catch him. I need to check on the other driver."

As Tanner struggled to get the other driver's door open, I brushed the shattered glass off my lap and did my best to ignore the faces pressed to the bus window and the reek of gasoline.

A rubbernecker crawling by from the opposite direction flicked his cigarette out his window.

"Idiot." I jumped out of the car to ensure it wouldn't spark the leaking gasoline.

Flames licked the ground.

"Tanner, get her out of there. It's going to blow!" I waved to the people on the bus. "Get off the bus! Off the bus!" I raced around the car to give Tanner a hand with the trapped female driver.

He pulled out his Leatherman knife and sliced the seat belt at its base. "I got her. Go!"

I raced to the bus and steered escaping passengers toward a nearby parking lot.

The lady's car exploded in a fireball.

"Tanner!"

"You're, like, a magnet for trouble," my old high school friend Matt Speers said, sidling up to me next to the convenience store I'd chosen for a semblance of cover as I watched the tow truck load my blackened, crumpled car.

"Is that what they teach you to say in police school to cheer someone up?"

He chuckled. "No, I thought it up all by myself."

Manufacturing a smile, I wrapped my arms around my aching ribs. Airbags didn't feel so pillowy when they exploded into your chest. I shifted my focus from my car to Tanner talking animatedly on his cell phone as an EMT wrapped gauze around the burn on his arm. He'd insisted on being the last person they attended to, saying he'd had worse sunburns, but that hadn't stopped *tough guy* from wincing as the gauze hit his skin.

Thankfully, no one was seriously injured. They transported the other driver to the hospital because she was in shock, but she hadn't appeared to have any injuries.

Tanner pocketed his phone, thanked the EMT, and then joined Matt and me. "XYZ Inc. reported the car as stolen a few minutes before I phoned 911 to report the hit-and-run on a federal agent. Police found its burned-out remains ten minutes ago behind an abandoned factory in North Riverfront."

"And let me guess. No one saw the driver?"

"Bingo."

"Do you think the car was stolen?"

"Not a chance. XYZ Inc. is one of Dmitri's holding companies. He's got to be behind the attack."

"Or someone wants you to think he is," Matt interjected.

"What did the police learn about Saturday's shooter?" I asked.

"Nothing helpful," Tanner said. "Every witness disagreed on the make, model, and color of the gunman's vehicle, and no one saw the gunman."

"You think you were the shooter's target too?" Matt asked.

I gave him my best *duh?* look.

He shrugged. "Ramming your car is a big step down from a drive-by shooting, don't you think?"

"I don't know what to think. For all we know, the guy with the cigarette was in on it."

"Bad guys are only that coordinated in the movies. But trust me, there are plenty of screw-looses who'd flick a cigarette without thinking."

"Or to see if they could cause chaos."

"That too." Matt looked from Tanner to me. "If you don't need me to give you a lift home, I've got to get back to work."

The accident reconstruction team was still

taking photographs and measurements on the pavement, even though the last of the vehicles had been towed.

"I'll take her home," Tanner said, then cocked his head at me. "Is that your phone chirping?"

"Oh, with all this traffic noise, it didn't register." I dug it out of my purse. "Six missed messages." *All from Nate.* I thumbed through them.

Is everything okay? Did you get called out? Just heard about a traffic accident. Please tell me that wasn't you. Serena, I'm getting really worried. Praying you just got sidetracked and your phone's lost its charge.

"Your aunt?" Tanner asked.

"Nate. He drove Aunt Martha home from Capone's in her car, and I said I'd give him a ride back to the apartment." I glanced at my watch. "Over an hour ago."

"We can swing by and pick him up."

I tapped in *Sorry for the delay. On my way now.*

On the drive to my parents', I caught Tanner up on why Aunt Martha had been at Capone's and about Detective Richards's investigation and on what we found in Capone's apartment—the evidence that had been destroyed.

At the mention of the photograph of my grandfather's painting, he reached across the console and squeezed my hand. "I'm sorry."

Tears burned my eyes at the warmth in his voice, his touch. But I managed to hold it together.

Forced out a chuckle even. Nana would be proud. "We may have lost the ledger, but I snapped a picture of the photograph of Granddad's painting. That's something. It's one more piece of the puzzle, and one way or another, I'll figure out how it fits."

19

The next morning, Harold was still giving me the cold shoulder for reaming him out for breaking into his bag of cat food and spilling it all over the counter and floor.

"Look, I'm sorry I yelled at you. I had a rough day, okay? It's not like I remembered to feed *myself* supper either." Cupping my hand, I brushed what was still scattered on the counter into his bowl and plopped it on the floor beside his water dish.

He sniffed at it and stalked back to the bedroom.

"You're the one who left it out all night to get stale," I called after him.

I downed a protein shake and left for my morning run. The sky was already a light blue, but the sun hadn't peeked above the trees bordering Forest Park yet. My apartment building was just off Skinker Boulevard, west of the park, so even moving a little slower thanks to last night's accident, I'd reach its relative serenity within a few minutes.

I paused to adjust the ankle holster I'd worn under my loose-legged track pants. I didn't usually carry a gun for my morning runs, but with Tanner's *friends* still on the prowl, I wasn't taking any chances. I scanned the street. No sign of anyone watching me. I skipped my usual entrance to the park anyway and turned in onto the road farther up. The smell of autumn was in the air, and it didn't take long for the steady rhythm of my pounding feet to lull me into a better mood.

I'd spent half the night reliving finding Capone's dead body and the car crash, and the other half rehashing my conversation with Nana. The evidence may have been blown up, but I still had the photos I'd snapped. If I could track down the owners of the original paintings, I could potentially come up with a lot of leads. Nana might not be happy if the police started sniffing around, but I'd come too far to give up now. In the long run, when Granddad's murderer was behind bars, she'd thank me.

A vehicle slowed behind me.

I glanced over my shoulder. Didn't recognize the silver Ford Escape and picked up my pace. I was about forty-five seconds away from the next path that cut through the woods.

The whir of a window motor reached my ears above the purr of the engine.

I broke into a sprint, turned onto the path, and

ten feet in, ducked behind a tree and palmed my gun.

"Serena, it's me!" Tanner called.

I shoved my gun back in the holster and stalked out of the trees. "What are you trying to do? Give me a heart attack? Where's your Bronco?"

"At work. This is yours. One of the SWAT guys is picking me up at your place in ten minutes. We've got another training exercise scheduled."

"They're giving me an SUV?"

"I advised Benton it might be safer until we nail Dmitri. One more attempt and Benton's going to be tempted to transfer you to Alaska."

I laughed.

Tanner didn't.

"You're serious?"

"We're talking the Russian mob, Serena. Dmitri's got too many henchmen on his payroll for us to have eyes on all of them 24/7. You shouldn't be running out here by yourself. Get in."

I did, but only because he needed to get back to my apartment to catch his ride. "Where are you off to today?"

"The shoot house. We're practicing CQB."

CQB was *close quarter battle*. "Fun."

He grinned. "It's starting to get same old, same old, but the captain promised a surprise or two today."

• • •

I spent the morning at headquarters, tabulating the paintings I'd snapped photos of from Capone's file and trying to track down their owners. I managed to get hold of one woman in University City who said, "When I read in the newspaper about that theft where someone swapped out the painting they stole with a forgery, I told my husband I thought someone had swapped out our O'Keeffe too."

"What did he say?"

"That I was daft."

"Do you mind if I come and take a look at it?"

"You come right on over. There's nothing I'd love more than to make him eat his words."

"I have a few other stops to make first. Is later this afternoon okay?"

"Perfect."

I stopped by Gladys's first to test the paint on her forged Dali.

"Oh"—she glanced toward the street as I explained the reason for my visit—"Pete usually stops in on Tuesday afternoons."

"It won't take long," I assured.

After one last glance up the street, she motioned me inside. "Your grandmother told me you'd tracked down the forger."

"Maybe. My plan is to compare the composition of the paints in your copy to the paints in his studio to see if they match." Assuming they hadn't all been removed and burned up with the police van.

"You can do that?" She led me into the room with the Dali.

"Yes, it's pretty impressive what we can find out with technology these days." I lifted the Dali off the wall and laid it on a side table for easier testing.

Gladys paced the room as I worked, glancing out the window every half minute or so.

The data for the blue color on Gladys's painting matched that in the painting Tyrone had sold Aunt Martha. My heart ticked up a notch. I didn't want Tyrone to be an accomplice. The two lived in the same town, so they both could've merely bought the same paint brand and batch. I wrote a memo on my notepad to remind myself to ask Tyrone where he bought his paint.

At the sound of a car pulling into the driveway, Gladys flapped her arms like a frightened bird. "Oh dear, could you put that gadget away now? I still haven't told Pete about the painting being swapped."

"I think it's time you do, don't you? Your daughter and son-in-law know—your housekeeper and your neighbors' housekeeper too. How do you think he'll feel if he finds out about it from someone else?"

Gladys wrung her hands as Pete's hello boomed through the hall. The housekeeper must've bustled out to welcome him, because he said, "Whose SUV is that in the driveway?"

Gladys popped her head out the door before Ruby could answer. "Hi, Pete. Look who dropped by to say hello."

Pete stepped into view, and his head cocked as his gaze drifted from the Dali on the table to the gadget in my hand. His gaze lifted to mine and locked.

Nope, he wasn't buying the *dropped by* line. Not for a second.

"What's going on?" he asked.

Gladys clung to the pearls at her neck and worked them in her hands like a stress ball. "What do you mean?" she squeaked.

"Hey, Pete." I set down the paint tester and flipped to the page in my notebook where I'd noted details of the art theft-swap Detective Richards was investigating. "I'm glad I ran into you again. Are you familiar with the Stanfords' place in Westmoreland?"

"The Stanfords' place?" Pete repeated, clearly hedging. "It's a little outside an FBI agent's price range, I'd think."

"So you are familiar with it?"

His eye twitched. "I've shown it to a client or two, sure. Why?" He was dressed in crisply pressed black slacks and a tailored polo shirt, apparently not on police duty today.

"Are you aware a painting was stolen from the

premises? Or more precisely, swapped out for a fake?"

He planted a hand on the back of the upholstered chair nearest the door and shifted his weight to a more casual stance that might've been believable if it didn't appear so stiff. "You scored that case? I thought the theft squad had it."

"I'm consulting."

Gladys gasped. "There have been other thefts like mine?"

"What do you mean *like yours?*" Pete's stance reverted to ramrod-straight. "You were robbed and didn't tell me?"

"Burglarized," I corrected, which earned me a glare that had me thinking Pete might be innocent after all. Or a stellar actor.

"When did this happen?" he bellowed.

Gladys fielded his questions, apologizing after every other sentence for keeping him in the dark, and not once did Pete suggest she move out of her home as she'd feared. When he turned his questions to me, I answered without apology and fired back with a few of my own. His surprise about the theft seemed genuine, but I still had the distinct sense he was withholding something important.

"What do you know about your hit-and-run driver?" he suddenly asked.

"That has nothing to do with this case."

"Weren't you at the scene of that murdered artist not long before?"

My gaze dropped to the Dali lying on the table in front of me. Its dreamlike depictions of a place that held sinister secrets seemed to morph into something all too real. I wasn't sure how much to make of Pete's knowledge of my whereabouts yesterday.

Then again, both the hit-and-run and the murder had been big scenes for St. Louis PD. So it should be no surprise he'd heard about them.

Pete closed the distance between us. "I heard that's where the Lexus picked up your tail— outside Capone's apartment." Pete moved my purse off the end of the table and picked up my electronic gadget. "And you just said this test could prove he's our forger."

"Your mother isn't in any danger, if that's what you're worried about."

"How do you know? Do you know what kind of danger you're in? Who's after you?"

I danced around his questions for a good fifteen minutes, being careful not to give away anything connected to Tanner's investigation and still eventually managing to allay his concerns for his mother.

Next I drove over to Truman Capone's apartment building, where St. Louis PD said I'd find Detective Irwin, the man in charge of the homicide investigation. Two heavily armed officers stood guard at the front of the apartment building.

I lifted the flap of my jacket with two fingers so they wouldn't assume I was reaching for a gun as I revealed my badge. "Special Agent Serena Jones here to see Detective Irwin."

The officer repeated my request into his radio.

"What does she want?" Irwin barked back.

The officer looked to me for an answer.

I reached for the radio. "May I?"

He hesitated a moment, then handed it over.

"Sir, this is Special Agent Jones. I've brought an electronic device that will enable us to test the composition of the paint in Capone's studio and compare it to the forgeries swapped out in a couple of local art theft cases."

The detective used some colorful language to tell me what I could do with the device. Apparently, thanks to last night's car explosion on the heels of the murder-scene evidence being rocket-launched into oblivion, the rumor mill was blaming me for the fallout. "This is a murder investigation. When I release the scene, you can do whatever you want with it—and not before."

"But I have—"

"Are you hard of hearing? Just because they call you a *special* agent doesn't give you special privileges. I don't want you anywhere near my crime scene. You've done enough damage already."

"Fine." If he didn't want my copies of the paintings Capone almost certainly forged, it was his loss, not mine. I handed the radio back to the officer. "Have a good day, gentlemen."

I turned on my heels and walked back to my car to the mutters of "First Bunch of Idiots"—the local police department's term of *endearment* for FBI agents. Hopefully Detective Richards would be more cooperative.

I circled back to police headquarters, where Detective Richards begrudgingly accompanied me to evidence lockup to sign out the Margaret Keane forgery and supervise my test.

"What is this supposed to prove?" Richards asked.

"Paint is made out of a mixture of basic elements. Some elements are distinctive to certain time periods or regions or commercial paints. If we find the same distinctive elements in Capone's paint bottles"—*when Irwin gets around to releasing the scene*—"it will corroborate our theory he painted the forgery the thief swapped in."

"Him or anyone else who shopped at the same art store."

"Perhaps. But if there are elements in the paint that aren't in Capone's, we can be fairly certain he isn't our forger."

"So what if Capone's the forger? Dead men don't talk."

By the time I stopped by the home of the woman I'd talked to on the phone this morning to test the

O'Keeffe, and one look at the back confirmed it was a forgery, I suspected the test results weren't going to tell me anything definitive, except that the forger made no attempt to use historically accurate paint. There were certain elements used in paints in Dali's time that were no longer in use in O'Keeffe's years. And sure enough there was virtually no difference in the results on the two forgeries.

The Basquiat and the Keane were another story. Their results were very similar to each other but had notable differences to the Dali and the O'Keeffe, perhaps due to color choices. But a lawyer would argue that, since we know Tyrone, not Capone, painted the Basquiat-style painting, the similarity in results offered no proof Capone painted any of them.

Since I was already in University City, I stopped by my parents' to see how Aunt Martha was doing.

"Detective Irwin is a twit," Aunt Martha said after I gave her the lowdown on the tests and Irwin's refusal to allow me on scene to test Capone's. "But I know where you can go to test Capone's paintings."

"Where?" I asked, despite my growing doubts any of the results would prove useful.

"The We're All Legit Flea Market, of course. Lots of vendors leave their wares onsite."

"You're brilliant! Yes, his neighbor said he

leaves his paintings set up. So if I can get a search warrant . . ."

"Pfft." Aunt Martha swatted her hand. "Livvy— you know, the garage-sale lady who lives down the street—she can get us in. It's her brother-in-law who runs the place, and if he gives you permission, you don't need a search warrant, right?"

"Right."

Within minutes, Aunt Martha had made arrangements for Livvy's brother-in-law to meet us at the flea market.

"Are you sure you're up to walking around?" I asked Aunt Martha as we headed for my new SUV. "Your ankle still looks swollen."

"Nonsense, I can't let you have all the fun."

The flea market was located in the burbs twenty minutes north of downtown. Or rather, in a dicey-looking industrial strip on its outskirts. Aunt Martha grabbed the dash as I turned into the parking lot. "Good thing you got this fancy schmancy new vehicle. The parking lot has more potholes than Beirut."

And she would know. She'd traveled just about everywhere in her years as an assistant to some bigwig corporate exec.

The building was a long, low, steel-clad affair with three wings branching off like a capital *E*. A burly man waved us over to a door at the tip of the middle branch.

"There's Dan," Aunt Martha said and pushed open the SUV's door.

Dan had long, gray hair tied in a ponytail with a red bandanna and a tattoo of a snake hiding in the fuzzy hair covering his arms.

"He's Mom and Dad's *neighbor?*" Nana would have a meltdown on the spot if he happened by to borrow a cup of sugar while she was around.

Aunt Martha grinned. "The coolest chap on the street. A regular Willie Nelson." She made introductions, and Dan led us through the maze of booths featuring everything from T-shirts to shoes, books to DVDs, antiques to small firearms. I paused in front of a glass case displaying a collection of knives, pepper spray, and stun guns. A sign at the back of the booth proclaimed, *If you don't see what you want, ask.* No wonder Benton kept an eye on this place.

"Isn't this place a hoot?" Aunt Martha said. "You should've seen what one vendor tried to sell me when I was shopping for my gun."

"You bought your gun at a flea market?"

My exasperation must've made the question sound a tad judgmental, because Dan turned around and said, "All my vendors are legit."

Yeah, right, and there really is a Santa Claus, Virginia. To Aunt Martha, I whispered, "Did you make sure the serial number on the gun you bought wasn't filed off?"

She giggled.

"I'm not kidding!"

"Here you go." Dan stopped in front of a ten-by-ten booth adorned with portraits and sketches and an eclectic mix of art, from impressionistic landscapes to modern pop art. "I'll leave you girls to it," he said, walking backward down the aisle. "I'll be in my office up front if you need anything."

"Thanks!" The paintings all hung askew. "It looks as if an earthquake rumbled through the place and threw everything off-kilter," I said, pulling the paint tester from my purse.

"Probably from the cars rumbling through the car park," Aunt Martha quipped. "The holes are big enough to swallow small children." She squinted at a few paintings. "What do you want me to do?"

"See if you can find Capone's initials hidden in any of the paintings that are copies of famous ones. That's how the owners of the Keane figured out their original was replaced."

"TC?"

"Yeah."

"We've got *T* people coming out of our ears on this case—Tyrone, Tasha, Truman . . ."

Ted. I opted not to disclose that suspect to Aunt Martha. "Only one with the initials TC, though."

"You're forgetting Tanner. His last name is Calhoun, right?"

"I'm confident he's not our forger."

She shrugged. "You never can tell about people. Just because someone's in law enforcement doesn't mean he's honest."

I grinned. "Trust me. I've seen him play Pictionary." It wasn't Tanner I was worried about being honest. It was Pete blipping my radar.

"Did you find a TC on Gladys's painting?"

"No." Not on the O'Keeffe forgery I'd looked at this afternoon either. "But my theory is that it's his trademark, or a prideful touch or something, and the ability to skillfully hide it is part of the allure."

She pulled a magnifying glass out of her suitcase-sized purse. "Sounds believable."

While Aunt Martha scrutinized the other paintings, I gathered data from two painted in colors similar to the Dali and to the Keane Detective Richards was investigating.

"I can't find his initials hidden in any of these," Aunt Martha complained. "Did they look like the *T* and *C* in his signatures on the portraits?"

I glanced at the signature on the nearest portrait, and the next, and then the next. "You know what? It didn't look anything like these." Truman signed his name with an almost calligraphic beauty. "The initials were in plain print on a slight slant that blended with the design."

She took a second gander at the painting in front of her, then shook her head. "I don't think he made a habit of secretly initialing his work."

"You're probably right. If he was selling to criminals who wanted to pass them off as the genuine article, they wouldn't appreciate the tell."

"Or maybe he was basically honest, and once he realized what his client was doing with the commissioned paintings, added his initials so he could point to them later as proof he wasn't in on the scam. Or at least didn't want to be." Aunt Martha sucked in a sudden breath. "Ooh, maybe that's why they killed him, because he refused to paint for them anymore and knew too much."

"Could be." Satisfied with the data I'd collected, I packed my paint tester back in my purse. "I wondered why they would kill the most important cog in their scheme, but yeah, if he'd become uncooperative—"

"And a liability, sneaking his initials into his paintings," Aunt Martha added.

"Then it would make sense. Except you'd think they'd have confiscated any evidence on the spot."

"Maybe the neighbor was wrong about the men in the van. They could've been collecting the evidence and got spooked."

A thud came from a booth down the main aisle.

"Did you hear that?" I asked, pushing Aunt Martha behind me.

"It's probably Dan coming back to see—uh-oh."

I snapped my gaze in the other direction to see

what had Aunt Martha worried. Dan was heading up the aisle, followed by Detective Irwin and a couple of uniformed officers.

Aunt Martha yanked me behind the cover of a display stand. "Can they arrest us for being here?"

"No, we had permission." Although I wouldn't put it past Irwin to try to charge me with interfering with a police investigation. "But that doesn't mean we have to stick around." I ushered Aunt Martha through an opening in the back of the booth and out another aisle before he caught sight of us. "I've got what I came for." Only . . . what or who made the thud?

Chances were slim one of Dmitri's goons had picked up my tail in the new SUV without me noticing, but I didn't want to take any chances. "Wait here a second," I said to Aunt Martha as we reached the back exit. I glimpsed movement in the shadows to the right.

I palmed my gun and edged around a bookshelf that doubled as a booth divider.

A black cat scrambled across the open floor and under a table. I scanned the area for potential hiding places for something bigger and, seeing no one, I returned to Aunt Martha. "All clear. Let's go."

I hurried her to the SUV and gunned it out of the parking lot.

"Woohoo, that was fun," Aunt Martha whooped.

Glad she thought so. I kept my gaze glued to the rearview mirror the entire drive back to my parents' place.

Aunt Martha texted a thank-you to Dan, no doubt with some creative story about why we'd left in such a hurry. "Where are you off to now?" she asked.

"Back to headquarters," I fibbed, knowing she'd want to tag along if I admitted I planned to speak to Tyrone.

Mom was home by the time I dropped off Aunt Martha and came out on the porch as I gave Aunt Martha a hand down from her seat.

"Did you see the new vehicle Tanner gave Serena?" Aunt Martha said to Mom. "He wanted to make sure she'd be safe. Isn't that sweet?" Aunt Martha flounced inside, leaving Mom to glower at me.

"What's wrong?"

"I don't know what kind of nonsense she's been feeding you, but playing one man against another is not a good strategy for landing a husband."

"Landing a husband? What are you talking about?"

"Nate and Tanner. Aunt Martha's been rooting for Nate from day one, so if she's singing Tanner's praises, I can only imagine she thinks it'll some-how turn things in Nate's favor."

I rolled my eyes. "Tanner is a colleague, and Nate is my building superintendent who happens to be good friends with Aunt Martha." And okay, who shares my love of old movies and art.

Mom folded her arms. "First of all, any man who buys a woman a fancy new SUV because he's concerned for her safety is hearing wedding bells."

I let out a strangled sound halfway between a laugh and a gasp. "Mom, it's a work vehicle."

"A work vehicle Tanner handpicked and delivered to your house in person."

"How do you know that?" Was everyone and their grandmother spying on me?

"I stopped by the apartment to drop off the notepad that fell out of Nate's jacket when he was here last night and he mentioned seeing Tanner this morning, looking for you. And don't think Nate just sat around here last night, waiting for you to answer the half-dozen text messages he left you. He hopped back in Aunt Martha's car and drove around looking for you. Then phoned every cop and official he knew to track you down."

Warmth spread through my chest. Nate was an all around nice guy. He'd drive tenants to the ER in emergencies. Send out the cavalry, aka me, to hunt down the never-late Aunt Martha. It was no surprise he'd pull out all the stops to make sure I was okay.

But it still felt nice. Really nice.

20

Tyrone wasn't at home or at the drop-in center, so I decided to stop by the art museum and knock two things off my to-do list in one visit—make peace with Zoe and make sure the museum didn't have any of Capone's forgeries hanging on their walls.

I spotted Matt strolling out of the nearby zoo with his wife and little boy and pulled over. "Hey," I called out my window, "good to see you enjoying some time off with the family."

His wife, Tracey, wrapped her arm around his waist and grinned. "We're off to have a picnic in Turtle Park now."

"Ooh," I said to their toddler, making my eyes go wide. "Fun."

"By the way," Matt said to me, "we did get some good news last night. A traffic cam got the license plate number of the driver who flicked the cigarette at you. He claims he didn't do it deliberately."

"You believe him?"

"Yeah, I do. He doesn't have a record. And no known ties to XYZ Inc. or any of its employees."

"That's great." I shot Tracey an apologetic look for interrupting their family time with work. "Now get back to enjoying yourselves."

I shifted the SUV back into drive and parked it along the street in front of the museum. It was a sweet ride. I took a few minutes to experiment with all the bells and whistles and to ensure no one had followed me. The love song Zoe had picked for her wedding played on the radio, and Mom's words echoed through my brain. *Any man who buys a woman a fancy new SUV because he's concerned for her safety is hearing wedding bells.*

I shook my head. Mom was seeing what she wanted to see. Tanner was married to his job.

I strode in the front doors of the art museum and showed my ID to bypass the metal detectors, then headed straight to the security room.

As Zoe opened the door, she said to the man surveying the line of monitors, "If you see anyone watching or following her or doing anything suspicious, radio me immediately."

"I'm sorry. Are you in the middle of a situation? I can come back."

Zoe grinned. *"You're* the situation."

I groaned. "You heard about the bus incident?" Zoe had a tendency to joke about things she was especially worried about. Maybe that was why we got along so well. We shared the same deranged sense of humor.

"Oh yeah. The phone lines around the neighborhood were buzzing all night."

"I guess that means Jax won't want you rescheduling our shopping trip anytime soon."

"Ha, we're thinking of ordering online from the security of a heavily guarded conference room."

I frowned. She wasn't being serious. But she probably should be.

Zoe pulled me into a hug. "I'm glad you're okay. I tried calling, but the phone was busy all night."

"Reporters," I said, giving her a quick hug, then stepping back to avoid attracting unwanted attention. We were still standing in the short hall outside the security room, within view of the museum's main lobby. "Eventually I just left my apartment phone off the hook and turned off my cell phone."

"Well, don't worry about the dress shopping. We'll figure something out."

I ignored the twinge of guilt that worrying about dress shopping had been the furthest thing from my mind and steered her toward the Impressionists' gallery. "I also needed to talk to you about some paintings." I explained the situation with Capone and his photographs of pieces from the museum.

"Oh sure, I remember him. He came here a lot. Painted fabulous reproductions."

"Yes." I stopped in front of the Pissarro I'd recognized in one of Capone's pictures and handed Zoe the contact sheet I'd made of his photos of museum pieces. "Like this one." I scrutinized the painting more closely but didn't notice any telltale signs it was fake. Then again, I was no expert. "To be on the safe side, you might want to check to make sure they're all still the originals."

A shudder reverberated down her arms. "Absolutely, we don't want a repeat of what happened at Caracas Museum in Venezuela," she said, referring to a Matisse, stolen and replaced with a forgery, that remained undetected for two years.

"Hey, the FBI recovered it for them."

"Ten years later. I'd be out of a job by then for letting it happen on my watch." Zoe's radio buzzed, and I automatically scanned the area. Zoe laughed. "That's the code for a problem with the bathroom, not for someone following the FBI agent." She winked.

"I'll leave you to deal with that, but let me know if you turn up any iffy paintings."

"Will do."

I headed straight home from Forest Park. The street was quiet. No suspicious vehicles lurking outside my apartment building. I parked in the small lot behind the red brick three-story and scrutinized my door and window, accessible from the outside metal staircase. No sign of tampering, so I walked around to the front of the building to collect my mail and check the inside door.

Mr. Sutton, my next-door neighbor, was just locking up his box. "Evening. You use today's word of the day?"

"Um, I think I missed catching today's. What is it?"

"Pettifogger. A person who tries to befuddle others with their speech."

"Hmm, if I could master all the words you're teaching us, I'd make a good pettifogger."

He laughed. "That's the idea. Yes." He pushed the elevator button and then held the door for me when it opened.

"You go ahead," I said, opening my mailbox. "I'll be a bit."

Nate rounded the corner, carrying a ladder, a tool belt slung low over his hips like a gunslinger. "Planning on reading your mail in the lobby, are you?" Amusement twinkled in his eyes.

"No, I was going to talk to you."

"Uh-huh, and did that idea come to you before or after the thought of being closeted in an eight-by-eight box suspended by a thin metal cable?"

I stuck out my tongue at him. I'd never broadcast the fact I might be slightly . . . somewhat . . . horribly claustrophobic, but he'd apparently figured it out.

He grinned. "You interested in watching that DVD tonight?"

"That's a great idea." In fact, it sounded really safe and normal. I could use some normal.

"I could come up around eight. Work for you?"

"Perfect." I jogged up to my second-floor apartment. No note on the door. Looking good so far. I scanned the edges from top to bottom. No signs of trip wires. I cocked my ear to the door.

Meow.

Harold's paw shot out under the hall door and swatted my foot.

Okay, that was a good sign. Maybe Tanner's *pals* decided to take the day off from terrorizing me. I unlocked the door and, pushing it open, scooped up Harold before he could scoot out. "Hey, buddy, you talking to me again?" I eyeballed the parts of the kitchen and living room I could see from the doorway. No sign anything had been moved.

I closed the door, released Harold, and did a thorough check of all the rooms. "We're good. And guess what? Your pal Nate is coming up to watch a movie with us tonight."

Mom's pettifogging on Nate's apparent romantic interest whispered through my mind—*he phoned every cop and official he knew to track you down.* Uh, boy. What was I supposed to do with that?

Harold twined around my legs, meowing and nudging me closer to his bowl.

"Okay, okay, don't worry. I won't forget your dinner tonight." I filled his bowl with kibbles and tossed a frozen TV dinner into the microwave. Mom would cringe if she knew, but I actually kind of liked them. Well, okay, I liked pretty much anything I didn't have to cook, except maybe frog legs. Not that I couldn't cook. There were just a lot of other things I'd rather do.

While my food was being nuked, I changed into jeans and my favorite Wash U sweatshirt and debated what to do with the couple of hours I had before Nate arrived. Paint? I wasn't really in the mood. Laundry? I still had two clean white blouses. Research the case more?

I clicked on the computer.

The microwave beeped. I grabbed a fork and brought my dinner to my desk. Harold had already commandeered my chair and was swatting at the mouse, his eyes fixed on the screen.

"You want to watch more cat videos, do you?"

I clicked onto his favorite site and found a video of a cat sneaking up on a dog and pouncing on it. Harold was mesmerized. No doubt wishing he could have such a fun playmate to terrorize.

Pounding erupted on my door.

"Hold your horses," I called out, then checked the peephole because it wasn't like Nate to hammer my door, and he wasn't due for half an hour.

Matt Speers stood in the hall, looking haggard, his two-year-old son on his hip.

I yanked open the door. "What's wrong?"

"Good, you're home." Matt shoved a diaper bag at my chest. "I need you to take care of Jed until my mother-in-law can get here to pick him up."

"What? Uh, Matt, someone tried to make a bus sandwich out of my car last night. You don't want me anywhere near your child right now."

Matt's face went pasty, but he shook his head. "It can't be helped. I've got no one else close enough. I've got to get Tracey to the hospital. There's something wrong, but she refuses to go in with Jed along. She doesn't want him to be frightened. She almost died with the last—" His voice faltered.

I scooped Jed into my arms. "Okay, go. Go."

"Thank you. And pray. *Please.*" He raced off without any further instructions.

Jed looked at me as if he might burst into tears at any second, and my heart did a nervous flutter.

"Hey, buddy," I said, bouncing him in my arms. "We'll have fun. Wait until you meet Harold."

Harold took one look at the little guy and darted under the couch.

"Chicken," I said. I shut the door behind us and glanced around my living room. I only had a few breakables I'd have to put up. Hopefully the new surroundings to explore would distract him from his parents' panic.

"Uh!" Jed pointed to the replica of my grand-father's old Ford pickup I had sitting on the bookshelf.

"You want to play with the truck?" I asked.

He eagerly reached for it.

"Okay." I set him and the truck on the floor and

then grabbed a box to collect everything potentially dangerous that looked too enticing to a twenty-month-old.

Jed happily pushed his toy truck around my living room floor as Harold watched suspiciously from under the sofa and occasionally took a swat at the truck's wheels when it got too close. I locked the box in my spare room and shut the other doors to be on the safe side, then checked out the diaper bag Matt had left. It contained all the paraphernalia I could possibly need—diapers, PJs, a well-loved teddy and blanket, and—"Ooh, animal crackers."

I peeked around the corner at Jed and snuck a sample. "Yum." Taking a seat in the living room, I finished eating my dinner while watching Jed muscle his car around my coffee table. He was adorable, with curly blond hair and the cutest dimple in his left cheek when he smiled, which he seemed to do often. And it was one contagious smile. I could see why Mom was so eager for grandkids.

I slipped into the kitchen, rinsed out my frozen dinner container for recycling, and poured myself a glass of juice.

Crash!

I dashed back to the living room. "Jed? Where are you?" My heavy coasters were scattered across the wood floor—the crash. "Jed?"

"Uh." The sound came from under my desk,

264

where Jed had his little hands fisted around the dangling wires.

"Oh no, no, no." I grabbed the keyboard and mouse inches before they hit the floor.

Thankfully, Jed didn't cry the way my cousin's daughter did when you told her no. He just toddled off to the sofa as I set the keyboard and mouse back in place, fished the dangling wires up to the top of the desk, and then wedged the chair into the opening so he wouldn't be able to crawl under again.

I spun toward him and clapped my hands. "Okay, what do you say we—oh no, Jed!"

He was happily plucking items out of my purse.

"Let's put those back in," I said in my best isn't-this-a-fun-game voice.

He fell for it and stuffed my comb and then my pack of gum back inside as I dug my keys out from behind the cushion.

"What's in your mouth?"

He grinned up at me with that adorable dimple, his lips clamped tight.

I held out my hand. "Let me see."

His lips pinched tighter.

"Je-e-ed," I said sternly.

He scampered to the other end of the couch.

I grabbed his foot. "I gotcha. Now let me see." I forced my fingers into his mouth and pulled out what looked like—I gasped. "Where did you find this?"

He pointed to the purse. "Uuuuh."

I grabbed my phone and called Tanner. "You'll never guess what I just found in my purse. A GPS tracker."

"That explains how our Lexus driver tracked you down."

"Yeah, and now he knows I'm home." My voice rose a tad hysterically. Checking it, I glanced back at Jed a second before he disappeared into the kitchen. "And I'm babysitting Matt's little boy."

"I'll come over and pick it up," Tanner said, sounding as if he was already jogging out the door. "We can devise a trap to lure him into."

Crash!

"I gotta go." I thumbed End on the phone and dashed into the kitchen. "Ah, so you think my pot cupboard needs rearranging, do you?" I said sweetly, willing my racing heart down a couple hundred beats. "You're probably right. You go right ahead." I didn't have anything breakable in my lower cupboards. "Oh." Then again . . . I snatched my cleaning supplies out from under the sink and pushed them to the back of the counter. "There, now you should be okay."

He held up a pot with holes in the bottom. "Uh?" His little voice modulated up on his three-syllable version of the word, which I took to mean "What's this?"

"That's a steamer."

He held up a circular pan that folded in half. "Uh?"

"That's to make omelets."

He pushed to his feet and toddled back to the living room, leaving the pots strewn across the kitchen floor.

"Are you done?" I called after him. "We should clean these up before you play with something else." I stacked them back in the cupboard. "I could read you a book. Would you like that?"

Silence.

I hurried back into the living room. "Jed?"

The smell hit me two feet in. "Whoa, Jed. You little stinker."

He was back at his truck and grinned up at me. "Uh."

"Uh is right. We need to change you." I fished through the diaper bag and found the wipes and a clean diaper. "C'mon, mister, we'll do this in the bathroom where we can put on the ventilation fan." If I'd had a clothespin, I might've even clipped it on my nose. How did mothers do this every day?

But I had to chuckle when I saw what else was in the diaper. He'd pooped out a smiley face sticker! Then again, I sure hoped his parents didn't find something of mine in there tomorrow.

The instant I got his bum wiped, Jed twisted off the clean diaper I'd set under him.

"Hey, hey, we're not done yet."

He twisted the other way as I tried to figure out how to open the tape. "Uh!"

Apparently *uh* was the only word he knew, but he said it with a dozen different inflections I couldn't translate. "You're a regular pettifogger, aren't you?"

He slipped out of my fingers and made for the hall.

I slung the diaper on him on the run and had two of the three snaps snapped on the diaper shirt by the time he hit the living room. "And I thought suspects were slippery!" I hurried back to the bathroom to bag up the foul-smelling diaper before it polluted the whole building and then slipped out to drop it directly down the garbage chute. As I stepped back inside, I glimpsed a dark shadow cross the window.

I snatched up Jed and doused the light.

"Waaah," he wailed.

"Shh, shh, it's okay, baby," I whispered, edging toward the hall door. No way could Tanner have gotten here this quickly. It had to be one of Dmitri's guys monitoring the tracker.

Pounding erupted at the kitchen's exterior door.

Jed abruptly stopped crying. "Uh?"

I reached for the doorknob of the door that opened into the building's central hallway. "C'mon, bud, let's get you to safety."

"Serena?" The shout came from outside the kitchen door.

Billy? I flipped on the outside lights, and my *prowler* knocked off his night-vision goggles. I yanked open the door. "Are you crazy? I could've shot you." He was wearing black camo from head to toe and had a gun and a billy club slung on his hip and night-vision goggles dangling around his neck. "What are you doing out here?"

"Zoe was worried about you. Suggested I keep an eye on the place. I heard crying and thought you were in trouble."

"That was Jed." Who was now straining to get back to his exploring. I set him on the floor, and he went back to the pot cupboard. "You're lucky I had Jed to worry about or I might've shot first and asked questions later." Billy was ex-military and apparently had become his family's own personal peacekeeper.

"Should he be in there?" Billy looked seriously concerned.

My gaze dropped to the pot cupboard. *No Jed.* I spun around. "Jed, no!" I pulled him out from under the kitchen sink and yanked the cleanser-laden steel wool he was clutching from his hand. "Did you put that in your mouth?"

He burst into tears.

Billy backed toward the door. "Is he okay?"

I pried open Jed's mouth and saw no sign of foreign stuff inside. "I think so." I bounced him in my arms. "Shh, you're okay. I'm sorry I scared you. You scared me."

"I'll go now," Billy said, backing out the door, his gaze fixed on Jed like he might be the IED that would finally take him out.

"Right, thanks for"—Jed wailed louder—"shh, shh, it's okay. The scary man is going."

I locked the door behind Billy and startled at the sound of someone tromping through the main door. I spun around. "Nate!"

"What's going on? I heard screaming and crying and no one answered the door, so I used my passkey. Who's the kid?"

"A friend's. I'm sorry. I should've called." I lifted my voice higher to be heard over Jed's fussing. "I don't think we'll be able to watch the movie."

Nate made a goofy face and even goofier noises.

Jed laughed and stretched his arms toward Nate.

Nate scooped him up and blew a big raspberry on his belly, which sent Jed into rip-roaring peals of laughter.

My smile must've wobbled because Nate threw me a concerned look. "Hey, you alright?"

"No. He's adorable, but he gets into everything. A second ago he almost ate a pot scrubber. Who knows what chemicals they put in those things."

Man, people think my job is scary. Being responsible for a baby is way scarier.

Tanner stepped inside my kitchen door and took the small microchip-sized tracker from my fingers, his gaze straying to Nate bouncing Jed.

"Matt's wife had a sudden complication with her pregnancy, and they needed a babysitter fast," I explained.

Tanner's expression didn't betray what he was thinking. He studied the gadget. "It's the same model as the one they found on your car."

"What? They found a tracker on my car? Why didn't anyone tell me?"

"Sorry, did I forget to mention it when I delivered the SUV?"

"Yeah! I'm sure I would've remembered if you had."

"I wish I'd thought of planting one on you after last night's scare," Nate chimed in from behind me. Jed was now perched on his shoulders, playing the drum on the top of Nate's head.

Tanner's lips twitched into an almost-smile, as if he agreed but didn't want to admit it. "I'll take it. I already talked to Benton. We're going to set up a sting."

Matt appeared at the kitchen door, rapped his knuckles on the window, and immediately let himself in. "What's going on? Did something happen?" His gaze zinged to Jed. "Jed's okay?"

I lifted him from Nate's shoulders and handed him to Matt. "He's fine. Was as good as gold. How's Tracey? I didn't expect you back. I thought your mother-in-law would be coming."

"Tracey's stable. Her mother's with her at the

hospital. They admitted Tracey and then she started worrying about Jed being here."

"Ah, I'm sorry." I patted Jed's back and gave Matt an encouraging smile. "It's all good. Haven't heard a peep from any bad guys."

Matt looked skeptically from Tanner to Nate. "Then why the bodyguards?"

I shrugged. "You know what they say. It takes a village to raise a child."

Tanner showed him the tracker. "Your kid found this in Serena's purse. You ever see one like this?"

"Sure, it's the model our detectives use."

"You aware of anyone having Serena under surveillance?"

"Only me. I asked a buddy to cruise by every half hour."

A lot of good that did me. He hadn't spotted Billy skulking around the place.

Nate backed toward the door. "I'll get out of your hair. Maybe we can catch the movie tomorrow night?"

"Yes, I'll call you." So much for my *normal* evening.

Matt gathered up Jed's paraphernalia. "I better go too."

I closed the door behind him. "Why would a cop be following me?" I asked Tanner. "Do you think a cop's in cahoots with the Russian mob?"

"Wouldn't be the first time cops were on the mob's payroll. Sloppy of them to use department-issued equipment, though."

"I guess anyone could pick up this kind of thing at a high-tech store. Even Aunt Martha was checking them out one day online."

Tanner eyeballed the piece again, a smile stretching his lips. "You don't think she or your mom planted it, do you? Because they might go ballistic on me if they see it spend the night at my place."

I laughed. "It would serve them right."

21

The next morning, Lucas's financials were waiting for me when I arrived at headquarters. Tanner and Benton weren't. I texted Tanner to find out if their plan to lure Lexus Guy worked.

Not yet, he texted back. *More SWAT training today. Have the tracker with me. If he shows up here, he'll be sorry.* He added a winking emoticon.

Perfect. I set to work analyzing Lucas Watson's financial data. It didn't take long to confirm he'd needed a serious influx of cash to cover the calls on some bad investments. And he'd made three large cash deposits within the last twelve weeks. The last deposit fit the potential time frame for a windfall from fencing his mother-in-law's painting. The deposit before that fit the time frame for the stolen Keane. The first deposit didn't fit the time frame of any other known art thefts, but I wasn't ready to rule it out.

On the strength of the data, I prepared a search warrant for Lucas's phone and email records, along with a search of his house, in particular his computer and printer. I hadn't seen a printer at Capone's place, so his customers must've provided him with the photographs of work they wanted copied. As I recalled, several of those photographs had seemed to be homegrown print jobs.

An hour later, I stood in the prosecuting attorney's office at the courthouse, straining to unclench my fists. "What do you mean the judge won't sign the warrant?"

"He says your evidence is circumstantial and conjecture."

"Would he feel the same if Watson wasn't CFO of the bank?"

The attorney handed back the papers. "I suggest you ask Watson's wife to show you what you're after. If she thinks he's cheating on her, she'll probably relish the thought of sticking it to him."

I groaned. I'd hoped to orchestrate a no-knock warrant so if nothing came of the search, Gladys wouldn't have to know about it. I returned to headquarters to find Tanner back from his training. "I need to sweet talk a beautiful woman into letting me search her house. Wanna help?"

He grinned. "Sure thing."

Tasha answered the door in a filmy sea-green number that left little to the imagination. "Oh, Miss Jones, I didn't expect—" Her gaze shifted to Tanner.

"I hope we're not interrupting anything," I said.

Tasha blushed. "No, no. What can I do for you?"

"Do you have a computer in the house?"

"Yes, in my husband's den."

"May we look at it?"

"What's this about?"

"At the hospital the other day, you said you wouldn't be surprised if your husband took your mother's painting. I want to see if he printed a photograph of it from his computer."

Tasha's eyes widened. "You think I'm right about him?"

"He's a strong suspect."

She swung the door wide and invited us in. "It's this way." She led us into a small, dark room that smelled faintly of cigar smoke and motioned toward the computer sitting in the center of a heavy walnut desk. "There you go. Have at it."

Tanner edged past her to sit at the computer. "Could you enter the password for me?"

"Oh." She flipped the desk calendar to the last page and pointed to the letters scrawled there. "We got hacked a while back, and when my brother Pete fixed it for us, he said we needed a stronger password, but I can never remember it." She stood at the corner of the desk, nibbling her fingernail, and anxiously watched the screen as Tanner's fingers flew over the keyboard.

"Could we have something to drink? Ice water, perhaps?" I asked to give her something to do.

"Yes, of course. Where are my manners?" She strode out of the room in long, graceful strides.

Tanner clicked on file after file. After his seventeenth or eighteenth, he smiled. "We hit the jackpot."

I rounded the desk. "You found the picture?"

"Yup, he deleted it, but he never emptied his virtual trash bin."

I snapped a picture of the image on the screen, desk and computer included. "We're going to need to take the computer in as evidence. Can you start unhooking it while I find Tasha?"

I opened the door and came face to face with Gladys. "Oh, hi."

"Serena? What are you doing here?"

"Collecting evidence, I'm afraid."

"Evidence of *what?*" Her voice shot up faster than a squealing toddler's.

"The theft of your Dali."

"That's ridiculous. Wait until your grand-mother hears about this." She bustled back to the kitchen, and voices rose exponentially.

Tasha scurried out of the kitchen a moment later

and stopped me in the hall. "I'm sorry. I need to ask you to leave."

Tanner strode out of the den. "Doesn't matter. We're done. There's nothing here." He caught me by the upper arm and gave me a silent *play along* signal. "Let's go."

"Right. Uh, thank you for your cooperation." I let Tanner hurry me outside and turned on him once we were in his truck. "What are you doing? She could destroy the evidence before we get back with a warrant."

"Not if she thinks we didn't find anything. He deleted the files, so he'll have no reason to think we found them if she happens to tell him about our visit." Tanner backed out of the driveway and headed toward downtown.

My phone rang before we were three blocks out. My heart sank. "It's Nana."

Tanner flashed me an empathetic look.

I opened the call, and Nana lit into me before I could eke out a hello. "I'm sorry I upset her. That wasn't my intention."

"If you'd been any less discreet, you might've ruined the reputation of a perfectly good man," Nana went on, apparently not privy to his wife's suspicions.

"Perhaps."

"What's that supposed to mean?"

"It means I was following the leads. And they don't always lead to palatable ends."

"Are you telling me Lucas stole the painting?" Nana's voice pitched so high it pinged off the roof of Tanner's SUV.

He sliced his fingers across his throat, signaling me to end the call.

"I'm sorry, Nana. I need to go. I'll talk to you later."

Tanner drove straight to the courthouse, and a police cruiser swerved to a stop in front of him as he parked.

Gladys's son Pete jumped out. "What's going on? Mom called me in a tizzy. Afraid you're going to arrest Tasha's husband. Did he do it?"

"I can't discuss the investigation." I headed toward the front door with Tanner at my side.

Pete chased after us. "She won't press charges if it's him, so why put them through the embarrassment?"

I stopped and whirled to face him. "Does your mother want me to drop the case? Is that what she said?"

"No, she didn't say that. But she's certain Lucas isn't the thief, and she doesn't want Tasha's world turned upside down in the time it takes you to realize it."

"We have nothing to discuss." I turned on my heel and headed inside. Behind me, I could hear Pete on his cell phone, probably delivering his mother the ultimatum—drop the case or face the fact Lucas would likely be arrested.

When we reached the prosecuting attorney's office on the third floor, he seemed to be expecting us. I took a seat and filled him in on what had transpired since the judge refused to sign the search warrant this morning, then requested he reconsider based on the new information.

The receptionist buzzed the PA's intercom. "Detective Briggs is here."

"Show him in," the attorney said.

"Who's Briggs?" Tanner asked me.

"I have no idea."

Briggs strode in looking like a disgruntled Tommy Lee Jones on the trail of Harrison Ford in *The Fugitive*.

"You're the detective from the hospital," I said, remembering him now.

"And you're the agent jeopardizing the well-being of my CI."

"What? Lucas is your confidential informant? Why didn't you tell me that Saturday?"

"You didn't need to know."

"What do you mean, I didn't need to know?" Tanner tapped my hand, and I hauled down my voice a few decibels. "I thought the shooter was targeting *me!* That Lucas was collateral damage!"

Briggs shrugged. "It's possible."

"But you don't think so."

"I wasn't sure at the time, and I'm still not. But I do know we can't afford to have you sniffing around his business."

I crossed my arms over my rampaging heart. Okay, if Lucas is a CI, that might explain the phone calls and other suspicious behavior that had been bothering his wife, but it didn't explain the photo of the Dali on his computer. "Did he steal the painting?"

"He swears he didn't."

"We found a digital image of it in his computer's trash bin, and his bank records showed influxes of cash corresponding to the dates of two separate art thefts in the city."

"A coincidence. When he couldn't raise the money he needed by hocking his wife's jewelry, the pawnshop clerk put a dealer on to him who offered him a job transporting drugs. They loaded the delivery into the panels of his old sports car at a car show in New Mexico, and he drove it to St. Louis."

"And you found the drugs when you pulled him over for a traffic violation?" The so-called "witness to a crime" report in his files.

"That's right. His brother-in-law, Pete Hoffemeier, was on duty and got the full story out of him and then suggested we make him a deal. So we flipped him. He gave us the dealers. We dropped all charges."

"And you let him keep the money the dealer paid him for being a mule?"

"If he didn't pay off his bills, his new *employer* might've gotten suspicious."

I took a deep breath and held it for a full three seconds as I met Tanner's gaze, hoping to read his take on the situation. His slight shrug seemed to say, *It is what it is.*

I let out the breath with a slow groan. "So you're asking me to shelve my investigation?" Nana might actually be happy about that since she didn't like the direction it'd been headed.

"Of Lucas, yes," Briggs said. "He swears he didn't swap out the painting, and I think he's too afraid of screwing up his deal to lie."

I surged to my feet. "Fine. I'll drop the investigation into Lucas. But I still need the search warrant, because if Lucas isn't my thief, his wife must be."

"Not going to happen," Briggs said. "If word gets out his wife is being investigated, Lucas's money-making opportunities will dry up faster than a puddle in the desert."

"Besides," the prosecutor cut in, "if she was behind the theft, do you think she'd have let you search the computer's files?"

"Sure. The file was deleted. She probably didn't know the trash bin has to be emptied too. It's a common mistake."

Tanner shook his head. "She also said she'd been hacked and that her brother had fixed the problem."

I glared at him. He was supposed to be on my side, not theirs. "C'mon, you honestly think a hacker *planted* the image in her trash bin?"

Tanner shot Detective Briggs a sideways glance, his jaw muscles tightening.

"I believe," Briggs interjected, "the agent is suggesting her brother planted it."

"What?" My gaze shot back to Tanner, who seemed hesitant to admit the suspicion in front of Briggs. But it fit. Pete had access to both his mother's house to pull the switch and his sister's computer to print the photograph. And as a cop, he had to know a fence or two who could've disposed of the painting quickly.

Briggs opened the door and paused. "Who better to frame than a fall guy who won't get prosecuted?"

I stared at the empty doorway for a full two seconds after Briggs exited. "Did he just agree with you and point a finger at Pete?"

"Sounds like it to me," the prosecutor said.

"Yeah." Tanner sounded skeptical. "When's the last time you've known a cop to turn on a fellow officer?" He pulled his hand from his pocket, the police-issue GPS transmitter lying on his flattened palm.

A chill shivered down my arms. Was Pete the one tracking me? He'd been turning up like a dirty penny ever since Friday's luncheon at the MAC.

22

I spent the rest of the afternoon discreetly chasing down information on Pete. And came up with *nada*.

Tanner stopped by my cubicle and tossed the newspaper on my desk. "Check it out. Pete Hoffemeier's got an Open House tonight down at your end of town."

"And what? You think if I waltz in showing an interest in the property, he'll admit to stealing his mother's painting?"

"Nope, but I'm sure you could think of some way to weasel information out of him."

"Aren't you worried he might try to hurt me? I mean, I'm assuming you think he planted the GPS tracker in my purse."

Tanner's jaw muscle flexed. He clearly didn't like the odds that *both* Pete and Dmitri's guys were following me. "I'll sit in a car outside and keep watch."

"Okay, yes, this could work. Let me make a call."

Tanner nodded. "Let me know when you want to leave."

I rang up Zoe. Because as much as Saturday's shooting had freaked her out, she was a security officer by trade. She knew how to take care of herself. And the fact she was my best friend and getting married in a few months was the perfect excuse for me to be house shopping with her.

She picked up on the third ring. "What's up?"

"How would you like to go house shopping with me tonight?"

"You're thinking of buying a house?"

"No, you are. And I've found a perfect one for you to see."

"You have? You who breaks out in hives at the mere thought of shopping?"

"Okay, okay, the real estate agent might be a suspect, and I might need the cover of a soon-to-be-married friend who's looking for a house."

"Uh-huh. And have you locked up your stalker—attacker, bad guy, dude—yet?"

"No, but Tanner's going to act as lookout."

"I'm afraid I'm busy tonight."

"With Jax? Because he could come too."

"No, with the will to live."

"Ha, the engagement's made you soft," I goaded.

"No, the desire to see my wedding day has."

The memory of her blanched face after Saturday's shooting pinged my conscience. Maybe it had been too much to ask.

"Why don't you ask your Aunt Martha?" she suggested. "She's always up for an adventure."

"Hmm, yeah, maybe." I blew out a breath. Aunt Martha would agree in a heartbeat, but I hated to involve her, potentially put her in danger. *Right, like I'd had qualms about putting Zoe in danger.* At least it was conceivable Aunt Martha would be interested in house shopping again. My parents' place had to feel tiny at times. I dialed her cell number before I lost my nerve.

Aunt Martha answered on the third ring. "What can I do for you?"

"Want to go house shopping with me? It's a cover," I added, before she could fret that I was leaving the apartment and . . . Nate.

"I'd love to. What time?"

"I'll pick you up at six."

"I'll be ready."

Three hours later, I pulled up outside my parents' nondescript two-story, and Aunt Martha emerged looking as if she was dressed for the Kentucky Derby in her wide-brimmed, brightly decorated hat and polka-dot dress. "How do I look?" she asked, slipping into the passenger seat.

"Like a woman with money to spend." I grinned.

"Good, that's what I was going for."

As I pulled away from the curb with Tanner following at a discreet distance, a call came in from Zoe.

"I've changed my mind. I'll go house shopping with you."

"That's okay. I've already picked up Aunt Martha."

"All the more reason I should join you too."
Her voice hiccupped.

"Zoe? Is something wrong?"

She sniffled. "Jax and I had a fight."

"About what?"

"Doesn't matter. I just need to get out. Can you come pick me up?"

"Sure thing. I'll be there in ten minutes." I texted Tanner the details of the temporary detour. As I pulled up to Zoe's house eight minutes later, Billy came striding out at Zoe's side, dressed in camo.

I jumped out of the car. "Whoa. Is Billy coming too?"

"I'm the bodyguard," he said.

I hitched my thumb to Tanner idling at the end of the block. "We're covered."

Zoe caught his hand and dragged him into the backseat. "This way, we'll be doubly covered." Her eyes were red-rimmed, and I didn't feel like arguing.

"Okeydokey. The more the merrier. But"—I held an empty chicken bucket toward them—"everyone's phone goes in here and stays in the car. My plan won't work otherwise."

Aunt Martha oohed. "Isn't this fun?"

I caught Billy's eye roll in my rearview mirror as he tossed his smartphone into the bucket.

Zoe clutched her phone a little too maniacally. "What if Jax calls?"

"Then you make the dear boy sweat by not answering," Aunt Martha said. "Trust me, he'll come around to your way of thinking soon enough."

Zoe's shoulders relaxed. "You think so?"

"Absolutely," Aunt Martha said as if she had infinite experience with men, despite being a happily unmarried woman.

Billy plucked the phone from Zoe's fingers and plunked it in the bucket. "She's right. Make him sweat."

A few minutes later, we parked in front of a rambling two-story in Clayton. It had a mix of stucco and stone finishes and a gorgeous gabled roofline. "Follow my lead," I said. As I climbed out of the car, Tanner rolled to a stop in front of a house several yards down the block.

Pete greeted us at the door, appearing thrilled and not the least bit suspicious that I'd brought people to check out the place. We wandered through, listening to his spiel, supplying appropriate oohs and aahs, which were totally real considering the place had an open floor plan with Italian porcelain tile flooring flowing through the foyer, entry hall, and the gourmet kitchen that was a chef's dream, with state-of-the-art appliances and granite countertops and eat-in seating. The separate formal dining room opened into a large living room with a fireplace and a study that adjoined an exquisite sunroom. And that was only the main floor! After we returned from viewing the upstairs bedrooms, den, and two and a half more bathrooms, I stopped outside the kitchen and pretended to fuss with my phone. "Figures. The battery's dead."

"Here, use mine," Aunt Martha piped up, and like a born actress she reached into her pocket and came up empty, then frantically checked her other pockets. "Oh dear, I must've left it behind."

Zoe disappeared into the washroom before I could put her on the spot.

I looked to Billy, who raised his hands. "Don't look at me. I dropped mine in my coffee yesterday. It's on the fritz."

A tinge of guilt niggled me at prodding them to lie to play their parts, but wow, were they ever good at hamming it up.

"Go ahead and use the house phone," Pete suggested. "As long as it's not a long-distance call."

"Actually, I need to look something up online. Could I borrow your phone for a minute?"

Pete searched my gaze, almost as if he suspected my ulterior motive. Finding an image of the Dali or any of the other missing paintings on his phone or a record of a call to Capone's apartment could wrap the case into a nice bow . . . if I had enough evidence for a warrant. This way, at least, I could see if I was on the right track.

"Please," I prompted.

He pulled his phone out of his pocket and pressed a few buttons, presumably to unlock it, then handed it over.

Aunt Martha caught his attention and directed it toward the kitchen cupboards.

Thank you, Aunt Martha! I pulled up the icons and clicked on the photos app. The file was empty. I immediately clicked out and checked the call history. Also empty. Pete must've guessed my plan and deleted everything with all that button pushing.

I went online and did a search on flooring options so if he bothered to check my history, at least he'd find I did look something up—something pertinent to the house. Gritting my teeth, I clicked through to a couple of related articles, then exited and handed back the phone. "Thanks so much. So what do you think, Zoe? Does it look like a possibility?"

"I'm not sure. It's quite a bit over the budget."

Pete nodded. "I'm afraid I can't help you with that. The house has been getting a lot of interest, so I don't think it'll sell for much less than the asking price."

Zoe sighed and flounced toward the door. "Oh well, thank you for your time."

Pete caught me by the arm as the others headed out the door. "I wanted to thank you for not arresting Lucas."

"Thank Detective Briggs. I assume you're the one who alerted him?"

Pete shrugged.

"My grandmother won't be happy about me dropping your mother's case."

"Why would you?"

I exaggeratedly arched an eyebrow.

"You still think Lucas stole the painting?"

Billy rushed back through the door, looking ready to rip Pete limb from limb if warranted. "Everything okay?" he asked, as if I'd been forcibly held up for more than a mere minute or two.

"Yeah, I was just coming."

As I stepped outside, I glimpsed Tanner halt his sprint toward the yard and dart behind a hedge. I smiled. *Nice to know people worry about me.* I beeped the SUV to unlock it, and everyone piled in from the sidewalk side, while I rounded the hood to climb in the driver's side.

I opened my door, and an engine gunned.

Gunfire erupted.

Aunt Martha reached over the seat and yanked me inside a nanosecond before a speeding pickup took off my door.

"I can't die before my wedding," Zoe wailed from the backseat.

Tanner ran up from behind my truck to the space where my door used to be, his gun gripped in both hands, aimed at the ground. "You okay?"

"Yeah, I think so."

He reached across my lap, snagged my radio,

and relayed a description of the pickup—decorated with a few bullet holes, courtesy of his Glock—and our location.

"You were the one shooting?" Zoe asked, sounding relieved it wasn't the pickup guy.

Pete ran out of the house, his cell phone pressed to his ear. Aunt Martha rolled down her window, and Pete stuck his head through. "I got 911 on the line. Do you need an ambulance?"

"I'm good."

"We're good," the rest echoed.

"Did you get the license plate?" he asked.

"No, I was kind of busy jumping out of the way!"

Tanner squeezed my arm. "I'm sorry. If I'd stayed in my truck, I might've been able to—" He glanced at Pete and clamped his mouth shut.

Right, Pete didn't need to know I'd brought Tanner along to watch my back.

A couple parked behind us and strolled toward the house.

"I've got to go," Pete said. "Police are on their way."

"Great," I said once he was out of earshot. "The last thing I want to do is answer a gazillion more questions."

"At least we know Pete wasn't driving the truck," Aunt Martha said. "He was who you were worried about, wasn't he?"

"He could've alerted the driver to her location," Tanner countered.

"Or used the GPS tracker," I added. "You still have it with you?"

Tanner grimaced, which I took to mean yes.

"Someone's tracking you?" Zoe's voice edged back up a few hundred decibels. "I don't believe this. I knew I shouldn't have come. I mean, I love you, but . . . Jax wants me to have all my limbs intact for the wedding. And I want to be able to *walk* down the aisle!"

23

The next day passed quietly, with no new developments in Gladys's or the other art theft cases. Detective Irwin continued to stonewall me out of access to Capone's apartment, while Tanner turned over every rock, log, and snitch for a lead on who was bent on terrorizing me. I mean, we were both pretty sure the order came from Dmitri, but we didn't have a sliver of proof and every known slimeball goon who did his bidding had a solid alibi.

So I caught up on all my reports in the relative safety of FBI headquarters and then tugged a little more on the Lucille Horvak thread. Nana's reaction to the photograph I'd found in Capone's apartment was bugging me, and I had a hunch Nana's fired housekeeper might offer some insight. If I could find her.

Tanner stopped by my desk at the end of the day and must've read my failure to turn up any leads on my face. "I guess you're wishing you had a hotline to the legendary Madame M?"

I laughed. "Yeah, she would've tracked Horvak down days ago." Madame M was a CIA operative who in her day, if the rumors could be believed, helped ferret out countless cases of international espionage.

"The woman could squeeze information out of stone."

I grinned at the reference to an exploit in which she found a secret message etched into the side of an Italian statue by a suspect she'd been tailing. "I want to be just like her when I grow up."

Unfortunately, I didn't feel so grown up with Tanner insisting on following me home. Yeah, he had a vested interest in nailing Dmitri's guys if they happened to pick up my tail, but if I'd been a guy, I was pretty sure he'd have just told me to be careful out there.

After supper, Nate and I finally sat down and watched *How to Steal a Million*. It helped me take my mind off my unproductive day, but despite the perfect segue of the hero helping the heroine steal her father's fake masterpiece, it hadn't loosened Nate's tongue about his brother's relationship with the unsavory side of the art world. Or, come to think of it, prompted him to tell me whatever it was Randy had asked him if I "knew."

But by Friday morning, things started looking up. Aunt Martha called before I left my apartment for work. "I found Lucille Horvak!"

"How? Where?" As it turned out, Aunt Martha had had the same idea about finding the gossipy housekeeper as I had, although her motives probably swayed more toward digging up dirt on Nana. And thanks to the connections Aunt Martha had cultivated during her globetrotting years, she'd managed to track down the since-married-and-widowed woman, who now went by the name Lucy Rice, to a retirement home in St. Louis County.

"I'll be there in ten minutes," Aunt Martha concluded.

"What? Why?"

"You can't go in there spouting you're an FBI agent or Stella Jones's granddaughter or she'll never talk to you. She hated the woman."

"How do you know that?"

"Stella fired her!"

Okay, she had a point.

Aunt Martha's voice lowered to that conspiratorial tone that always made me a tad nervous. "We can pretend we're assessing the place as a possible home for me."

"I appreciate the offer, but look what pretending to house shop got us last time—a busted car door. Besides, *my favorite great-aunt* once told me honesty is the best policy."

Aunt Martha snorted. "I believe what I said is the closer you stick to the truth, the less chance you'll get caught in a lie."

"Hmm." Given Aunt Martha's maxims, I sometimes wondered just what kind of *assisting* she used to do for her boss on all those business trips.

An hour later, I sat across from Lucille Horvak, aka Lucy Rice, in the empty dining room of New Life Retirement Home, minus Aunt Martha. Lucille eyed me over her cup of coffee. Her hands circling the cup were covered in age spots and fine lines. Her fingers, gnarled with arthritis, looked nothing like the ones I remembered replacing the book on Granddad's shelf. Although after all these years, they wouldn't resemble them, would they?

If she'd been in his office that night.

Her salt-and-pepper hair was cropped just below her ears. "You don't look like I remember," she said.

She was one up on me. I hadn't remembered her at all, even though she'd cleaned at my grandparents' house three mornings a week. "Could you tell me what you remember about the day my grandfather was murdered?"

Her gaze dropped to her coffee. "I didn't work at their house that day. When I showed up the next morning, the police questioned me, then your grandmother fired me."

Just like that? "Why?" Did Nana suspect Lucy

of being involved somehow? Maybe tipping off the burglars about when the house would be empty? Supplying a photograph of the painting so it could be replaced with a forgery?

"She told her old biddies I was a lazy gossip. None of them wanted to hire me then."

Hmm. Keeping up appearances *was* everything to Nana. She probably feared Lucy might let something untoward slip if she stayed on and was privy to investigators' questions.

"She'd been setting me up for weeks," Lucy went on. "She'd made irate comments about my work every time someone stopped by for tea, when the truth was, she couldn't afford to pay me, and she was too proud to admit it."

I found that hard to believe. Not the pride part, but Nana and Granddad had been very wealthy. Or so I'd always thought. "Did you tell the police?"

"Right, and give them a reason to think *I* had motive to steal the painting myself? Not likely."

I fell silent, a confusion of emotions churning up my insides.

"I didn't kill your grandfather, if that's what you're thinking," Lucy said, pushing her untouched coffee aside. "The painting the thief stole wasn't even real. Although I'm sure your grandmother didn't mention that to her insurance company."

My heart jumped to my throat, making my next question sound a little breathless. "How do you know that?"

Her lips squished from side to side as she retrieved the coffee mug and once again twisted it in her hands. "Because I'd already contemplated stealing it myself. For my retirement money."

My mouth gaped. In my experience, only suspects with guilty consciences admitted to things they weren't being accused of. Suspects with *very* guilty consciences.

She shrugged. "I figured I'd replace the painting with a photo reproduction and by the time they noticed the switch, I'd be long gone, but the joke was on me, because when I took a photo of it to an out-of-town dealer to find out what he'd give me, he told me it was a fake."

"A fake?" My pulse rioted. Could I believe her? Or was this some elaborate ruse to hide her crime? Or a trick to get back at the old lady's granddaughter? "And you think my grandmother knew?"

"Sure, I confronted her about it. Didn't tell her how I knew, of course. She fired me on the spot."

Ah. That I could see. "Did you tell anyone else what you knew?"

She shook her head.

"How about Petra Horvak?"

She smiled, clearly recognizing the name. "Yeah, I met her when we were both working in housekeeping at a hotel."

"You weren't related?"

"Not that we could trace. But it was the common

last name that sparked our drumming up a friendship." Lucy's gaze drifted, her finger absently tapping her lips. "I think I did mention your grandfather's murder to her. She was a talkative one, that one. Always asking lots of questions."

That sounded like Petra, always looking for information to prove her thesis that anyone could be bought. I braced myself. "Did you tell her who you thought killed my grandfather?"

"No, how would I know?"

I scrutinized Lucy for a full thirty seconds and saw no signs of deception. Chances were, if she'd implicated Nana in swapping out the painting, Petra had automatically figured Nana had also arranged for it to be stolen for the insurance money.

Nana's proclamation—*I trust you will ensure the police don't reopen the investigation*—whispered through my mind, and the churning in my gut grew downright choppy.

What was Nana hiding?

Hours later, the question continued to haunt me as I slid into my black cocktail dress for the evening's fundraising gala. I shoved it to the back of my mind to deal with tomorrow and put on my favorite dangly gold-and-rhinestone earrings. Harold sat on my dresser, eyeballing them with a curious glint in his eyes.

"Don't even think about it, buster."

His responding *meow* sounded like a *who, me?*

"Yeah, you." I dumped the contents of my purse onto the bed and transferred the bare essentials into my black clutch. The gun didn't fit. I studied the reflection of my clingy, knee-length dress in the mirror and contemplated pulling a *Miss Congeniality*, gun-strapped-to-the-thigh scenario. *Nah*. There'd be enough armed fellow FBI agents at the event to handle any problem that might arise.

I grabbed my ringing phone.

"The bad guys make any more plays for you?" Zoe asked.

"With Bulldozer Billy camped on my fire escape? They wouldn't dare." Billy and Tanner had tag-teamed keeping an eye on the place.

"So you haven't seen any more guys following you in pickup trucks or anything else?"

"No." Pete hadn't even gotten the color of my assailant's pickup truck right, when he put in the 911 call, and by the time we figured out his mistake—if that's what it was—the assailant was long gone. Not that they'd been on my mind since my visit with Lucille Horvak, aka Lucy Rice.

"Then I suppose I can risk showing up at the gala, but don't take it personally if I don't get within twenty feet of you."

I laughed aloud. "No problem. So you and Jax patched things up?"

"Yes," she said with a smile in her voice. "How

about you? Is Nate driving you tonight? I heard the two of you had a movie night last night."

"Who told you we watched a movie?"

"Your Aunt Martha. She visited the art museum yesterday."

Yesterday? As in *before* our movie night? Not to mention before we'd even made the plans.

"No, Nate's not driving me. I need to drive myself. Nana asked me to pick up some last-minute donations on my way to the silent auction."

Thankfully, handling details for the fundraising gala this past week had kept Nana too busy to chide me over the stalled case. I supposed that reprieve would end after the gala tonight.

"Are you sure that's the only reason? Or would a handsome, dark-haired federal agent have something to do with it?"

"Zoe!"

"Just saying. He looked pretty shook up Wednesday night after that pickup truck took off your door."

"Uh, yeah. Because a pickup took out my door!"

"You know what I mean. I may have been a tad hysterical, but I saw the way he squeezed your arm after you ripped into Pete."

"Was there anything else you needed?" I asked.

Zoe laughed. "No, my work here is done."

I clicked off the phone and stuffed it into my clutch, then gave Harold a rubdown. "You be

300

good, and I'll bring you home some caviar. Deal?"

Harold cocked his head.

"They're fish eggs. You'll like them."

He pawed my hand as if to say, *deal.*

I hurried out to my newest company vehicle. This one, another sedan. An ancient, bare-bones one. I guess the powers-that-be decided the SUV only made me a bigger target. And that I'd already gone through my annual quota of vehicles. I punched the address Nana had given me into my GPS and set out.

As I wound through the shadowed streets of Soulard in St. Louis's east end, it occurred to me the last-minute donation call might be a setup. My fingers tightened around the steering wheel. "Don't be ridiculous. The donor had no way of knowing Nana would send me to pick it up."

"Call Nana," I said to my phone.

"Where are you?" Nana asked, forgoing preliminaries. "Mr. Bateman had to give up waiting for you and leave his donation with the babysitter."

"So he knew it was *me specifically* coming?"

"Yes, of course. What happened?"

"I'm almost there. See you soon." I turned onto Bateman's street, my palms sweating. The area was known for its pub crawls and Mardi Gras, although the extent of my familiarity with the neighborhood was the farmers' market—the oldest one west of the Mississippi.

Several houses from the address Nana had given me, I pulled to the curb and called Tanner. I filled him in on Nana's request. "You think it's a setup?"

"Give me a second, and I'll run the address."

Three minutes later, he came back on the line. "The address is legit. A business owner. A member of the MAC. Clean record."

"No connection to Dmitri?"

"Not that I know of."

Okay, that didn't sound as reassuring as it should have.

"If you can wait, I can be there in fifteen minutes."

"That's okay. Nana won't be happy if I'm late for the gala." I did a visual scan of the area. The blue flicker of TV screens lit the windows of most of the nearby houses, including the one I wanted. I climbed out of the car and walked to the house.

A freckle-faced teenager with spiky hair and a couple of nose rings answered the doorbell. "You here for the clock?"

"Uh, is it the silent auction donation?"

She shoved a toaster-sized cardboard box into my arms with a nod, and at the sound of a deep male voice, turned her attention back to the TV in the corner.

"Thanks."

"Sure thing," she said, her eyes still glued to the heartthrob on the screen as she shut the door in my face.

"Okay then. Lots of worrying for nothing." I strode back to my car and opened the trunk. But as I set the donation inside, the rhythmic *tick tock* kicked my heart into a not-so-rhythmic frenzy.

I whipped out my phone. "Tanner, it's ticking. She said it was a clock, but what if it's a bomb?"

"Bateman owns an antique store. It's probably fine."

"Or maybe that's just what Dmitri wants us to think." An SUV pulled up behind me, and I jumped to the side of the car to put as much of it between me and the SUV as I could manage.

"*Serene* . . . uh." Tanner's gaze met mine through his windshield, and he waggled his phone at me teasingly.

"You could have warned me it was you!" I yelled over the roaring in my ears, then clicked off the phone.

Tanner joined me behind my car, a dimple winking in his cheek. "I could get used to seeing you in dresses."

The blood pulsing past my ears slowed to a dull roar. "I'll take that as a compliment." He was wearing a black tux and looked ten times better than any James Bond actor ever. "You look nice too," I conceded.

The only hint he'd caught on to the huge under-statement was a slight deepening of his dimples. He peered into the trunk. "The bomb squad is on its way."

"Are you sure that's necessary? Nana will kill me if I'm late for the gala."

"Better her than Dmitri." Tanner closed the trunk lid and took my keys.

I groaned.

"It's no problem." He steered me away from the vehicle. "I'll drive you, and we'll leave the package with Douglas. If it's safe, he'll deliver it to the MAC."

"I'm probably being paranoid."

"Trust me. Benton would rather you be paranoid than lose you . . . or another vehicle."

Douglas pulled up a minute later, and Tanner handed him the keys. "The clock is in the trunk."

By the time we arrived at the gala, most of the guests were already there, and with the backdrop of the MAC's opulent ballroom, it had all the ambience of the nineteenth-century painter Gaston La Touche's *The Ball*. Tanner strode by my side through the large foyer and then urged me into the ballroom ahead of him. His light touch sent a tingle down my spine—a sensation that morphed into a different kind of tingle at the attention our appearance seemed to generate.

Numerous colleagues were congregated around the punch bowl, and one by one their gazes snapped our way, followed by fevered whispering. Aunt Martha stood with Nate beside an easel featuring one of the silent auction items. She cast me a sour look, but that didn't bother me as much as Nate's frown. What must he think of me—showing up with Tanner after I declined his offer of a ride with the lame picking up donations excuse?

Mom and Dad crossed the dance floor toward us. Dad thrust out his hand to Tanner. "Good to see you."

Mom beamed at me with a knowing smile.

I shifted uncomfortably. Clearly she thought I'd drunk her find-a-man-and-get-married Kool-Aid. Maybe I shouldn't have whitewashed the details of my recent "collisions." Then she wouldn't be so pleased to see me with a fellow agent. Not that I was *with* him.

She leaned over and kissed my cheek. "You two make a handsome couple."

Tanner's dimple winked.

At least he didn't embarrass me by busting a gut laughing. I glimpsed Nana instructing one of the waiters. "Excuse me," I said to Mom, Dad, and Tanner. "I need to speak to Nana about the donation she was expecting." I headed her way, greeting guests as I passed.

Aunt Martha and Nate intercepted me before I reached Nana. Aunt Martha wore a stylish lavender dress suit with a floral blouse that made her look fifteen years younger. Nate wore a tuxedo and looked like a movie star walking the red carpet. Namely, Bradley Cooper.

"You look stunning," Nate said.

"Thank you. You clean up pretty nice yourself." I bit my lip. Oh man, was I flirting? His wide smile did funny things to my tummy.

Nana materialized at my side. "There you are. Where's the clock?"

"It's coming. I had a bit of a concern about the way it was tick—uh, working, and asked an expert to have a quick look at it before we set it out."

Aunt Martha's eyes flared as if she'd guessed what the concern might be. Not surprising since she'd had a front-row seat to my pickup truck encounter. Even Nate seemed to sense I was sugarcoating, if his furrowed brow was anything to go by.

Nana let out an unladylike snort. "Russell would've ensured it was working to perfection before handing it over."

I didn't doubt it. The question was to *whose* perfection. "Then I'm sure my friend will arrive with it in no time."

The music swelled, and Nate extended a hand. "Care to dance?"

I must've nodded, because he swept me onto the dance floor before Nana could say anything more. "Thanks for the rescue," I whispered. Oh, wow, did he ever smell good—a spicy, masculine, forest-like scent.

His fingers splayed across my back and drew me a fraction of an inch closer. "I suspect I wasn't the first *rescue* of the evening. What happened with the clock?"

"I was probably being paranoid, but between the collisions and drive-by shooting and—"

"Wait. Collision*s*? There's been more than one?"

I let out a humorless laugh. "Aunt Martha didn't mention it? A guy in a black pickup took off my door. So needless to say, when I heard the ticking, I had a sudden vision of a bomb."

He stiffened. "So I take it your *expert* friend is a bomb specialist?"

I grinned. "You're quick."

His grip on my hand tightened. "Is that why you arrived with Tanner?"

"Yes."

"And these"—his voice seemed to get squeezed off. He cleared his throat—"these incidents, are they all connected to the art thefts you're investigating?"

My mind did a sort of double take. Were they? We'd assumed the threat left scrawled on a restaurant napkin on my door had been courtesy of one of Dmitri's goons. And we knew the Lexus that followed me belonged to one of his companies, although maybe it really was stolen. After all, two of my suspects in Gladys's case—Ted and Lucas—were connected to the pawnshop. Not to mention, the Lexus driver had picked up my tail outside Capone's—the suspected forger supplying the thief. And the pickup driver targeted me after I met with Pete—another suspect in the case. Maybe the scares were meant to derail *my* investigation.

24

"You know you can't string them both along forever," Zoe oozed in a hushed whisper as Nate left me at the edge of the dance floor.

"What?" I spluttered, turning my attention away from watching him saunter to the punch bowl to fetch me a drink. "I'm not stringing anyone along."

"Uh-huh. None of my colleagues would escort me into a room the way Tanner did you. And let me tell you, he was shooting daggers at Nate's back the entire time you two were dancing."

"You're imagining things! We're just friends. Both of them."

"Okay, that's good. Then you won't mind introducing Terri to one of them."

"What?" My voice might've spiked a tad high. "Aren't you worried about taking your life into your own hands standing so close to me?" I deflected in a whisper.

Zoe laughed. "With every male FBI agent in the place watching you? Not a chance."

I glanced around and shrank a little at the

realization she wasn't exaggerating. Even Tanner, his curious gaze straying my way, seemed to be only half listening to my dad. Whereas Nate, two punch glasses in hand, had gotten snagged into a conversation with Aunt Martha and . . . was that the governor?

"Terri's latest internet date reneged on coming tonight," Zoe went on. "So the instant she saw you come in with Tanner, she started drooling and it got worse when you started dancing with Nate." Zoe's gaze shifted, and her voice quieted. "Here she comes."

Nate chose that moment to start our way too, with my glass of punch.

"I scarcely know Terri," I hissed to Zoe. "I can't fling someone I scarcely know on Nate or Tanner."

Zoe's eyes twinkled. "Uh-huh."

"I can't!" I waved over Ron, from the terrorist squad. When he'd bought the gala ticket from me, Yvonne said he'd expect a dance for the favor.

Zoe must've clued in to my plan because she headed Nate off, allowing Ron and Terri to reach me at the same time with no Nate to complicate the introductions. "Hey, Ron, I'd like you to meet Terri Weldon, my fellow bridesmaid in my best friend's upcoming wedding."

At the mention of a wedding, interest flared in his eyes. Apparently Mom's Kool-Aid was getting around. Ron clasped Terri's hand. "Pleased to meet you. Would you like to dance?"

For a couple of seconds, her mouth pulled a guppy routine, and I thought she was going to blow it. But she rallied and, after a quick glance in Nate's direction, gave Ron her full attention. "I'd love to."

They swirled off, and Zoe returned with Nate in tow. "I'd better go find Jax before he sends out a posse for me."

Nate sipped his punch as Zoe scurried away. "Your friend is quite a character."

My heart seesawed. "What did she say to you?" If she said something she shouldn't, she'd better keep that twenty-foot perimeter, or I might be the one to hurt her.

"She mentioned you were her maid of honor and—"

"I wasn't going to invite a date to the wedding because it wouldn't be fair with me stuck at the head table," I rushed to explain, then gulped down my punch to cool my heated face.

"O-kay. She didn't mention—"

Tanner plucked the empty punch glass from my hand. "Care to dance?"

"Oh. I—" I looked at Nate.

He smiled magnanimously and relieved Tanner of my glass. "We'll talk later."

Tanner prodded me onto the dance floor before I got my tongue untied. "What are you doing?"

Tanner drew me close—waltz-style. "You looked like you needed backup."

I did? He must've noticed my mortification when Nate brought up his conversation with Zoe, which meant Tanner had been watching me. I shoved away the thought that it could be for any other reason than he was watching out for me—safety-wise. Physical safety. Not emotional.

Tanner chuckled.

"What's so funny?"

"You. Your expression. What's the matter? Didn't you think I knew how to dance?" He twirled me under his arm and then drew me back against his rock-hard chest. *Oh boy. I shouldn't be noticing things like that.*

"You all right?" Serious concern shadowed his gaze.

"Yes. Absolutely. You just surprised me is all. Have you heard from Douglas?"

"Yes, the clock was clean. No bomb. I handed it off to your grandmother."

The heat returned to my face. "So I overreacted big-time."

"Better safe than sorry." He swung me in a circle, making me feel more breathless than safe.

As one song transitioned into the next, another field agent tapped Tanner on the shoulder. "My turn," he said.

Tanner halted our movement but didn't relinquish his hold on me. "Is cutting in still a thing?" he asked me, brows raised.

The agent, whose name I couldn't remember,

held out his hand to me. "Afraid so, buddy. She promised us each a dance."

"Did you now?" Tanner said, releasing me slowly. A teasing glint slipped into his brown eyes. "All of them, huh?"

"K-kind of," I stammered, inwardly sighing. I couldn't admit in front of Agent . . . Whatshisname that I'd shamelessly hustled the charity tickets any way I could, but Tanner knew me well.

Tanner stepped back. "Okay, she's all yours." His lips twitched into a smirkish smile. "You kids have fun."

Six dances with six different agents later, I begged for a reprieve and headed for the punch bowl.

Mom was there and handed me a glass. "You're popular tonight," she said, not sounding as if it made her happy.

"Colleagues," I explained.

"Hmm."

I took the punch and meandered around the silent auction tables but had the flesh-crawling feeling I was being watched. And not in a can-I-have-this-dance kind of way. I surreptitiously glanced around.

Gladys's son, Pete, stood at the far end of the auction tables, leaning against the wall, and nodded as our eyes met, not betraying a stitch of discomfort at being caught staring. In fact, he kept right on watching me.

Remembering the misleading description he'd

given the 911 operator after the hit and run, I bristled.

Tanner came up behind me and whispered close to my ear. "He's not the only one who's watching you."

I sighed, pretty sure he intended to tease me about bribing our colleagues to buy gala tickets. "I don't know what you're talking about," I said, all innocence.

Tanner jerked his head toward my grandmother sitting at a table near the front of the room. Her friend Gladys, Gladys's daughter Tasha, and Tasha's husband, Lucas, were all seated with her but diverted their attention toward the musicians when my gaze drifted their way.

"It feels a little like an Agatha Christie novel," I quipped.

Tanner gave me a blank look.

"You know. She gathers all the suspects in one room for the great reveal."

"But you don't know who done it."

I snorted. "I'm not even sure I know what all's been done."

Tanner slanted a glance at his cell phone screen, and his face clouded.

"What's wrong?"

He scanned the room. "Two of Dmitri's guys are here." He steered me behind a statue being auctioned off and jerked his chin toward three guys standing in front of an art easel.

313

Dmitri's bouncers in the black polos . . . "Isn't that Ted?" I asked.

"Yeah," Tanner practically growled, "and he's talking to them."

Ted pointed to the bottom corner of the painting on the easel.

"Whose painting is that?" Tanner asked.

"Tyrone's. I don't like this. Ted showed an interest in his art the day he showed up at the drop-in center too. What's going on? Does Dmitri deal in art?"

"Not that I've observed. Although you know as well as I do that it can be a convenient currency."

Ted pointed to someone across the room, and Dmitri's guys' gazes followed the direction of his fingers.

I scrutinized the throng of people. "He's pointing out Tyrone to them."

The men said something to Ted, who then crossed the room in Tyrone's direction.

Malgucci—an enigmatic member of an Italian mob family who'd wiggled his way into my aunt's good books (okay, probably mine too) by donating a kidney to a dying woman—sidled up to Dmitri's men and started talking.

"Since when do Russian crime families chitchat with Italians?" I asked.

"Since I asked him to question them," Aunt Martha interjected, joining us.

"Why?"

"I noticed their interest in Tyrone's painting and pointed them out to Malgucci. I'm so proud of how well Tyrone's doing."

"Only Malgucci questioned the nature of their interest," Tanner guessed.

"Yes."

"He's heading this way," I whispered, pulling Aunt Martha out of view of Dmitri's men. It was bad enough they were going after me to control Tanner. I didn't need to give them any more targets—especially my loved ones.

"What did they have to say?" Tanner asked, turning his attention toward the silent auction tables instead of Malgucci.

Malgucci glanced at Aunt Martha, who gave him an encouraging nod, then followed Tanner's lead and placed a bid on a nearby auction item as he answered. "They said the guy's name is Ted—a wannabe criminal who's tried to brown-nose up to them before."

"He's worked for them?" I asked.

"No, they said he's too green."

But ambitious. *Interesting.* Between Ted's connection to Tasha and his connection to the Russian mob and the pawnshop, he could've masterminded the theft of Gladys's Dali. Maybe coaxed Tasha to pull off the switch and took care of the rest himself.

I scanned the ballroom for Tasha. Lucas was still sitting with Nana and his mother-in-law, but

Tasha had left the table. I glanced back to where I'd last seen Ted. Not with him. Restroom, perhaps? I excused myself and headed for the ballroom door. It opened to an expansive lobby. The aroma of cigar smoke—reminiscent of my grandfather—wisped from the smoking lounge to the left. A small group of people had congregated in the sitting area at the far side of the lobby. The grand central staircase that led to the powder room on the second floor was empty. I strolled past it and found Tasha and Pete just beyond the reception desk, having a heated discussion.

Pete glanced up and immediately ended the conversation and strode out the back.

Tasha let out a long-suffering sigh as I approached. "I don't know why Mother favors him so. Blind to his faults, I suppose."

"What faults would those be?"

She opened her beaded clutch, extracted a cosmetic case, and right there in the center of the hallway proceeded to powder her nose as she peered in the tiny accompanying mirror. "He's a dreamer. He comes up with all these money-making schemes, and when they don't pan out, he goes running to Mother for another bailout."

"Like when he can't sell a piece of real estate?"

"Exactly."

"And your mother always helps him?"

"She'd never refuse her golden boy."

Okay, if that were true, Pete would've had no

reason to abscond with his mother's Dali. Unless he was too ashamed to ask for money again. But if it wasn't Pete or Lucas, that left Tasha or Ted. Or both.

"How well do you know Ted?"

She snapped her cosmetic case closed. "This is hardly an appropriate time to discuss my lover," she said, her voice low. "My husband is in the next room, not to mention my mother and umpteen of her cronies."

Yet, somehow I suspected she'd wandered out of the ballroom, hoping to meet up with Ted, not her brother. "He seems to have a keen interest in art," I said, making it sound as if it was an off-the-cuff observation, even as I gauged her reaction.

Her lips quirked into the slightest of smiles. "It's not so much the art as the subject." She stroked her neckline suggestively.

"He would've appreciated Truman Capone's work, then," I segued and didn't miss her infinitesimal flinch. "He did a lot of commissioned portraits. You know his work?"

She tapped a blood-red fingernail to her pursed lips. "Ca-po-ne. The name sounds familiar."

"It's been all over the papers. He was found murdered in his apartment a few days ago."

She flushed and dropped her hand. "That's right. Killed while sitting in his apartment, minding his own business. Tragic."

317

Aunt Martha tootled her fingers at us from the staircase. "Did you see where Tyrone went?"

I looked around the lobby. "No, why?"

"He seemed upset after that Ted fellow talked to him. Stormed off before I could catch up to him."

Tasha started to walk away, but I caught her arm. "Do you know why Ted would talk to Tyrone?"

She shrugged. "Don't even know who Tyrone is."

I released her arm and trailed her back into the ballroom with Aunt Martha at my side. Tasha glanced Ted's way but returned to her mother's table. Her husband stood and escorted her to the dance floor.

"How does she know Ted?" Aunt Martha asked.

"He sold her jewelry." Aunt Martha didn't need to know it was hocked or that Tasha and Ted were having an affair.

Aunt Martha glanced back out into the lobby. "I hope Tyrone didn't leave already."

"All the pomp might've been overwhelming." I looked around for Tanner but couldn't spot him, either. "Did you see where Tanner went?"

"No."

Dmitri's goons were nowhere to be seen, either. I returned to the lobby and peeked out the front door. A few of the teens from the drop-in center were loitering on the sidewalk, passing around a cigarette. "Anyone seen Tyrone?"

"He said he was going home."

There was no sign of Tanner or the Russians, so I slipped back inside and checked out the side door that opened onto the parking lot.

A familiar voice caught my attention. "I don't renegotiate."

Pete? I squinted into the shadows but couldn't make out who he was talking to.

"Now, keep your mouth shut and your ears open," Pete went on.

A lanky figure in a black hoodie slunk off into the night.

The mugger who'd grabbed the Degas last week? Sure, lots of creeps wore hoodies, but Pete had been around that day too.

Pete strode to his car and sped away, tires squealing.

I sensed movement behind me and spun around, one fist pulled back, ready to let loose, my other arm raised to block a blow.

Tanner smiled. "Everything okay?"

"No!" I dropped my arms with a huff. "I wish my grandmother had never asked me to find Gladys's stolen painting. My prime suspects are her children, and Nana will never speak to me again if I arrest one of them!"

"So don't arrest them. Quietly share your suspicions with Gladys and ask if she wants you to keep digging."

"She'll refuse to believe it. I know she will. And she'd never press charges against one of her own."

"Then that will be the end of it."

"I can't drop the case!"

"You can still keep a lookout for her missing Dali."

"It's not just the Dali. Capone had—"

Tanner raised his hand. "Dozens of photographs of paintings. I remember."

"Including my grandfather's," I reminded him.

"Yes." He gripped my upper arms and held my gaze. "But *not* Gladys's."

I opened my mouth, the need to justify continuing the investigation surging up my throat.

"Two different investigations," Tanner added.

I clapped shut my mouth. Okay, that made sense. Pete, or Tasha and Ted, could've been mimicking the MO of thefts they'd read about in the papers.

Then again . . . I filled Tanner in on the exchange I overheard between Pete and the guy in the black hoodie. "If Pete's behind more than the theft of his mother's Dali, I can't turn a blind eye."

Tanner grimaced, no doubt thinking of the GPS locator I'd found in my purse. "He won't be easy to nail."

Anxiety churned in my chest. "And my grandmother will hate me if I manage it."

25

The next morning crawled in gray and gloomy, which pretty much matched my optimism about the way the day would go. "Should I do what Tanner said and talk to Gladys about my suspicions?" I asked Harold as I fitted my gun into my shoulder holster. Yes, it was Saturday, but until my suspicions were settled one way or the other, I'd be an even lousier shopping partner than I was on a good day.

Harold circled his spot on the bed a couple of times and plopped back down without responding.

"Yeah, I feel like I'm running in circles. But the photograph of the Dali was on Lucas's computer, so it's got to be Tasha's doing, maybe with Ted's help, or Pete's, or Lucas's, if his handler is wrong about him." I sat on the edge of the bed to pull on my shoes. "I don't have anything to connect any of them, or the Dali, to Capone though. So Tanner's probably right about Gladys's theft being a copycat."

Harold let out an indignant throat warble at the word *copycat*.

"Trust me. The idea doesn't sit well with me either." I pulled out my phone and thumbed through the pics I'd snapped of Capone's photographs. I paused on the one of Granddad's

321

painting, thought about the explosion that took out the originals. "Somebody didn't want the police examining these. Which means he had to be afraid they'd give him away."

Tasha wasn't old enough to have been involved in Granddad's murder, but Pete would've been eighteen, maybe nineteen at the time, old enough to concoct a scheme to steal the painting, or to be cajoled into helping. And savvy enough now to know the best time to destroy the evidence. "Maybe I'll dig a little deeper into Pete's activities before I speak with Gladys."

I tapped in Matt Speers's number. "Hey, can we meet for coffee?" The best way to gain insider information on a cop was to talk to his colleagues.

"Too busy today. Haven't you heard?"

"Heard what?"

"We've got a warrant for Tyrone Gaines's arrest."

"What? Why?"

"His prints were all over Capone's apartment. I'm sorry." Matt knew Tyrone was one of my art students because he was the one who'd introduced him to the drop-in center after picking him up for painting graffiti on the side of a bank.

"They can't think he'd kill Capone. Why would he?"

"I don't know, but Capone's neighbor recognized his picture and remembers hearing yelling coming from Capone's apartment not long before he saw Tyrone leave last Friday. The neighbor said he glimpsed Capone through the open door, and he looked like he'd been punched in the face." He paused. "And now they can't find Tyrone."

"Which only makes him look more guilty." I heaved a sigh. "Okay, thanks for the heads-up, Matt. By the way, how's Tracey doing?"

"Much better. On bed rest, but home at least."

"Good to hear."

I patted Harold's head. "Looks like I'm paying Tyrone's mother a visit."

When I parked my car outside Tyrone's parents' place twenty minutes later, I couldn't help but notice the guys sitting in a green sedan across the street perk up. My heart did a quick dip, until I realized Dmitri's goons had no reason to watch for me here. They had to be plainclothes officers hoping to spy Ty sneaking home.

I crossed the street, shifting my coat so they'd see my badge clipped to my waistband as I approached. "St. Louis PD?"

"That's right. And you are?"

I glanced into their vehicle and spotted the police radio and other hardware confirming their admission. "Special Agent Serena Jones. Tyrone is one of my art students at the drop-in center where I volunteer."

"Thanks for letting us know."

"No problem." Unless they informed Detective Irwin. He wouldn't be happy about my being here.

Tyrone's crumbling brick two-story sat on a narrow lot. A curtain in the neighboring house slid back as I approached the covered porch. I couldn't see who was looking out but nodded anyway. The curtain immediately swung back into place. I rapped on the door and waited on the small covered porch as multiple locks slid open.

Tyrone's mom didn't even wait for me to introduce myself, although I suspected she recognized me from the drop-in center. "Like I told them other po-lice," Tyrone's mom railed, "he didn't come home last night. Said he was staying at a friend's."

"Which friend's?"

"Don't matter. He ain't there. He ain't anywhere. Them po-lice already came back and told me that much." Even her dark complexion didn't hide the tired circles under her eyes.

"I'm sorry, you must be terribly worried." She was hiding it behind anger, but I remembered my mom doing the same thing when my brother would stay out all night without calling.

She collapsed into a chair, her hands fisted against her thighs. "It ain't like him. Ty's a good boy."

"What was the nature of his relationship with Truman Capone?" I asked gently.

"That artist?"

"Yes."

"He was tutorin' Ty. Sold some of his paintings too."

"Did they have a disagreement recently?"

She shrugged. "Ty stomped around here the Friday before last after seein' him."

The Friday before last? Ty had been at the Boathouse that night, watching a couple of Dmitri's goons.

"But when he came by Sunday to pick up one of Ty's paintings, they seemed square. Mr. Capone even gave us a nice portrait he did of Ty. Had nothing but good things to say about our boy."

"Okay, thank you for your time," I said and stepped out of the house. My gaze drifted to the officers still sitting in the nondescript sedan. *Lord, please let me find Ty. Please let this all be a big mistake. But if it isn't, please compel Ty to come clean.*

Catching the attention of the officers, I gave my head a small shake to let them know I came up empty talking to Ty's mom. Then I climbed into my car and began trolling the streets. A lot of the places in this neighborhood were rentals, and it showed. Perched on scant patches of grass that didn't seem to grow, they had zero adornment. Broken windows went unrepaired. Peeling porch rails had settled into a uniform gray. I spotted one of Ty's friends near the drop-in center and pulled over. "Hey, Jamal, you seen Tyrone?"

"No," he spat in that indignant tone teens seemed to have down to a fine art. "TC didn't do what those po-lice are saying he did."

I blinked. "You call Tyrone TC?"

"Sure, we all do."

Oh, this was so not good. The initials TC had been what tipped off one forgery victim. Was that what Capone had been tutoring Ty in? Painting forgeries? "But Ty's last name doesn't start with a *C*."

"His dad's name does."

But he goes by his mom's name.

A police cruiser turned onto the street and slowed beside us.

"Act cool," I whispered to Jamal as the driver's window whirred down.

Pete Hoffemeier sat behind the wheel. "Kind of early to see you in this end of town, isn't it?" he said, obliquely referring to my volunteering at the drop-in center down the street, but clearly fishing.

"Always things to follow up on after a big fundraiser," I said, not about to be baited.

He squinted at Jamal. "And what are you doing here?"

"It's a free country. I can be wherever I want."

"You know a kid named Tyrone Gaines?" Pete asked Jamal, wisely not rising to Jamal's taunting tone.

"Sure, he goes to my school."

"You seen him today?"

"No," Jamal barked back with a heavy dose of like-I'd-tell-you sauciness in his tone.

Pete offered me a tight smile and cruised on.

"You'd better go easy on that attitude," I said to Jamal, "before the police get on your case too."

He shrugged and skulked off in the opposite direction from Officer Hoffemeier.

As I returned to my car, I glanced toward the drop-in center, wondering if I should let myself inside for a few minutes for appearance's sake. The basement windows were the old, wooden-framed type that opened like a hatch, and the one nearest the back looked as if it wasn't closed properly. I strode over to investigate.

The edge of the window near the lock was dented, as if crushed by a pry bar. I squinted through the glass but couldn't make out anything in the dark basement.

I returned to the front of the building and casually glanced up and down the street. No sign of Pete's cruiser. A green sedan rounded the corner and parked in front of the convenience store at the next corner. I let myself in through the center's front door and locked it behind me.

"Tyrone? It's Miss Jones. Are you in here? I want to help you," I called out. Only after the words were out did it occur to me someone other than Tyrone might've broken in. I palmed my gun and scanned the large, open main room. No one. I glanced in the office, under the desk. No one. I checked the bathroom, the storage closet. No one. I flipped on the basement light. "Ty? Talk to me."

Silence.

I hesitated. It would be too easy for whoever was down there to waylay me or shoot me as I descended the stairs.

A shadow detached itself from the wall and stepped into the light, arms raised.

"Ty, what's going on? They think you killed Truman Capone."

"They who?"

"The police. Is it true?"

"No! I'd never hurt him."

"Then why are you hiding?"

He shifted from foot to foot, his gaze bouncing about the floor, the muscles in his cheek flinching every couple of seconds. "I didn't know what he was doin' with the paintings. I swear."

I holstered my gun. "Okay, calm down. Start at the beginning."

"Tru was teaching me how to paint. Then he offered to sell my paintings from his booth. You know, like on consignment."

"What kind of paintings?" I asked, already guessing the answer.

"Copies of masterpieces. He gave me photos of the ones he wanted. Said his customers ate that kind of thing up. I swear I didn't know what he was really doin' with them."

"Which was?"

"Sellin' them to a couple of goons who'd swap them out for the real thing. Except one of the homeys they hit spotted my initials. My mark, you know? I hid them in my copies, didn't even tell Tru. The goons freaked on him. Accused Tru of setting them up."

"What did Capone do?"

"He told me to hide as soon as he saw 'em coming. And he didn't give me up. Just took the beating."

So that explained the yellowed bruises on Capone's face. "Why didn't you call the police?"

"He would've gotten in trouble. We both would've."

It beats being dead. I didn't say it aloud. Tyrone looked eaten up enough with the guilt as it was.

"After they left, I told him I wouldn't paint no more copies if he was gonna sell them to criminals. Then I followed the guys."

"To the Boathouse."

"Right, so I guess you know about the Russian mob guys?"

"You're saying they bought the paintings from Capone?"

"Why else would they beat him up?"

"He wasn't just *beaten*."

"Don't you think I know that? He got beaten up 'cause of me." Tears sprang to Ty's eyes. He swiped at them, shook his head. "It don't make no sense. They had a bunch more orders Tru was supposed to do for them. I even finished the one I'd started for him because he was so desperate."

The painting I'd witnessed Capone picking up Sunday afternoon?

"They sent someone to talk to you at the gala. What did he want?"

"For me to take over Tru's business." Tyrone lifted his chin, squared his jaw. "I told that"—he slicked over a colorful description of Ted— "I wasn't interested. But he said if I knew what was good for me, I'd change my mind."

"Why didn't you come to me?"

Silence.

Not that he needed to spell it out. Most kids in this neighborhood didn't see law enforcement as the kind of people who had their best interests at heart.

My cell phone rang. I glanced at the display. *Nate.* I dismissed the call without answering. A few moments later, a text alert came through— *Randy has vital info for you. We need to talk.*

"Excuse me a second," I said to Ty and then called Nate. "Can this wait? I'm a little busy right now."

"Where are you? We'll come to you. We might know who killed Capone."

My heart missed a full beat. "Who? How?"

"We'll explain everything when we see you."

"Okay, I'm at the drop-in center in north St. Louis."

Ty tapped my shoulder and shrank back into the shadows.

"I know it," Nate said on the other end of the line. "We'll be there in ten minutes."

I clicked off and turned to Ty. "You don't have to worry about Na—"

Ty cut me off with a slice of his hand. "Someone's trying to get in upstairs," he whispered.

I cocked my ear toward the stairwell. "Stay here," I whispered and hurried up the stairs two at a time. At the top, I slapped off the light switch.

The doorknob rattled, followed by knocking. "Miss Jones, you okay in there?" Pete's voice boomed through the door.

I opened it. "I'm fine," I said, although I suspected he was more concerned about what I might be up to than my welfare. "What's going on?"

He looked around without moving from the doorway. "I noticed the light on in the basement when I drove by and then you didn't answer when I first knocked."

"Oh, sorry. I must've still been downstairs at the time."

"Do you mind if I look around?" He moved to the front of the room and glanced under the supply table. "It occurred to me that if Tyrone is familiar with the center, he might decide it's a good place to hide out from the police."

"I'm actually glad you came back," I deflected, heading him off before he made it to the stairs. "I wanted to ask you about the guy in the black hoodie I saw you talking to outside the MAC last night."

"What about him?"

Interesting. So he didn't deny meeting the guy. "He fits the description of the guy who mugged me in that neighborhood last week. What's his name?"

"What was the description? Tall, white guy in a black hoodie?"

"Pretty much," I acknowledged, not missing that he'd avoided supplying a name as deftly as I'd omitted mentioning Tyrone was indeed hiding in the basement. "Do you know his name?"

"Afraid I can't tell you that." He headed toward the basement stairs.

"Let me guess. Another informant?"

He paused at the head of the stairs and pivoted on his heels. "Yes, as a matter of fact, he is."

Or a cohort in crime and Pete was afraid the guy would give him up faster than a wooden nickel?

Nate and Randy rushed into the center, minutes faster than predicted. But my relief was short-lived.

"Randy? What are you doing here?" Pete asked.

I'd momentarily forgotten they knew each other, and it occurred to me Randy's new information might've been fabricated for Pete's benefit. Only if that was the case, Nate wasn't in the loop, because he immediately jumped in with a cover story. "I recruited him to help me help Serena"—

he looked around the room—"with this place."

"That's great. I'll just check the basement, then be out of your hair." Pete descended the stairs.

Stop him, I mouthed to Nate.

"What you looking for down there?" Nate trailed after him. "Maybe I can help."

"A fugitive. You best stay put."

Nate flicked on the light at the stairs. "You don't want to go down there without backup, then."

The front door opened again, and Aunt Martha trundled in. "What is this? A party?"

"Aunt Martha, what are you doing here? Did you come with Nate?" I asked.

"Followed in my own car."

Pete paused on the bottom step and did a slow three sixty, shining his flashlight into the corners, then came back up. "All clear. I'll see you around."

I squelched the relieved sigh that squeezed from my chest and turned to Nate as the door closed behind Pete. "What's going on?"

"Randy has something to tell you," Nate said, sounding less-than-happy about it.

Randy paced.

"We think the guy who beat Randy up outside his apartment might be the same guy that went after you," Nate began.

Jolted by the unexpected connection, I gripped the back of the nearest chair. "Who's that?"

Randy stopped pacing and met my gaze, his own filled with apology. "He said he was a friend of Tasha's who wanted to make sure I kept my mouth shut."

My heart burst into an erratic pulse. "About the Dali theft?"

"I guess."

"You guess?" I didn't bother keeping the exasperation from my voice.

"I didn't know anything about any theft at the time. A couple of months ago, Tasha looked me up and asked if I could recommend a good artist who could make a copy of a painting for her. It never occurred to me she planned to do anything illegal."

"So you recommended Capone?"

"Yeah. Then when Tasha saw me at the MAC that day you were there, she asked me not to mention our conversation to her family, or you. I didn't think anything of it. Not until her *friend* beat me up."

I glanced at Aunt Martha, but she showed no sign of surprise. In fact, besides being unusually quiet, she seemed more interested in what might be going on outside than what Randy had to say.

"So why didn't you say anything that night?" I asked Randy.

"I like my face the way it is!" He scraped his hand over his chin and gave his head a shake. "And I didn't see the point. Gladys would never have let you arrest Tasha anyway. But I didn't think her rent-a-thug would come after you too."

I fisted my hands and somehow managed to keep my tone neutral. "Did you get his name?"

"No. He just told me if I knew what was good for me, I'd keep my mouth shut."

"What did he look like?"

"Five eleven, average build, shaggy blond hair, and he had a real distinctive voice. A strong Texas drawl, but he paused on words so long I wasn't sure if he was on something or thought the pauses made him sound more ominous. You know what I mean?"

Yeah, he'd described Ted to a *T*.

I questioned Randy a few minutes longer, but he didn't have anything more useful to add, except his apologies for not speaking up sooner.

"Do you think he killed Capone?" Randy asked. "I mean, if he was worried about me talking, he must've been worried about Capone too, right?"

"Hmm." Unlike Ted's strong-arm approach to Randy, the trauma to Capone's body—the broken fingers on his left hand, the purple eye—had been days old, the work of Dmitri's goons, according to Tyrone. Had Ted gotten smart and gone prepared to off him with some sort of drug?

Unfortunately, Detective Irwin wasn't keen about sharing information, so I still had no idea what the actual cause of death was.

"I can't believe Tasha's mixed up with that fellow," Aunt Martha piped up, breaking her unusual stretch of silence. "I saw you talking to her in the lobby last night, and she seemed so nice."

The reminder of that conversation twigged another memory. Tasha had said Capone was killed while sitting in his apartment minding his own business. I hurried over to the supply table and riffled through the stack of newspapers. Finding one reporting Capone's death, I scanned the article. No mention of him being found sitting in a chair. I pulled out my phone and checked the online articles.

"What is it?" Aunt Martha asked.

"Something Tasha said," I mumbled absently as I scanned articles. "It could've been more than she should've known. Unless she was there." I clicked Play on the TV news report. No mention of Capone dying in his chair. "I appreciate you bringing this to my attention," I said, moving everyone toward the door. Tyrone would be getting antsy, and I clearly needed to get the ball rolling on bringing in Ted and Tasha.

Randy and Aunt Martha ambled outside, but Nate lingered. "Do you know who this guy is that beat up Randy?"

"Yeah, I do."

"Do you think he's the one who rammed your car?"

"I'm not sure. In my job, you make a few enemies."

Nate's mouth was a grim line—the quintessential picture of why I wasn't likely to find a quiet, hearth-and-home kind of guy to settle down with as long as I worked this job.

"You won't go question him alone, will you?"

"No."

His tense posture seemed to relax a fraction, and he trailed the others outside. Aunt Martha's car was parked in the narrow drive to the side of the building. I walked over and gave her a hug before she climbed in. "Thanks for coming."

"Nonsense, you know I like to help." She glanced surreptitiously around, then opened her door and, looking at me, tilted her head toward the backseat.

My eyes widened at the sight of Tyrone hunkered down on the floor between the front and back seats.

26

Aunt Martha pulled me into another hug next to her car outside the drop-in center. "Give me a call when it's safe for Tyrone to turn himself in."

I wanted to protest, but a cruiser chose that moment to round the corner, not to mention the two familiar-looking guys standing outside the convenience store on the corner eyeballing us. *What is wrong with me? I'm a federal agent and my aunt is harboring a fugitive. We're talking serious jail time if she's caught.*

"By the way," Aunt Martha said, sliding behind the wheel, "you'll find Tasha at Gladys's. Last night at the gala, I overheard her volunteer to fill in for one of their Saturday morning bridge players who's sick."

I grabbed the car door before she could pull it closed, but then the cruiser slowed to a crawl, the officer inside rubbernecking in our direction. I firmly closed the door. "Thanks, Aunt Martha. I'll be in touch."

She drove off as I locked up the center. The cruiser disappeared around the corner with her. The curious guys hanging out at the corner store, who I now recognized as the pair of plainclothes cops from outside Ty's place, climbed into their car and pulled in behind me as I passed.

They must've alerted Detective Irwin to my visit, and he probably figured following me was their best shot at finding the kid. Too bad they had no clue Aunt Martha was my ace in the hole. Of course, if the detective had been interested in sharing information, I'd be calling him to share Randy's tip.

Instead, I phoned my supervisor to request surveillance on Ted while I rounded up Tasha.

"The guys aren't going to be happy about being pulled in on a Saturday. You got enough on these two to get arrest warrants?" Benton questioned.

"I could get Ted on assault, no problem, but I suspect Tasha will roll on him for the murder

338

charge, if I can get to her first. I just want to make sure he doesn't run."

"Okay, I'll put a couple of guys on him. Keep me posted."

"Will do." Next, I called Tanner, who was always game to get the bad guys no matter the day of the week, and asked him to meet me at Gladys's for the interview.

"I'm afraid I'll be at least forty minutes. We had an operation this morning, and we're still mopping up."

"That's okay. I can't see Tasha giving me any trouble in front of her mother." I filled him in on Ted's and Tasha's run-ins with Randy and their connection to Capone.

"So you think Ted killed Capone?"

"He's a hothead if the number he did on Randy's face is anything to go by. And he's got to be in cahoots with Tasha, or why would he have bothered with Randy?"

"Okay, I'll meet you at Gladys's as soon as I can."

The cops followed me to Gladys's circle and parked at the opening when I pulled to the curb in front of her house. I resisted the temptation to sashay back to them and give them a rundown on the how-tos of Covert Surveillance 101. Except they probably couldn't care less whether I spotted them or not.

Gladys, not her housekeeper, opened the door.

"Oh, Serena, it's you." She poked her head out the door and glanced up and down the street. "We're waiting on our fourth for bridge, and I thought you'd be her."

"Sorry to disappoint. May I come in?"

She teetered on the threshold a moment as if she might say no, then stepped back and motioned me in. "I trust you're satisfied now that my son-in-law wasn't behind the theft. If I'd known you were going to investigate my family, I wouldn't have agreed with your grandmother to involve you. After the way the police went after her when your grandfather was killed, I would've thought you'd be more sensitive."

My pulse kicked up a few dozen notches. *So Nana really had been a suspect?* The official report had mentioned them questioning her, but not the investigators' apparent dissatisfaction with her answers. "The last thing I want to do is hurt you," I heard myself saying. I bit my lip, knowing it would happen anyway. "Sometimes the truth can be something we don't want to hear."

Her eyes flared. "What are you saying?"

"I need to speak with Tasha," I said, suddenly wishing I'd waited until she was at her own house. "I understand she's here."

Nana and Tasha joined us in the foyer, Nana looking expectant, Tasha looking worried.

I kissed Nana's cheek and wished her good morning.

"I think I want you to drop the investigation," Gladys blurted. "I don't care about pressing charges anyway. I'd just hoped you might locate the painting."

"I understand," I said sympathetically, "but I still need to speak with Tasha."

"Why? I just said—"

Tasha laid a hand on her mother's arm. "It's okay, Mom. I'm happy to talk to her." She motioned toward the room where the Dali had hung. "Shall we go in here?"

I stepped inside ahead of her as she gently dissuaded her mom from joining us. Nana glared at me over their heads. So much for my solving this case earning me a place in her good books.

There was no door on the room, so Tasha waited at the doorway until Nana and Gladys left the foyer, before turning my way. "How may I help you?"

"Randy told me everything."

"I see." She sat on the sofa and clasped her hands in her lap. "Thank goodness Mom doesn't want to press charges." She shook her head. "It was Ted's idea. I heard Mom talking about getting the painting appraised, and I knew what she was up to. I knew she'd sell it so she could help her beloved Peter out of yet another one of his financial pits. Everything is Pete this and Pete that. I swear, half the time I'm invisible. And at the rate she was going, she'd have sold herself out

341

of house and home to help Pete, and where would that leave me? With a cheating husband who burns through money faster than he makes it?"

"Your husband *isn't* cheating on you."

"What? How would you know?"

"I know."

"Oh yeah? So how do you explain the late-night phone calls? The secret rendezvouses? He had a woman bring a paternity suit against him for goodness' sake."

"Since nothing came of the suit, I assume testing proved her wrong. As for the rest, there is an explanation," I said firmly, wishing I were at liberty to divulge it.

Tasha burst into tears and buried her face in her hands. "Ted is no better. He's a hothead. I told him Randy wouldn't say anything, but no . . . he had to *make sure*. As if beating the poor guy is going to make him want to keep quiet. I knew it was a mistake, but Ted's so . . . so . . . obsessed with the idea of being someone. You know what I mean?"

"I think I do, yes." I waited, hoping she'd keep talking. I was itching to ask questions, but since I planned to arrest her, I'd need to read her her rights first.

She swiped at her damp cheeks. "Is Randy going to press charges against him? I mean, I know he has every right to, but then everything else might come out in the papers and I don't want to put Mom through the embarrassment."

"A man is dead. That can't be swept under the rug."

Her face blanched. "I . . . I don't understand."

I unzipped my purse and pulled out my Miranda Warning card. "The victim was the man Randy referred you to."

"But"—her gaze dropped to the card—"what . . . what's that?"

"I need to read you your rights before I ask you any questions."

"But Mom doesn't want you to arrest me. Mom!" she screamed as I read the card.

Gladys rushed in with Nana on her heels.

"Tell her you won't press charges. Please," Tasha pleaded. "I admit I switched the Dali. And I'm sorry. I was just so jealous. You're always doing things for Pete and . . ." Her explanation petered out in a fashion befitting a drama queen.

Gladys stroked Tasha's hair from her face. "Oh, sweetheart, I'm sorry," she cooed. "I didn't mean to make you feel left out." Gladys turned to me, her voice cooling considerably. "I'm sorry we've put you to so much trouble. I won't press charges."

"I understand that, Mrs. Hoffemeier," I said, feeling Nana's heated glare scorch the side of my face. "However, Tasha has been implicated in a larger investigation."

"What's this about?" Nana demanded. "You were asked to find the missing Dali, not dig up trouble for the sake of trouble."

"I didn't hurt that man, I swear," Tasha blurted.

"Of course you didn't," her mother said.

"How did you know he died sitting in a chair?" I asked.

"She would've read it in the newspaper like the rest of us," Nana interjected.

"It wasn't reported," I said, not taking my gaze off Tasha.

She squirmed.

Her mother looked taken aback. "What is she talking about?"

Tasha shook her head. "It was Ted. He went crazy. It was all his idea. When he heard about Serena talking to Randy, he insisted on beating him up to make sure he kept his mouth shut about referring us to Capone. Then when he heard Serena was looking at Capone, he was so afraid the old man would snitch on us that he said we had to silence him. Of course I said no, we should just come clean." Tasha squeezed her mother's hands. "I knew you would forgive me."

"Of course," Gladys confirmed. "I had no idea how you felt." Gladys turned to me. "Can't you see she was lashing out because she didn't feel loved?"

I crossed my arms, sickened by Tasha's display. "I don't feel loved by my grandmother, but you don't see me stealing the art off her walls."

Gladys's eyes widened.

Oh no. Did I just say what I think I just said?

"What utter nonsense," Nana said.

My face heated, and I didn't dare chance a sideways glance in Nana's direction. What was it about Tasha that pushed all my buttons? She was a spoiled brat.

But yeah, I knew how it felt to be ignored. Maybe even loathed. I stuffed away that thought to examine later, or maybe not, and focused on why I was here. "So you're telling me Ted killed Capone?" I asked, my pen poised over my notepad.

Tasha swallowed hard. "Injected him with insulin. Said it couldn't be detected. I know I should've said something right away. Does that make me an accessory? I didn't see him do it. I just assumed it must've been him after the way he went on and on and even went after you."

Whoa, back up the bus. "When did Ted come after me?" I'd assumed all the *special* attention given to me lately was courtesy of Dmitri's goons, or Pete's.

"He said he almost ran you over."

"Who is Ted?" Gladys and Nana demanded in unison.

"He works in the pawnshop where Lucas sold her jewelry to pay for his drugs," I barked, then clapped my mouth shut at the slip.

Gladys's face darkened five shades, and she looked as if she might burst an artery. "You took up with a man from a pawnshop?" she asked

Tasha, the part about Lucas and drugs apparently going *whoosh,* right over her head.

My jaw slacked. Now I knew where her daughter got her messed-up priorities.

The ringing doorbell spared Tasha from answering.

"That'll be Betty. We're supposed to play bridge," Gladys said.

Okay, this was crazy. I'd completely lost control of this interrogation. "I'm afraid Tasha needs to come with me."

"Is that really necessary?" Nana asked impatiently.

"Yes." I snapped cuffs on Tasha, and Gladys's face paled to a ghastly gray. "I'm sorry this didn't work out the way either of us hoped."

Nana sniffed. "You always were such a contrary child."

Talk about not working out the way I'd hoped. I took Tasha out the side door to spare Gladys the embarrassment of passing her guest with her daughter in handcuffs. Technically, I was supposed to have a second agent along to sit with Tasha in my backseat, but I didn't want to stick around longer than necessary, and I was pretty sure Tasha wouldn't give me any trouble.

As we stepped outside, my cell phone chimed the theme song for *Murder, She Wrote*—a sound I hadn't heard for a few days. Then the mother of the sticky-fingered girl who found Aunt Martha's phone in the bush clued in to why her daughter was suddenly so self-entertaining and made the girl return it.

I helped Tasha into the passenger seat and buckled her in, before glancing at the text.

Please come quickly. Got car trouble. I'm in the back parking lot at CCVac.

Ugh, what else was new? She should've traded that old clunker in years ago. Except . . . *What on earth is she doing at the old vacuum cleaner factory?* I paused outside the car, debating what to do. She probably figured the deserted industrial area was the safest place to hide out until the heat died down. A gray-haired, white senior with a black teen hanging out at the mall or Forest Park would attract unwanted attention. And she had to know Mom wouldn't stand for a fugitive in the house, so she couldn't call Dad about the car, let alone roadside assistance. Unless . . .

What if car trouble was code for trouble with Ty?

The cops in the car at the corner sat up and took notice of my hovering outside my car.

Terrific. I'd have to lose them before I saw to Aunt Martha. I climbed in my car, my mind racing. With any luck, the trip to the marshal's office would convince the cops that tailing me was a waste of time. But what if Aunt Martha *wasn't* just being her usual dramatic self and needed me *now?* It would take me half an hour, minimum, to get Tasha squared away.

I took a deep breath. *Okay, this isn't a ticking clock that can't tell me if it's a bomb. I can just call her already.* "I'll just be a minute," I said to Tasha and dialed Aunt Martha's number.

The call went immediately to voice mail.

I texted her back. *Can you give me 45 minutes?* I reversed out of the driveway and tipped an imaginary hat to the pair of cops at the corner as I passed.

Aunt Martha's response—*No. I need you now*—came in as I was about to notify dispatch I was transporting a suspect.

I hit Redial, but my call went to voice mail again. At the stop sign, I fired back another text. *Why aren't you answering your phone?* I wavered at the corner. This sounded more serious than car trouble. Did she not want Ty to overhear her on the phone? Or someone else?

Sorry. Have the ringer off.

But she got the text alert? This was starting to feel fishier than the ticking clock.

I don't feel well. Might need to go to the hospital.

Wow, okay, major red flag. Aunt Martha loathed going to the doctor. This had to be code for "I can't talk, but you need to get your buns over here."

Only . . . it was the *why* she couldn't talk that had me antsy. Especially when I needed to unload Tasha. I couldn't exactly ask the cops now trailing behind me to take over the transport. It'd probably make them so suspicious they'd keep following me with Tasha in tow. And it'd take just as long to call in another agent or marshal to pick her up as to take her myself. I made a quick turn and then another. The factory was five, six minutes away, tops. I could drive by first, and if the situation looked dicey, I'd pull back. If it was nothing, the pit stop wouldn't matter. If it was something, I'd be glad I went. But first I needed to lose Starsky and Hutch trailing behind me.

Of course, backup would be good. Just not them. I veered into a mini-mart lot and stopped behind a delivery truck. As the green sedan sailed by, my thumb hovered over Tanner's name in my contact list.

No, it was one thing to put my job on the line by failing to turn Ty in. I couldn't ask Tanner to take the same risk. Nate?

He'd be game to help. But . . . the thought of him finding out I knowingly let Aunt Martha harbor a fugitive didn't sit so well. I bypassed his name and kept scrolling through my contact list. Malgucci. Of course. Helping a fugitive wouldn't compromise his morals one iota. Especially a fugitive Aunt Martha was fond of.

I clicked on his name and pressed Call, then scouted the street for the green sedan and turned back toward the factory.

"Why are those men after you?" Tasha asked.

"Who knows?" I said. She'd been surprisingly quiet while I did my disappearing act. From the way she was chewing on her lip, she was probably relieved by the delay.

"Carmen here," he answered on the second ring.

I quickly brought him up to speed on what was going on and the potential trouble I *thought* Aunt Martha might be in, beyond "car trouble."

"On my way," he said without questioning me.

I smiled. He was the third cousin, twice removed on his mother's side, to one of the most notorious crime bosses in the country, and purported to have his fingers in the business. Although Aunt Martha claimed he just enjoyed flaunting the persona. Either way, it was handy to have him on speed dial.

"We need to make a quick stop before we go to the marshal's office," I said to Tasha.

"What's going to happen to me?" she asked.

"Tell the truth and be as cooperative as possible, and I imagine the prosecutor could be persuaded to be lenient." Considering we had no physical evidence, as far as I knew, tying Ted to the murder scene, it was far from a done deal that even her testimony would clinch that conviction.

My phone rang. Tanner. I tapped it on.

"Where are you? I'm outside the Hoffemeier place, and your car's not here."

Right. I'd forgotten he said he'd meet me there

when he got done. "Uh, I'm taking Tasha to the marshal's office." In a roundabout way. "I'll meet you back at headquarters. I asked Benton to put surveillance on Ted. Could you look into it? See where he's at?"

"Sure. See you in a bit."

I swiped a sweaty palm down my slacks. Omitting mention of the pit stop I was making en route wasn't really lying. Was it? My heart twinged.

Or maybe my conscience.

It's not like I don't plan to encourage Tyrone to turn himself in. I just don't think he's guilty, and if I can prove it before he goes in, it'll save him a lot of undeserved grief.

I slowed as I neared the industrial park that housed the now-defunct Cleaner Carpets Vacuum factory. I squinted at the rooftops, down the side alleys. My chest tightened. "You see a car anywhere?" I asked Tasha. "It's powder-blue."

As we coasted past the next building, she jutted her chin toward the lot behind it. "There. At the back."

The car was parked facing away from the road, overlooking a steep hill littered with garbage of every description. Aunt Martha was in the driver's seat, hands on the wheel, but there was no sign of Tyrone.

I drove a little farther to scout the area. Seeing no signs of anyone lurking nearby, I turned and slowly crossed the parking lot.

Aunt Martha's head whipped around, and the panic in her gaze sent my heart slamming into my ribs.

"It's a trap!"

27

Before I could ram the shifter into reverse and stomp on the gas, my car door burst open and a rifle muzzle plowed into my cheek.

"Get out. Nice and slow," the gunman said in a gravelly voice.

Okay, I had to admit losing those two plainclothes cops who were tailing me was *not* the brightest move. But . . . my gun was holstered on my right hip next to the seat-belt latch, and Rifleman looked egotistical enough to think I wouldn't give him any trouble. Holding up quivering arms, I babbled hysterically to aid the impression.

"Out," he ordered.

The ever-obedient hostage, I meekly unlatched my seat belt, then discreetly palmed my gun.

The rifle came down hard on my arm, knocking my gun to the floor.

"Ow!" I screamed at an ear-bursting pitch and grabbed the rifle barrel with my other hand. I jerked hard.

The gunman toppled toward me, but before I could wrestle the gun out of his hold, a second guy reached across Tasha and snatched it from the both of us.

I scrambled for my Glock, but just as my fingertips grazed the steel, the first gunman grabbed me by the collar and yanked me out of the vehicle. The second guy pocketed my gun and hauled Tasha out the other side of the car.

Inside her car, parked just ahead of us, Aunt Martha screamed like a wild woman. Her head bobbed frantically from side to side, but strangely she didn't jump out of the car, didn't even let go of the steering wheel.

As the jerk holding my arm slammed me face-first against the hood, I saw why. They'd duct-taped her hands to the steering wheel.

"Who are you? What do you want? Why are you doing this?" I demanded.

"We ask the questions."

I surreptitiously scanned the area. Rusting equipment littered the parking lot. Foot-high weeds pierced the cracked pavement, testifying to the lack of traffic. The closest warehouse was four hundred feet away, and based on the number of missing windowpanes, it'd been abandoned long ago. The good news was, there was no sign of any other bad guys skulking in the shadows.

And these guys weren't expecting Malgucci to show up any minute.

Hopefully packing.

"Do you know who I am?" I squinted at the guy

holding Tasha and instantly recognized him from the surveillance stint at the Boathouse—one of Dmitri's goons. One of the ones Tyrone had been spying on.

Rifleman yanked my face off the hood of my car, his hot, stinky breath slithering down my neck. "I said, we ask the questions."

Ow, ow, ow, ow, ow. I clearly should've paid more attention to the niggling voice that gave me such a hard time over keeping Tanner in the dark. And a buzz cut would've been smart too. "I'm just trying to help," I said, all innocence. But somehow pointing out that if they killed a federal agent, they'd have the rest of the agency breathing down their necks for the rest of their lives didn't seem as if it would faze them.

The second guy held my Glock to Tasha's temple. "Tell us where you put Capone's package, and we'll let you walk."

Black mascara streaked Tasha's ashen cheeks. "I . . . I don't know what you're talking about."

"Look, lady, we had a nice business going with Capone before you waltzed in. Be happy we don't pop you for that alone."

"She didn't kill him," I said.

"That's not the story her boyfriend tells."

Tasha gasped. "Ted told you I killed that man? He's lying. He's crazy."

"Look, he didn't have it. And it wasn't in Capone's apartment after you offed him."

"I didn't off him!"

The guy twisted his fist in her hair and got in her face. "Whatever. It wasn't there. And no one's going anywhere until we get it."

"What does this package look like?" I asked, stalling for time. Where was Malgucci?

The guy holding Tasha, who seemed to be the spokesman for the pair, squinted at me. "Documents, photographs, tapes maybe. I don't know. Trust me, we would've offed him ourselves after the stunt he pulled, if it weren't for that package."

"So these documents? They're incriminating?"

"I said, we're asking the questions," my handler bellowed, twisting my hair in his fist.

I gritted my teeth against the pain. If I wasn't expecting Malgucci any minute, the creep would've learned what a hoof to the kneecap felt like, followed by an elbow to the nose and capped with a knee to the groin. Out of the corner of my eye, I could make out Aunt Martha working at the duct tape binding her wrists to the steering wheel, and she seemed to be talking to someone. Herself? Or was Tyrone still hiding in the car?

"I don't know anything about any package," Tasha wailed.

"Ted says you went through Capone's desk and grabbed some stuff."

"The photo of my mother's painting. That's all."

So she'd been at Capone's apartment with Ted, after all. So much for her truthfulness.

The creep twisted his gun—correction, my gun—in front of Tasha's face. "I don't believe you."

Mascara-streaked tears streamed down Tasha's face.

"Why would she lie?" I screamed.

A cruiser raced into the parking lot, but my elation quickly deflated when it whipped around in a dust-stirring donut before squealing to a stop in front of us, and the bad guys didn't blink an eye.

Pete jumped out of the car, showing no emotion, save for a flinch in his cheek when his gaze landed on his sister.

"Pete! How did you find us? Tell these guys I don't have what they're after," his sister screeched.

Pete offered me a nod, which I responded to with an icy glare. Clearly he was in the organization's back pocket. "What's going on, fellas?" he said.

"This broad is your sister?"

"That's right."

"You got a problem with us roughing her up?"

Pete shrugged. "We've never been close."

"Pete!" Tasha wailed. "What are you saying? You know me. I don't have what they're after."

Pete's voice turned caustic. "You stole a painting from your own mother. I don't know you at all."

"I'm sorry. I told her I was sorry."

He shook his head, looking disgusted by her begging.

My stomach revolted at his coldness. And at the

realization that, unless Malgucci brought reinforcements, we'd be seriously outgunned. Worse than that, Pete was a dirty cop. And now that I knew it, there was no way on earth he'd let me live.

"How'd you get them here?" Pete asked.

"We followed the old bag in the car from her apartment to the drop-in center"—the guy hitched his chin in my direction—"and saw her exchange a hug with Jones and figured she'd be the ticket to lure her to us once we got word Jones had the woman."

Pete nodded. "Good work. But if you'd called me sooner, I could've saved you the trouble and gotten her myself."

Tasha let out a strangled sound.

"Sorry, Tash, I'm in a tight spot here. I was counting on the money from the painting you swiped. Then you had to go and compound the problem by killing Capone."

"I didn't kill him," she wailed.

"How could you sell your soul to a guy like Dmitri?" I hissed at him.

Pete cocked his head and narrowed his eyes. "I think Jones here knows a lot more than she's been saying." He pulled his gun and grabbed my arm, and with a jut of his chin, signaled my captor to release me.

"You kill a federal agent, Hoffemeier, and the agency will hunt you down for the rest of your life, if these guys don't throw you under the bus first."

He laughed. "Big talk for a woman in your position." He raised his voice. "You lost the cops tailing you. Bailed on your partner." He lowered his voice to a whisper. "Give me something to work with here, Jones. I'm on your side. Stall for time." His voice exploded louder. "Who's going to know? Huh?"

I blinked. Searched his eyes. Was he playing me?

"Talk to me," he barked. "Where'd Capone hide the documents?"

"Maybe they're behind one of his paintings," Tasha blurted. "Like you used to hide those girly photos behind your band posters on the wall."

Pete actually blushed as he tossed a glare at his sister.

My mind bobbed to the conversation with Tyrone's mom—the painting she'd mentioned Capone giving her. Could that be where he'd stashed the evidence?

Pete squinted at me as if he sensed I was connecting the dots. Then he shoved me back at my captor and opened the door of Aunt Martha's car. Pointed his gun at her head. "Tell us what we want to know."

"Pete, no!" Tasha screamed. Struggled to break free of her captor's hold.

Aunt Martha gnawed at the duct tape binding her hands, then shot her leg out sideways and caught Pete in the knee.

"Ow," he yelped. Then, scowling at her, he

stepped back a half pace, his gun still pointed at her.

Aunt Martha babbled something I couldn't make out as Tasha continued to wail.

Pete swung his attention back to me. "You have three seconds. One . . ."

"I don't know anything," I said with a stony calmness that belied the frenzy in my mind. Was this an act for the bad guys' benefit? What did Pete really expect me to do? Was he playing with my mind?

"Two . . ." Pete said louder.

Aunt Martha frantically strained at the duct tape binding her wrists, babbling at the rearview mirror.

I fought against the creep holding me. "Pete, you can't do this. You're not a murderer."

"Shoot her," the guy holding Tasha barked. "This isn't getting us anywhere." He pressed a gun to Tasha's temple. "Tell us what we want to know."

Pete's finger slipped inside the trigger guard. "Thr—"

"No, wait!"

He paused, cocked his ear as if to say, *I'm listening.*

"Capone has a booth at the flea market. Maybe the evidence is stashed there," I blurted, praying it wasn't.

"We already checked there," the other guy grunted, which explained why all the paintings had been askew. He raised his gun as if he intended to shoot Aunt Martha himself.

"No!" I screamed, and Pete glared at him.

But the instant the guy lowered his gun, Pete's gaze narrowed on me. "Three." He fired.

"No!" I rammed my elbow into my handler's gut. I never thought Pete would shoot. Not an unarmed victim. *Not Aunt Martha.*

28

Pete swung his gun in my direction. "Tell us. Or the next one goes in her head."

I froze. Blinked.

Aunt Martha was ranting at him, still struggling to break free.

He shot the dirt. *He shot the dirt.*

Then suddenly there was a second person crawling up between the seats, reaching for her duct-taped wrists. *Ty.* He must've hidden in the trunk. So far, no one else seemed to notice him.

Hoping to keep it that way, I screamed, "Okay, okay!" and allowed my fuming captor to grab my arm once more.

Malgucci materialized behind Pete, looking every inch hard-core Italian mob. He had a long-barreled pistol pushed into the front of his waistband and one in each hand at his sides. "I don't recommend that, son. It would be suicide," he said with a cool aloofness that left no doubt he'd see to it. His gaze skittered over each of Dmitri's guys. "You mess with her—you mess with the whole Malgucci family."

A hint of a smirk flitted over Pete's lips as he raised his hands and flattened his trigger finger along the side of his weapon.

I stilled. Was he on our side? Or not?

My captor shot a panicked glance at Tasha's captor. "What do we do?"

They outnumbered Malgucci three to one, but clearly they took his threat *very* seriously.

"Dmitri will kill us if we start a turf war."

Pete's gaze briefly shifted sideways. There was no way he couldn't have seen Ty. But he didn't let on.

The guy holding Tasha suddenly did a double take at the car's rear window. "Hey, it's the kid." He reached for the door with his gun hand, with Tasha in tow under his other arm.

Malgucci squeezed off a shot in his direction.

The guy yelped, dropping his hold on the door handle and on Tasha. A second shot sent his gun toppling to the tarmac.

I hammered a heel into my captor's kneecap and spun a left hook to his nose.

His hold dropped for a nanosecond, then he plowed into me, grabbing me around my arms and middle. Squeezed the air from my lungs.

A shot rang out, and his grip loosened.

My gaze slammed into Pete's. His chin dipped in the slightest nod. I shoved the creep off of me and scanned the scene.

Malgucci's aim veered from the guy who'd been trying to get into the car to Pete.

"Not him," I screamed as the guy he'd been watching rolled onto his belly, snatched up his fallen gun, and aimed at Tasha hysterically running back and forth like a duck in a shooting gallery, one three-inch heel on, one broken. "Tasha, down!" I dove toward her to take her down myself.

I didn't hear the shot.

No, that's not true. I heard an explosion of shots. And one of them ripped through my arm. I huddled over Tasha on the ground, shielding her body with mine. I could smell the blood spurting hot and sticky.

Someone lifted me to my feet. Tanner in full SWAT gear. A St. Louis police officer, also in SWAT gear, helped Tasha to her feet.

"How?" I babbled, not thinking clearly enough to form a complete question with Tasha wailing.

"What were you thinking, keeping me in the dark?" Tanner hissed through gritted teeth as he tied a band around my bleeding arm with jerky movements.

I bit down on a cry of pain.

"Ouch. Sorry." His hands gentled, but his tongue-lashing continued. "We're supposed to trust each other. Have each other's back. I was *five* minutes away when I called, and you sent me in the opposite direction. Then got yourself shot."

He exhaled, the rush of his pent-up breath stirring the ends of the bandage.

"I'm sorry." I cupped a hand over the seeping wound, fighting a wince. "I—"

He nailed me with a hard look. "You could've been killed!"

I swallowed miserably and looked away. I was an idiot. And I had the screaming pain to prove it. He had every right to be angry. "How did you"— I leaned heavily against him, feeling woozy— "know to come?"

"Pete called us before he engaged. He's on the joint task force investigating Dmitri's organization. He'd won their trust by pretending to be on their payroll, feeding them just enough police intelligence so they'd believe it, while collecting evidence against them."

"Oh," I said faintly, glad he was still holding me up, even though he'd clearly rather drop me on my sorry backside.

Tasha rushed into her brother's arms. "I knew you couldn't be dirty."

"Huh," I murmured. "That's not what she was babbling ten minutes ago. She thought he was ready to throw her under the bus." I managed a grin, albeit a weak one.

Tanner didn't return it. "Yeah," he said. "There

was a significant lack of trust going around, wasn't there?"

I winced.

The other SWAT members busied themselves trussing up Dmitri's guys.

I glanced around. "Where's—?" I swallowed Malgucci's name before saying it aloud. He'd disappeared. And considering the firepower he'd been packing, it was a good thing. He didn't deserve to be carted off to the station with this lot.

And something told me Dmitri's men wouldn't be too quick to explain the source of the unidentified bullet or two that were bound to be located by the evidence recovery team.

Aunt Martha hauled herself out of the car, along with her giant purse, and stalked over to the guy who'd tried to go after Ty, now lying facedown on the ground, getting his hands tie-wrapped. She kicked him in the hip. "Not such a bad guy now, are you? How does it feel to be the one getting tied up?"

She reached into her purse, and I had visions of her pulling her gun. "Aunt Martha," I cried out.

"Spoilsport." She closed up her purse with a pout.

Pete handed his clinging sister over to the waiting officer.

Her eyes widened. "I still have to go to jail?"

"You committed a crime," Pete said.

"I didn't kill that artist like they said. I didn't!"

"At this point, it's your word against Ted's. I suggest you tell the detectives everything you know." Pete nodded to the officer, who escorted her to a police car.

Another SWAT guy handcuffed Ty.

"Whoa, wait," Aunt Martha said. She swung around to face him, looking ready to club the muscle-bound officer with her gun-weighted handbag. "What are you doing, young man? Ty didn't do anything wrong."

"There's a warrant for his arrest."

She turned pleadingly toward Pete. "You know he didn't do it."

Pete stepped forward. "I'll take charge of the boy." To Aunt Martha, he added, "Don't worry, I'll see that the charges get dropped."

I hoped he could do that before the poor kid had to endure the humiliation of being processed like a common criminal. I turned to Tanner. "We need to go back to Tyrone's house. I think I know where Capone stashed the evidence on Dmitri's organization."

Tanner cupped my elbow. "You're not going anywhere until you get that gunshot wound tended."

As if on cue, an ambulance careened into the lot, and Tanner motioned them toward us.

Now that I thought about it, I was feeling more than just a little woozy, and my arm felt like it was on fire. Then a shadow dropped over my vision, and my knees crumpled.

"Whoa, hang on there," Tanner whispered, his breath stirring my hair.

My cheek lay against his solid chest. I blinked. "What . . . what happened?"

Tanner deposited me onto a gurney. "You passed out."

"Oh"—my mind felt as if it was slogging through murky water—"that's not good, huh?"

"No. Nothing about the way this went down was good."

29

"She's my granddaughter. You can't keep us away from her." Nana's angry voice carried down the hospital's hall.

I offered an apologetic smile to the nurse checking my IV. "That sounds like my grandmother. Would it be okay for her to come in?"

"Yes, of course." She made an adjustment on the IV, then left the room.

The bullet had gone clear through the fleshy part of my arm with minimal damage, but I'd apparently lost a lot of blood.

Mom and Dad piled into the room with Nana trailing. "Tanner called us."

"Oh." I mustered a smile.

Of course Tanner had called them. He was a decent guy. But he hadn't responded to my texts apologizing—again—for not calling him to back me up.

Mom stroked the hair from my face and kissed my cheek. "How do you feel?"

She looked like she'd been crying, and from the way she was plying the tissue in her other hand, it was taking every ounce of her self-control not to lecture me.

"I'm fine, Mom. We got the bad guys."

Trying to be unobtrusive, I reached for my phone on the nightstand and shifted it a little closer to me.

Dad came around to my other side and kissed my cheek. "From the sounds of it, you might've toppled a lot of bad guys." He smiled down at me, pride beaming in his eyes.

Nana stood at the foot of my bed, her fingertips grazing the sheet.

"I'm sorry about Tasha," I said. "I'm sure Pete will do all he can to get her a reduced sentence for her part in Capone's murder."

Nana dipped her chin in a single nod. "I'm sorry this happened to you," she said, her words shaky, her eyes red rimmed.

"It goes with the . . ." I was about to say *territory,* but one glance at Mom had me rethinking the pat response. I shrugged. "Things happen. I'm sorry we were too late to recover the Dali, but it's been logged into the Art Loss Register, so it might turn up yet."

Mom shook her head. "I can't believe Tasha knew that man was a murderer and didn't come forward."

"She was afraid." Probably as much of Ted's retaliation as of being socially humiliated if her theft came to light. I surreptitiously glanced at my phone to make sure I hadn't missed an alert.

"Being afraid is no excuse," Mom said, disgust coloring her voice.

I winced because the excuse was uncomfortably familiar.

Tell them, a still, small voice inside my head said.

I shrank at the idea. *I can't. They'd be more disappointed in me than Tanner is.*

Dad chucked my chin. "What's the matter?"

Tell them, the voice repeated, more forcefully this time.

I scrunched the bedsheets in my fists and gave my head a shake, as if that would silence it.

They won't hate you.

I stilled, because the voice sounded an awful lot like Granddad's. I blinked back tears. What had they put in my IV? Something that made me hallucinate? Hear voices?

"Serena?" Mom said gently. "Should we call the nurse?"

I closed my eyes and shook my head. "No, there's something I need to tell you. Something I should have told you a long time ago but was too afraid of what you would think of me."

Warm fingers curled around mine.

My eyes popped open, and Dad was gazing down at me, his expression serene. "We love you, sweetheart. You can tell us anything."

A lump lodged in my throat. They could say that now, but if I told them, it would always be there in the back of their minds—my failure, my selfishness, the what-ifs if I'd been brave enough to say something then, not eighteen years too late.

Mom looked worried. Dad didn't. His expression was resolute. I couldn't bring myself to glance Nana's way.

I took a deep breath, and the confession spewed out. "I was there the night Granddad died. I was hiding in the secret passage behind his office wall."

They gasped.

"We thought it was Nana coming home early," I rushed on before I lost my nerve. "Granddad didn't want me to get caught staying up past my bedtime, so he showed me the passage to sneak through to my bedroom. But as soon as I was inside, he must've realized it wasn't Nana coming in, and he told me to stay in the passage, to not come out, no matter what I heard."

Mom's hand flew to her mouth.

I didn't dare look at her, at any of them. I fixed my gaze on a spot on the wall and forged on. If they were going to be disappointed in me, they might as well hear the whole story. "I heard the person come into Granddad's office. Heard the struggle. I couldn't see anything. Didn't think I knew anything that would help the police. Except earlier this year I remembered one thing I'd seen that I must've blocked out all those years ago."

This time the sharp intake of breath came from Nana's direction.

"I saw a hand return a book to the shelf on the wall I was huddled behind. I don't know how long I sat behind the wall like Granddad told me, hugging my legs, gnawing on my sleeve to keep from screaming. I was sure he would get me when it was okay." Tears welled in my throat. I swallowed hard and forced myself to continue. "But later, much later, I think I must've fallen asleep. I heard Nana say I was in the bedroom. That's when I rushed out the other side of the passage and dove into bed and pretended I'd been there all along."

Dad pulled me into his arms and hugged me hard against his chest. "You must've been so scared when you learned what happened. I'm sorry we didn't know. We should've known. We could've helped you."

Tears streamed down my cheeks and soaked his shirt.

Mom patted my back. "That's why you're so afraid of enclosed spaces," she said as if it was the biggest revelation of what I'd said, not that I'd been a spineless wimp, too scared to come forward and help the police figure out who broke in and killed my grandfather.

I lifted my face from Dad's shoulder, and my gaze collided with Nana's.

"You saw? You heard?" she asked in halting sentences. "And you didn't tell anyone?" She turned away, and any hope she might forgive me vanished at the sight of her stiff back.

My heart shattered. "I'm sorry. I didn't know they suspected you. I could have spared you that." My voice broke. "I miss him so much. And I was so ashamed." I knew I was babbling, but I couldn't help myself. The sight of her rigid back undammed a lifetime of regret. "I know that if I hadn't begged you to let me stay over so I could paint with Granddad, he would've been out with you when the burglar came. I know that's why you hated me so. That's why I joined the FBI. I thought one day I'd track down his murderer, bring him to justice."

"It won't bring your grandfather back," she spat, her words as cold as ice. "Nothing can bring him back."

The breath seeped from my lungs.

Dad hugged me tighter. "It's okay."

"It's not. My work is pointless. She'll never be able to forgive me, and I don't blame her." For the first time, I admitted to myself what I'd really yearned for all these years. It wasn't really to bring Granddad's murderer to justice. It was absolution.

Absolution for my role in his death. Absolution for not somehow trying to stop the intruder. Absolution for not talking to the police.

Nana turned back toward my bed, and a tear splashed onto her cheek.

I froze. I'd never seen her cry.

Her lips quivered. She blinked rapidly, staving off the tears clinging to her lashes. "I never blamed you. Never. I just . . ." She looked away.

I shook my head. I wasn't ten years old anymore. I didn't need it sugarcoated. "You do. You can scarcely bear to look at me. It's okay. I understand."

"No, that's not why." She lifted her gaze back to mine, and the anguish in her eyes tore at my heart. "You remind me too much of your grandfather." She looked away. Inhaled, straightened her waist jacket as if refortifying the walls that had let too much undignified emotion seep through. "I'm sorry I hurt you." Her voice had turned cool once more. "That wasn't my intention."

Mom stroked my hair. "You always reminded me so much of your grandfather."

"You were the apple of his eye," Dad added, his smile tinged with sadness.

Was that why they'd never wanted to talk about him? Were they afraid it would make me too sad? Or maybe make them too sad?

"Blaming you for his death never crossed my mind," Nana added.

I squashed the cynical thought I'd just supplied her a reason and stole another glance at my mute phone.

"I was to blame." Nana glanced at Dad and swiped a tissue across her nose. "We should've sold that house years before, but I was too proud to let him."

My mind flashed to the photo at Capone's apartment and puzzle pieces started falling into place. "And the stolen painting?"

Pain flickered across Nana's face. "A copy. We paid Capone to copy our entire art collection, then quietly auctioned off the originals."

Looking deep in her eyes, I could see the grief she valiantly strained to hide. And for the first time, I realized that in my egocentric childhood world, I hadn't fathomed that it wasn't all about me. Much like Tasha's assumptions about her mother's affections.

"Knock, knock," Nate said from the doorway of my hospital room. He held a gigantic bouquet of at least a couple dozen red and yellow and peach roses.

My heart jumped at the sight of him. Them. Both him and the roses.

Mom's eyes popped. "Here"—she cleared her purse from the table next to my bed—"you can set them here. Isn't this lovely?"

Yes, it was. There was a man in my life who cared that I was lying in a hospital bed.

"A bunch of the residents chipped in when your aunt told us what happened."

My chest deflated just a tad.

"Aunt Martha told you? How did she hear about it?" Mom asked.

I exchanged an uneasy glance with Nate. Mom and Dad clearly hadn't heard about Aunt Martha's involvement in today's takedown. And I wasn't sure I wanted to break it to them.

"Oh, uh . . ." Nate stalled. "I think maybe . . ."

It was on the tip of my tongue to blurt "She's friends with Gladys's neighbor," but one glimpse at Nana squashed the notion. I'd already kept my family in the dark about one too many things. "Aunt Martha was there," I said solemnly. "The bad guys used her as bait to lure me to the ambush."

Nana let out a tiny chuckle.

Not Mom. Her face went white.

Dad moved to her side and wrapped an arm around her shoulders. "But she's fine, right? Everyone's fine."

"Not a scratch on her," Nate piped up as if it was no big deal.

I gave him a grateful smile.

Dad jostled Mom's arm. "Hear that, honey? Not a scratch."

"She was pumped," Nate went on. "You know how she likes an adventure."

374

Mom looked at me pleadingly. "Why can't you get a safe job? Settle down. Start a family"—she glanced at Nate—"with a nice young man."

"Um . . ." I floundered, not really up for fending off my mom's heavy-handed matchmaking.

Nate gave me a smile and a conspiratorial wink, then before I could come up with a suitably noncommittal response, a movement at the door caught my eye.

A stunning arrangement of purple roses and hydrangea, accented with hot pink roses and white freesia, hovered in the doorway, attached to a disembodied arm.

Then Tanner followed the spectacular bouquet into the room.

My heart skipped a beat.

He'd swapped out his SWAT gear for a handsome dress shirt and sports coat. Most importantly, he wore a smile.

"Hey, kiddo, brought something for you."

"Tanner, you shouldn't have," I said, but I could feel a big, goofy smile spread across my face.

"I didn't." He paused briefly at the sight of Nate's gorgeous roses, then edged them back to make room for his in front.

"Huh?" My smile slipped.

"All the agents chipped in."

"Oh." *Right. A lot of that going around*, I thought, then immediately felt ungrateful. I pasted my smile back on. "Tell everyone thanks."

"How are you feeling?" he asked.

"Sore," I admitted.

"Well, I have news that will cheer you up."

"Yes?"

"Ty has been released. And you were right about"—he glanced at my family, clearly hesitant to discuss the case in any kind of detail in front of them—"the missing evidence. And it's a goldmine."

"Awesome!"

"What about Tasha?" Nana asked.

"The last I heard, the attorneys are hammering out a deal. In return for her full cooperation, she might avoid jail time."

"Oh, that's good to hear," Mom said. "Isn't that good?" She turned to Nana.

Nana nodded. "For Gladys's sake."

Tanner's cell phone went off. He glanced at the screen. "Excuse me, I need to take this." He squeezed my hand. "I'll see you later."

Mom shot me a gleeful glance at his friendly touch, while the muscle in Nate's taut jaw twitched.

I mentally rolled my eyes, because hello? Translation: *I'll come back when we can discuss the case in private.*

"We should be going too," Nana said. "Serena needs her rest."

Neither Nate nor Mom made any move to leave. Dad cupped Mom's shoulders and prodded her away from the bed. "Mum's right. Can we get you anything before we go?" he asked me.

"Yeah, I'd love something to eat. I think I must've missed dinner."

Dad nodded and edged Mom toward the door. "We'll stop by the cafeteria and bring you up something."

Nana patted the blanket over my foot. "Take care." She held my gaze only a moment, but it seemed to say so much more than she'd voiced.

"I will. Thank you for coming."

With a quick nod, she trailed Mom and Dad from the room.

Nate tilted his head, curiosity lighting his eyes. "What just happened there?"

"Happened?"

"You're grinning like you just cracked the city's worst criminal organization."

My smile widened. "I did, as I'm sure you heard from Aunt Martha."

"Oh yeah, but I don't sense it's what has you skipping on clouds."

I didn't think I could grin any bigger, but I did. I had to give him credit for his perceptiveness. "Skipping on clouds, huh? Are you a closet poet on top of your many other interests?"

A smile lit his eyes. "I've been known to write a verse or two. What's the deal with your grandmother?"

"Well, let's just say I'm seeing her in a whole

new light. And it has made my heart much lighter."

"I'm glad. How long do you have to stay in here?"

"Just overnight." I glanced at the bandage covering the wound. "The recovery won't be nearly as trying as convincing my mother I don't have a death wish if I don't quit."

He chuckled. "Your aunt would be disappointed if you did. She thrives on the chance to get in on your escapades."

I groaned. "I thought today might've cured her of that. For a while there, it didn't look like we'd make it out alive."

Mom and Dad appeared at the door again, this time carrying a tray of food.

Nate offered me a wink. "I'd better get going. Don't worry about Harold. I'll see he gets fed and entertained."

"Oh! Thank you." I hadn't even given a thought to my cat shut up in the apartment with no one to feed him. And Mom thought me having kids was a good idea?

"Don't be so hard on yourself," Nate whispered as if he'd read my thoughts.

"Nice seeing you again, Nate," Mom said as he left. She moved the flower arrangements to the windowsill so Dad could set the dinner tray on the bedside table.

She spent a long time fussing with the blooms.

"Which one do you think is nicer?" she asked, her back still facing me.

"They are both lovely," I said, sipping the juice they'd brought.

Dad threw me a mischievous smirk.

Yeah, I was pretty sure she hadn't been comparing the flowers either, but it was safer to play dumb. When Mom turned around, she was positively glowing. I could hardly blame her. I was feeling pretty warm and fuzzy inside, myself.

Two lovely bouquets from two handsome, thoughtful men—okay, and from my colleagues and neighbors, but I was sure Mom wasn't remembering that part.

I was sure Mom never imagined I'd have days like this.

A NOTE FROM THE AUTHOR

Dear Reader,

In *Another Day, Another Dali*, Serena realizes her closely guarded secret has caused her to misinterpret her grandmother's feelings toward her for years. Too often we see only what we expect to see in situations and others—like Gladys does with both her painting and her children and Tasha does with both her husband and her mother's relationship with her brother. Aunt Martha sees Nate as the only option for Serena. Serena's mother sees Serena's job as a barrier to her happiness. The teens see the police as their enemy.

Sometimes it takes an appraiser's objective perspective to recognize the forgery, whether in art or life. But identifying the forgery is only the beginning. As Serena discovers, getting to the truth requires a willingness to search, no matter how painful the outcome might be.

I hope you had as much fun reading Serena's latest adventure as I had writing it. The enthusiastic response to my invitation at the end of *A Fool and His Monet* to vote for whom Serena should date has been eye-opening. The feedback will definitely shape Serena's destiny moving forward.

If you would like to add your comment to the discussion, visit http://www.SandraOrchard .com/vote-for-your-favorite/. Also find fun bonus features such as character interviews, deleted scenes, and setting pictures at http://www.Sandra Orchard.com/extras/bonus-book-features/.

Sincerely,
Sandra Orchard

Sandra Orchard is the award-winning author of many inspirational romantic suspense stories and mysteries, including *Deadly Devotion, Blind Trust,* and *Desperate Measures*. Her writing has garnered several Canadian Christian Writing Awards, a *Romantic Times* Reviewers' Choice Award, a National Readers' Choice Award, a HOLT Medallion Award of Merit, and a Daphne du Maurier Award for Excellence in Mystery/Suspense. In addition to her busy writing schedule, Sandra enjoys speaking at events and teaching writing workshops. She lives in Ontario, Canada. Learn more about Sandra's books and check out the special bonus features, such as deleted scenes and location pics, at sandraorchard.com.

Center Point Large Print
600 Brooks Road / PO Box 1
Thorndike, ME 04986-0001 USA

(207) 568-3717

US & Canada:
1 800 929-9108
www.centerpointlargeprint.com